Isle of Passion

AN IMPRINT OF HARPERCOLLINS*PUBLISHERS*

Isle of Passion

A NOVEL

Laura Restrepo

Translated by Dolores M. Koch

Originally published in Spanish as *La Isla de la Pasión*
by Editorial Norma, Colombia, 1999.

FIRST EDITION

Designed by Claire Vaccaro

Library of Congress Cataloging-in-Publication Data
Restrepo, Laura.
[La Isla de la pasión. English]
Isle of passion : a novel / Laura Restrepo ; translated by
Dolores M. Koch. — 1st ed.
p.   cm.
ISBN-10: 0-06-008898-2   ISBN-13: 978-0-06-008898-9
I. Koch, Dolores.   II. Title.
PQ8180.28.E7255I8513   2005
863'.64—dc22
2005045077

05 06 07 08 09 WBC/QWF 10 9 8 7 6 5 4 3 2 1

For my people: Pedro, Mamina,
Carmen, Monko, María, and Bebeño

ALL HISTORICAL FACTS, PLACES, NAMES, DATES,
DOCUMENTS, TESTIMONIES, CHARACTERS, PERSONS
LIVING OR DECEASED THAT APPEAR IN THIS STORY ARE REAL.
MINOR DETAILS ALSO ARE, SOMETIMES.

. . . and then, in a sort of ridiculous ceremony,
they gave him the keys to the town and
accepted him as the perpetual governor
of the Island of Barataria.

—MIGUEL DE CERVANTES
Don Quixote de la Mancha

Contents

Isle of Passion

Clipperton

A DOLL ABANDONED DECADES ago is lying on the rocks. Her eyelashes have faded as well as the color of her cheeks. Animals have nibbled at her porcelain skin. Dumbstruck, she seems to observe everything with her emptied eye sockets, and to register all in her head, now etched out in places by exposure to sea salts.

After all the events that took place, the doll is still there, bearing dead witness, surrounded by thousands upon thousands of crabs that cover the sand in their turmoil, piling on top of one another in a frenzy of nervously moving layers; always around her and watchful in their siege of her hairless head and dismembered torso, peeking out the holes left by the lost arms and disappearing between her broken thighs.

The army of crabs squirms in puzzlement at this remotely human presence. Perhaps because, together with other undefinable remnants, the doll is the only human vestige still left on Clipperton Island.

On this same beach, where the doll now reigns over her hysterical court of crabs, a while back there were children running after booby birds, and women lifting their skirts to wet their feet in the pleasantly warm waters, while sailors unloaded crates of oranges and lemons.

But this was all before tragedy struck.

Afterward, nobody was either able or willing to return to Clipperton, except maybe a guano trader, and the half-dozen French sailors landing there once a month who, lulled by indifference and by the soporific vapors emanating from the land, performed the ritual of hoisting their country's flag. Because Clipperton, which had been a Mexican territory in its golden age, had now become a French possession. This, too, in some way, as a result of the events that took place.

Including the French, whose names have long been forgotten, very few people have set foot on Clipperton throughout its history; so few, in fact, that by going carefully over the existing documents, and with only a small margin of error, a list of visitors could be drawn. Most stayed only a few hours, a few days maybe, and a very small number of people managed to stay there for years.

Those who have been there say that Clipperton is an unhealthy, unfriendly place. They claim that remnants of old shipwrecks surge onto its beaches with the tides and that there is an unpleasant smell of sulfur in the air, coming from a volcanic lagoon with poisoned water that neither tolerates animal life nor can be used to drink, and will burn the skin of anyone who attempts to bathe in it. This lagoon, nestled in an old crater, extends almost the full length of the atoll, about three miles, leaving as the only space for humans to tread a narrow ring of land around its brim, including beaches peppered with coarsely broken coral, and thirteen palm trees valiantly fighting the winds. Water surrounded by water; Clipperton is not much more than that.

One reason for Clipperton's isolation is that it is so far away from everything, and the other is its insignificant size and land conditions. It has been described as so small that one can walk all around it in a single morning, starting out leisurely at seven and returning full circle just before noon.

It is also known that it lies on the Pacific Ocean, at 10° 13' north latitude and 105° 26' west, and that the closest land to it is the Mexican port of Acapulco, which is 511 nautical miles, or 945 kilometers, away. If you pictured it on a world map, it would be at the intersection of a line drawn south from Acapulco and another one going west from San José, Costa Rica, at the same distance from the equator as the cities of Cartagena in Colombia, and Maracaibo in Venezuela. Those are the known facts. Nevertheless, some navigational charts relegate the isle to uncertainty, marking its location with the initials D.E. (doubtful existence).

The name of the isle is not even its real name. "Clipperton" is an alias, a sleight of hand. One of the many ways in which the isle hides and confuses. The real name, given to it between 1519 and 1521 when for the first time Ferdinand Magellan saw it from afar, is the sweet—and at the same time awesome—name of Isle of Passion. A suggestive name in a schizophrenic way because of its contradictory meanings: "passion," which may evoke love but also suffering, fervent enthusiasm as well as torment, affection, or, instead, lust. Anyone can verify, just by opening a dictionary of synonyms, the contrasting meanings of its name. The Isle of Passion was the name given to that atoll in the Pacific by Ferdinand Magellan, an old mariner who, by exploring so many unknown lands, learned to understand them at first sight.

Clipperton remains unpopulated not only because of its irrelevancy and isolation, but also, and above all, because the stubborn and angry isle has willed it that way. For centuries it has tried to become an unassailable fortress by building around itself, polyp by polyp, a living wall of coral reefs that lurks underwater with the intent of destroying any ship that comes near. This powerful reef is the only construction it tolerates, and in order to free itself from the others, from anything man-made, it acts as a magnet for hurricanes. Besides, the three large shoals that hug its coast will capsize every small boat and drown anyone who attempts to swim over them. And as for those who manage to land in spite of all hurdles and try to establish roots there in the illusion of having tamed it, the treacherous isle crushes them in the end with maledictions like scurvy, abandonment, and oblivion, and for every ounce of happiness it claims double in suffering.

Foul odors, pestilence, hurricanes, reefs, shoals—all true, but Clipperton cannot be as nefarious as it seems, because if it were, other events, equally true and historically undeniable, could not be justified: three-quarters of a century ago, a young officer of the Mexican Army, Captain Ramón Arnaud, and his new bride, Alicia Rovira, arrived there full of illusions, loaded with household items, and with the firm intention of populating the island with their descendants. The inhospitable Clipperton received them passively, allowed them to inhabit it without any fuss and be as happy there as Adam and Eve must have been in paradise.

Still an adolescent, Alicia found it a magical, romantic place, just as she had imagined it, and she fell in love with its sunsets and its peacefulness. Ramón Arnaud, an obscure character until then, who spoke French better than Spanish due to his ancestry, arrived at its shores hoping to start anew and erase his somewhat tarnished past. It was precisely there, in such a questionable, lost corner of the planet, that he was given the opportunity to make a heroic gesture defending Mexican sovereignty against real and imaginary enemies, the latter being no less formidable than the former.

That this story has a tragic ending does not belie the fact that Ramón and Alicia enjoyed a good life during their first five years on the Isle of Passion. So if it is true that this isle is neither hell nor paradise, if it evokes neither a joyous passion nor a painful one, then the remaining possibility is that Clipperton is nothing. Even its existence is doubtful: a tiny, imperceptible dot on the map, a place you may not find but from which you cannot escape. Storm swept, eroded by tides, erased from the charts, forgotten by men, lost in the middle of the ocean, once Mexican and now foreign, taken over, with its name changed and those who enacted its drama long dead. It just does not exist. There is no such place. An illusion at times, at others a nightmare, the isle is just that: a dream. Utopia.

Or is there someone who can attest to the contrary? Is there any survivor who still remembers, who could bear witness that it all happened?

MEXICO CITY, DECEMBER 1988

Today in
Orizaba, Mexico

❦

THE PENSIÓN LOYO IS in Orizaba, at 124 Calle Sur II. It is actually a boardinghouse for automobiles. A large parking garage, gray like any other, attached to a house. I haven't met the person who lives here, but it is the one I have been looking for in Manzanillo, in Mexico City, in Puebla, and beyond. Finally, after knocking on many wrong doors, poring through the telephone directories of those three cities, and consulting with public officials, admirals, deep-sea divers, pious church ladies, tarot card readers, and local historians, I came across someone on a street corner who, almost by chance, gave me this address. If it is correct, I will finally have found one of the last three survivors of the Clipperton tragedy.

It is Mrs. Alicia Arnaud, Mrs. Loyo until her husband died, who answers the door. As the second of the four children born to Captain Arnaud and his wife, Alicia, she is seventy-seven years old and does not at all want to remember. "Don't come to stir up memories," she says sweetly. But she knows the details; she can bear witness. In some dark corner of her mind this story that I am looking for is ensconced, well preserved. She knows, in her own flesh and bones, what happened there because when she was a child, early in the century, she lived through it all.

With its back to the parking area, her cool L-shaped house opens onto a patio. There are several rooms, though the only other person in the house is a domestic servant who has been helping her for several years. The walls are papered with photos of her children. "Let's rather talk about the present," she tells me, pointing at the photos, taking me through first communions, weddings, graduations. Then she has me sit at her kitchen table while she pours into several containers the milk that her oldest son, a rancher, has brought her from the hacienda. "Don't talk to me about the past, let me forget it," she repeats. "It's been so long since I talked about Clipperton. I was born on the island in 1911 and lived there until I was six or seven. What's the point of my telling you about those old things?"

While she keeps rejecting her memories, Clipperton begins to come back and quietly invades her kitchen, little by little. The more she talks, the more enthusiastic she grows. Her tone of voice gets more lively. She forgets about the milk.

"I only have good memories, happy memories, what can I tell you. What happened in Clipperton was a tragedy, but only for the grown-ups. We children were happy. The difficulties started later, when we returned. But while we were there, it was fine, we never wanted to leave. Sometimes we saw grown-ups crying, and we cried, too, for a little while and without knowing why, but soon we were carrying on as usual.

"We were playing all day long. As soon as a game ended, we started a new one, we never stopped playing. At the beginning we had reading and writing lessons. Father didn't want us to be uncivilized upon our return to Orizaba. Mother started a little schoolhouse where she was the teacher and the students were the little Irra brothers, the two Jensen girls, Jesusa Lacursa, and us, the Arnaud children—plus the other children who gradually joined us in Clipperton. But later, with so many things going on, the adults could no longer take care of the little ones, except for short whiles in order to feed us or tuck us in at night. During the rest of the time we were free, on our own, like wild animals. We played and played until we fell asleep out of exhaustion.

"You probably want me to talk about my father, but I remember little. There were times when he let himself be absorbed so much by his obsessions that he didn't see us even though we were right before his eyes. Like when he got the idea of trying to recover the sunken treasures of Clipperton the pirate from the bottom of the lake. For months he thought of nothing else. Other times we became his obsession, like when he spent days and days carving toy ships out of wood for us to play with. They were perfectly beautiful miniatures. We still had other toys brought from the mainland—I remember well a porcelain doll for which Altagracia Quiroz had made a wig of real hair the day all the women on the island cut their hair—but the ships that my father carved himself were always my favorites. Some were warships and others freighters. We set them sailing on the lagoon and made believe they had shipwrecked. And their passengers, at least some of them—poor things—were drowning. We allowed the rest to survive.

"My father was severe only when we were at the dinner table. He said that even though we were in the most remote corner of the world and only the crabs could see us, we had to eat like civilized people. Of course, after the calamities began he could not make the same demands, and we turned wild. After the hurricane swept away everything, including the china, the silverware, and the tablecloths, we soon forgot the good table manners he had taught us. All the better for us, we thought, for we felt freer and more relaxed. We ended up eating very fast with our hands, and taking big bites. The booby eggs had nice blue shells, and we loved them. Playing at the beach, we cooked them and sprinkled sea salt on them.

"We spent a lot of time with the crabs. There must be more of those crabs in Clipperton than in the rest of the world. There were so many, it was hard to walk anywhere. If the house had not been on higher ground, the crabs would have invaded it, just as they had invaded the beach, the reefs, the caves. Everything was blanketed with crabs. We liked to watch them fight. They are ferocious beasts and dismember each other with their pincers. We used to lock them in jars to start crab wars.

"This is how things were and we had a happy life. At the end, we were running barefoot and half naked, with some clothes Mom made out of sailcloth from ships' sails. We were so suntanned from so much sun exposure that we looked like Africans, and our hair was wild and spiky, since we could only bathe in saltwater and without soap.

"As children in Clipperton, we never knew the meaning of suffering. Perhaps only my brother Ramón, the oldest, did. I think that once in a while he realized that things were not going well at all. Ramón adored my mother, and when she cried, he clung desperately to her skirt.

"The day Dad died, we all—both the older children and the little ones—were standing on the beach and watching him sail away on a boat when suddenly a manta ray capsized his boat. We all saw him being swallowed by the waves. We also saw the manta ray, enormous and black like a shadow, coming out of the water. I am not quite sure we saw it, or just thought we did. We sometimes said it was black with blue stripes, and other times, that it was silvery and gave off electrical sparks.

"Part of our game was inventing our own stories, some out of fear, others about the grandparents we hardly knew, or about our cousins, from what our mother had told us. We had imaginary friends, as many as we wanted, so we didn't need any more. We invented a lot of stories about our father after he died. We liked to think that he had found some pirate's sunken treasure at the bottom of the sea and that he had given us the jewels and the crowns. Or that he had become the king of the deep and rode underwater on a carriage pulled by the manta ray. Sometimes we also said that he had not died, that he had just gone away and was coming back to bring us toys and oranges. Later at night we couldn't sleep, afraid that he would really appear.

"I remember all this because after everything happened, our mother kept retelling these stories to us, over and over, for years. Whenever she spoke of our father, she took out of her treasure chest a long necklace of gray pearls that he had brought her from Japan and allowed us to touch it.

"But none of this is important, you know, they are small, blurred memories, not good enough for you to write a book about. If you can afford the time, it would be better for you to come with me to the hacienda, only twenty minutes by car, and I'll take you to see my father."

In the outskirts of Orizaba, the two rancher sons of Señora Alicia Loyo, née Alicia Arnaud, are talking and resting on the porch of the hacienda after the day's work. They are eating nopal tacos with chiles and drinking expensive brandy with bottled water from Tehuacán. Facing them there is an expanse of land, all paved, where sheep, pigs, and hens surround a circular trough set right in the center. Señora Arnaud is pointing in its direction. At the center of the animals' drinking place, on top of a metal cask and accompanied by the chatter of his progeny and the din of the domestic animals, there is a bronze bust of Captain Ramón Nonato Arnaud Vignon, with a spiky Prussian helmet on his head.

Santiago Tlatelolco Prison, Mexico City, 1962

❦

Given name: Ramón Nonato

Family names: Arnaud Vignon

Date of birth: August 31, 1879

Place: Orizaba

Father: Angel Miguel Arnaud (French citizen)

Mother: Carlota Vignon (French citizen)

Height: 5' 7"

Color of hair: brown

Complexion: white

Forehead: ample

Mouth: regular, thin lips

Nose: chiseled

Distinctive markings: small scar in the middle of his forehead

THAT WAS RAMÓN ARNAUD'S personal description, July 8, 1901, as recorded in the enlistment papers of his troubled military career, when he was twenty-two years old. He started as a first sergeant in the Seventh Regiment cavalry of the Mexican Army. It is recorded in the archives of the National Defense Ministry.

His dossier even includes anthropometric notations, which indicate he was a man of medium height (67 inches), of small, almost feminine feet (left foot, 9.75 inches), normal-sized head, and small hands (his left hand, up to the tip of his middle finger, was 4.75 inches long).

Exactly a year after this dossier was recorded, on July 8, 1902, his rosy white skin had become mousy gray, his brown hair was jumping with lice, and the small scar on the waxen texture of his ample forehead stood out like a cross carved by fingernails. Lying on a cot in his cell in the Santiago Tlatelolco military prison, he left his ration of refried beans untouched on its pewter plate, and cried out of rage and humiliation.

A court-martial had dictated his sentence. Five and a half months of imprisonment for being an army deserter, and he had been stripped of rank, degraded to enlisted man. On the night of May 20 just seven weeks before, he had been waiting in a cold sweat for the right time to escape from the barracks, crouching behind some sacks of maize and anticipating with horror the moment that the news would reach his hometown, Orizaba: "Ramón Arnaud is an army deserter."

But he, poor devil, was incapable of enduring what his comrades in arms in the Seventh Regiment could easily bear. Those hungry, barefoot Indians were able to overcome the inhuman discipline, the kick in the ass, the filth, and the dire poverty that being an army trooper meant. But not he. And neither could he tolerate his comrades: he considered them backward, smelly, half naked in the rags they wore as uniforms, adrift in alcohol and marijuana.

While he, an Arnaud Vignon, a well-educated white man whose family influence had expeditiously advanced him to first sergeant, was more of a shit than all of that shit. And this would be the prized gossip in

Orizaba—whispers at the church portico, on the alameda boulevards, during the afternoon hot chocolate.

The town of Orizaba had a French gazebo in the center of the plaza, an Art Nouveau train station, a municipal palace with a wrought-iron facade designed by Eiffel himself—the man made famous by his tower—which had been brought disassembled, screw by screw, from France. The Orizaba families had a Gallic air and were industrious and prosperous. They had more faith in the progress achieved through violent force by their president, Don Porfirio Díaz, than in the heretical, nationalistic ideals of the Indian Benito Juárez. There were such families as the Legrands, who manufactured percale, piqués, calicos, blankets, and French linen in their Cocolapan Woven Goods Factory. And the Suberbies, whose fortune rose like the foam of their Moctezuma beer; Monsieur Chabrand, who sold fine silks and haberdashery in his store, which he had named The Factories of France. The society ladies wore silk *shantung* dresses embroidered with *soutache* to stroll down the alameda, and then had to lift their skirts and underskirts a bit to avoid soiling them in human excrement when crossing any of the other streets, used as public latrines by Orizaba's poor.

A few years earlier, Napoleon's invading troops had almost turned the city into their permanent headquarters, and the local gentlemen devoted themselves to the pastime of identifying their more exotic army uniforms. They could recognize the Vincennes hunters for their dark blue woolen jackets; the Zouaves, with their red britches, so wide they resembled skirts, and their yellow leather walking boots; the Algerian Zouaves, with their dark skin and white turbans; the Spanish soldiers under General Prim, for their light uniforms and straw hats, and their officers, who wore jaunty little caps they called "leopoldines."

Orizaba the Damned was condemned by the rest of the nation for its recent docility in the face of European domination and its fascination with the extravagant and phantasmagorical reign of Archduke Maximilian, who served as Emperor of Mexico for three years and seven days, until the Indian Juárez had him killed in the Cerro de las Campanas to prove that no blond-bearded Austrian would rule over the free men of his Aztec homeland. And to make sure this was completely understood, after he was shot, his body was returned to Europe in a rosewood coffin, properly embalmed, and having, instead of his own, the glass eyes from an image of Saint Ursula.

Ramón's French father, Angel Miguel Arnaud, had crossed the ocean and settled in Orizaba. He loved his new land more than his old one, toiled tirelessly, and managed to accumulate a sizable fortune. He took advantage of a transportation subsidy given to him by the Porfirio Díaz administration to build the local railroad. He became the owner of a hacienda and of a home on Calle Real. He was named Orizaba postmaster, and that was how he had turned into one of the thousands of bureaucrats supported by Don Porfirio in fulfillment of his political slogan, "Let's feed the donkey."

In spite of that slogan, life was not easy for these bureaucrats. Their salaries were usually not paid for months, and they were kept in a state of alert for fear of losing their posts at the slightest suspicion of disloyalty to the government. For self-preservation, they had to belong to the appropriate political club, contribute large sums for official holiday celebrations, buy presents for their superior's mistress, and march in all the parades.

Angel Miguel Arnaud understood these rules and knew how to play the game. During his lifetime, his family enjoyed a comfortable life, up to the provincial splendor customary in Orizaba. As soon as he died, his widow, Doña Carlota Vignon—who was until then a happy and carefree matron, famous for preparing the best homemade mayonnaise in town—squandered all of his fortune according to some, or fell victim to a greedy executor according to others, but with the same result: total ruin.

Ramón, their oldest child—by then a half-French, half-Mexican teenager with large, dreamy eyes and long, doll-like eyelashes—was so perplexed by this adversity that he had no idea of what to do with his life. He had been raised to count on an inheritance, not to deal with bankruptcy.

For a while he was an apothecary's apprentice. He memorized the formulas and names of all available medications, and he began providing first aid until the apothecary abandoned town, business, and all, and moved to the capital. After a chaotic period of doing nothing, Ramón opted for a military career.

If he could have afforded it, he would have paid for an officer's career with training at a military academy, as any son of a white man was wont to do, and would have received medals, honors, and all sorts of creature comforts for himself. But since he had no money, he had to become, like average Mexicans, just beaten-up army fodder. He did obtain one privilege in recognition of his social status, and that was to join with the rank of first sergeant.

At the first bitter taste of life in the barracks, young Ramón Arnaud regretted his decision and tried to change the course of his life a little too late, making his biggest error, the one that marked him, for better or for worse, till the end of his days.

It happened one night in the barracks, behind the sacks of maize. He started thinking about his life and that it was better to suffer humiliation than to be repelled by it all and be bored to death. He ran away.

After deserting, he went into hiding in Mexico City like an outlaw, ashamed like a sinner. He spent a month wandering in the sordid streets of Tepito, hiding in the warehouses of La Merced market, trying to avoid being doused by the locals emptying their chamber pots out the window. He took refuge in the whores' hovels in Calle del Organo, lived in the taverns together with suicidal bohemians and blind musicians, and vied for coins on street corners, like the fire-eaters, the poetry hawkers, and the cat hunters.

Then came his dark day, when he was found and jailed as an army deserter. On those humid and unbearable nights in Santiago Tlatelolco, while his crumbled honor tormented him even more than the cold in his cell or the lice on his head, he realized that he had made a terrible mistake, that it was better to be dead a hundred times than to suffer that humiliation just once.

In his feverish insomnia he thought of the worst possible forms of death: being consumed by fire, his body dismembered and roasted over a grill; trapped in miasmas, slowly sinking into a viscous and foul-smelling swamp; or being dumped into the ocean and menaced by the shadowy blue glimmers of a great black manta ray until finally drowning.

"Any of them," he said in his delirium, "I'll take any of those torments, anything but this dishonor."

The day he was set free, already recovered from his fevers and again in possession of his mental faculties, he made a sacred pact with himself. Once out of jail and looking back at the blackened pre-Columbian stone walls of Santiago Tlatelolco, he solemnly swore, on the memory of his father and on his mother's love, on the seven daggers that pierce the heart of Our Lady of Sorrows and on the love of his country, that never ever again, in his personal life or as an army man, would he go through the shame of another humiliation like this one.

Mexico City, 1907

COLONEL ABELARDO AVALOS of the engineering division, godfather and protector of the young junior officer Ramón Arnaud, made an appointment to speak with his godson in Mexico City.

"Ramón, you are going to Clipperton. With a detail of eleven soldiers under your command."

He was told just like that, no preambles.

When Arnaud heard the word "Clipperton," he felt a stab of pain behind his eyes. He knew all about that miserable atoll lost in the middle of the ocean because he had accompanied Colonel Avalos there a couple of times. While his guts froze, his face was burning; he wiped the sweat off with his hands, and onto his pants.

"Banished," he murmured almost imperceptibly, aware that with a desertion on his record he had no moral authority to protest.

Slouched in his chair, belittled, already twenty-seven years old, big and hirsute, but only a second lieutenant. His protest came almost in a whisper: going to that island would be like starting all over again, and for the third time. This was too much, it asked too much of him. How come nobody recognized that he did not deserve such an ill fate? Why was he being subjected to this third ordeal by fire when he was passing his second one with honors?

After serving his sentence at Santiago Tlatelolco, Arnaud, with a mule's obstinacy, had intended to go back, to retrace his path in order to show courage instead of fear, and to be decisive where before he had faltered. He would respect the solemn oath he had made to himself facing the blackened walls of the military prison, even at the cost of his life.

On December 16, 1902, he had rejoined the army, this time just as a recruit, in the Twenty-third Battalion in Veracruz. The conditions were tougher there than those that had broken him after his original enlistment as first sergeant, but in spite of this, he endured the second hitch. He endured it all with resignation and ate crow with a large spoon. In six months, he made corporal and, later, sergeant second class. Then he was again a first sergeant, just as before.

In July 1904, already a second lieutenant, he was transferred to the Tenth Battalion in Yucatán, with orders to quash an insurrection of the Maya Indians. It was an impossible objective. His mission was to do away with a cross that talked, someone known as Saint Talking Cross, who acted as the supreme commander of the Indians and incited them to rebellion. Arnaud tried to fulfill his duty. He demolished temple fortresses, and with his sword toppled many of those Talking Cross leaders, who were using their gift of speech not to call the Mayas to prayer but to encourage them to struggle. For each cross he struck down, another three new talking crosses sprang in place, and his mission turned into an inferno, an endless nightmare.

As a reward for his efforts, ineffectual though superhuman, he was given the medal of merit and courage, and his lost honor was restored.

If he had put his past behind him and was now in good standing with the army, distinguishing himself as a junior officer and even earning a medal, why then was he being forced to start all over again? Why was he being isolated in the remotest, most insignificant corner on the map?

"Besides, Godfather, I am getting married," Arnaud desperately pleaded to Colonel Avalos.

His wedding had already been arranged; he could not break his word and didn't want to. He had already asked for Alicia's hand in marriage, he was in love, and she was waiting for him. How could he explain to his fiancée that he was calling off their wedding? How to justify another failure to the people in his hometown of Orizaba? Everybody knew about his impending marriage. "Please understand," pleaded Arnaud, "please realize that this wedding cannot be postponed."

This merely served to free the torrent of Colonel Avalos's patriotic fervor. His words were gushing out in spurts. Ramón Arnaud could perceive only fragments, unconnected phrases that reached his ears slowly, as if deferred, moments after being uttered.

"There are issues that must take precedence," the colonel went on irrepressibly. "Now is the time for daring action . . . think of your country, your homeland . . . of defending this piece of Mexican soil from the French, who want to take possession . . . of taking up arms against historical injustice. . . . You speak French, and have the right qualifications . . . of giving up your life if necessary . . . Mexicans do answer the call to arms. . . ."

Arnaud was not concentrating on Avalos's words. These bastards, he thought. They really want to torture me. But anyway, he held on to his dejected mien and his pleading look, in the faint hope of softening Avalos with his victimized expression. The result was, though, that the persuasive, deliberate voice of the colonel began to ring with impatience, suddenly acquiring a metallic vibration, and, coming down like an ax, it struck this threat:

"If you refuse, the Mexican Army will consider it a second desertion."

"But, Godfather, if I accept, it will be close to a dishonorable discharge."

The obvious blackmail had sent a shot of adrenaline through Arnaud's brain, and, to his own amazement, his voice sounded virile and convincing, giving him strength to continue. "I'm not going to play the fool anymore; this one I am going to fight," he told himself, and he was already going to let his anger out in a barrage of words when Avalos stopped him cold.

"Easy, young man," he said. "If you stop taking it the hard way, I'll tell you what's good about it."

And then he began dribbling the encouraging news: that same day he would be promoted to lieutenant, and President Porfirio Díaz in person would name him governor of the island.

"If you want to get married, my dear Ramón, you can go to Clipperton with your wife, and we'll give you a good furlough to take care of the whole thing. I have met Alicia, and I know she will like that. I will put at your disposal whatever it is you need, so you'll have everything. What's more," added Avalos, "within a week, you and I will depart for Japan on a special mission that has to do with your appointment in Clipperton. I will explain later, very delicate matters of state, you know."

Clipperton, Japan, lieutenant, governor . . . Ramón did not quite understand. Then Avalos lunged upon him.

"You've got it made, my son. Congratulations," he heard him say, while getting a big bear hug, with big paws patting him on the back.

That was how Ramón received notice that the following day the president was to send for him and assign him to a delicate mission because he considered him the right man, recognized his merits, pardoned his misdemeanors, and was going to name him governor of Clipperton Island and raise his pay. Arnaud was still stunned by it all. What at first had sounded like a terrible disgrace and a punishment had suddenly turned into that golden and unique opportunity to change the course of his life.

When his appointment with Don Porfirio came to an end, he took his leave with a lot of genuflections, and left the splendidly luxurious billiards room of the Chapultepec Castle, completely sure he was, at last, going to be a happy man.

The blood throbbing in his temples drowned the sound of his own footsteps—too quick to be martial—and he had the sensation that his black shoes, meticulously polished very early that morning, scarcely touched the parquet, an ostentatious display of precious woods. For a moment he feared that the weight of the president's gaze on his back would make him lose control of his legs, and he anguished over the possibility of tripping and falling, but when at last he went through the door and heard it close behind him, he was finally able to breathe deeply and recover his composure. He looked up at the cherubs painted on the ceiling and felt that the smiles of their little rosy lips were for him.

After leaving the Chapultepec Castle, which was the presidential summer residence, Arnaud started walking aimlessly along the brand-new Paseo de la Reforma in total disbelief of the preceding events, and without seeing anything else but the two new resplendent metal bars on his army jacket that now accredited him as a lieutenant. He kept thinking that none of the pedestrians who crossed his way could help but admire them, and did not even notice that the unforgiving noonday sun was overheating him too much inside his dark woolen dress uniform.

He tried to reconstruct, word by word, his dialog with Porfirio Díaz, and mentally repeated each phrase about ten or twelve times. Though he did not say anything special to him, Arnaud made an effort to remember every word. Nor did the president receive him in his office, as anticipated, but instead, Arnaud was forced to walk around accompanying the president on an inspection tour of the esthetic reconstruction already under way at the castle.

In fact, the president had spoken only about furnishings: "Lovely brass candelabra. I had them brought in from Paris," or "Notice this Pompadour boudoir. Solid mahogany, feel it," or "Do you see the tapestry designs depicting the ancient Greek games? Thirty-five hundred pesos," or "Do you like the billiards room? Queen's style. The table is a Callender and the curtains are English." The president's comments were all of this nature, obsessed as he was with the restoration of his summer residence.

Walking ahead a few blocks, Arnaud remembered also his own answers: confused monosyllables, false exclamations of admiration. He could hear the exact tone of his voice repeating "I find everything just right for my taste, Your Excellency" whenever the president pointed at some object or piece of furniture. "Just right for my taste," he had said in a forced timbre, and recalling it now made him blush. Did His Excellency care about his taste? Probably his phrase was not even grammatically correct.

The evening before he had been carefully preparing to say different remarks, like, "When I was a child, my father used to tell me about your heroic campaigns," but when the time came, he had only come up with "Ohs!" and "Ahs!" and, to top it all, in that falsetto voice. He had lost sleep reviewing everything concerning Clipperton, its possibilities as a source for exporting guano, the many judicial facets of the litigation with France, its strategically important location in case of war. He could have gone on for hours discussing these things with Don Porfirio, and would have dazzled him with his factual knowledge, with his enthusiasm for the island, with his firm decision to establish himself there. But Don Porfirio gave him no opportunity to deal with those issues.

The fact was, the sole indication of the importance of his assignment, of the trust bestowed upon him, was the strong farewell pat on his shoulder, and the president's final words: "Good luck, young man." He did say that to him, "Good luck." Surely His Excellency meant good luck in Clipperton, the radiant Arnaud elaborated as he walked aimlessly, as if mesmerized, along the Paseo de la Reforma. Or maybe luck on the trip to Japan, luck in this difficult undertaking, luck in the defense of the national sovereignty. Or maybe not. Perhaps he had only wished him good luck.

But the meaninglessness of their dialogue was not enough to dampen Arnaud's joy. What he told the president did not matter; what counted was that Don Porfirio had called for him, that gesture was significant, that he had personally received him—him, of all people; him, Ramón Arnaud, in spite of everything. He had not been so brilliant in his interview, he had to admit, but that did not count. After all, Porfirio Díaz had not been so brilliant either, Ramón Arnaud thought, satisfied with himself.

Marble from Carrara, Baccarat lamps, Henry II furniture—or his fucking mother's, who gave a good goddamn, he had the lieutenant bars pinned on his jacket, his appointment had been signed, and in eight days he was leaving for Japan with Avalos, representing his government; he had been granted a face-to-face interview with none other than Don Porfirio himself, and, come what may, no one could take that away from him.

It all had happened as if by magic; literally from one day to the next he had gone from being a poor devil, an outlaw, a loser, a failed junior officer, a provincial nobody, and a deserter, to becoming a lieutenant and a governor, a man trusted by the establishment. Suddenly he had been graced by the gods.

"Some day a page will be written about me in the history of my homeland," he unexpectedly declared out loud.

That night in his room, while he unbuttoned his suffocating dress uniform jacket, and relaxed the muscles of his incipient belly, he added: "And if nothing gets written, at least I got a pay raise."

Orizaba, México, 1908

✦

A PHOTOGRAPH IN SEPIA, taken in an interior with printed velvet draperies in the background, and dated on the lower-right corner "May 1908"—that is, a few days before the wedding—shows Alicia the way she was then: with a gracefully dimpled chin, a porcelain complexion on her doll-like face, the light shadow of her straight eyebrows, and an adult gaze in her little girl's eyes.

It took her six months to do the twenty yards of lace for her wedding dress, and during this time she repeated the same operation a million times—hook in one hand and in the other the ball of linen thread from Holland—yarn over twice, insert hook, draw up a loop. Those were the last six months she spent at home with her parents in Orizaba, at number 30 Calle Tercera de la Reforma, while her fiancé, Ramón, was away on his military mission.

She, the child bride, was waiting for his return. At times she felt like an adult attending marriage preparation courses, where she learned that at the moment of the marital encounter, she should close her eyes and pray, "Oh Lord, make me not take pleasure in this." Or she would sit and visit with her relatives Dorita Rovira, now Mrs. Virgilio, and Esther Rovira, who was Mrs. Castillo. Or she would sit and sew clothes for the poor with Ramón's sister, Adelita, and with his aunts Trinidad Vignon, Maria Vignon Aspiri, and Leonor Arnaud, who was a widow.

At times she was just like a child running along the house corridors shaded by ferns, making sure she did not step on the yellow floor tiles, only the blue ones. Or without stepping on the blue ones, only on the yellow ones. She played wolf with her sisters, and cops and robbers, or pretended that the hallway was the ocean and that the pillows they laid on the floor were sharks. When she got tired, she sat on a bench under the palm tree in the patio to think about Ramón, or something else, or nothing at all. She liked to imagine lavish weddings, eternal loves, honeymoons on a deserted island.

Sunny mornings in Orizaba always had a warm fragrance, bittersweet and tropical green. It smelled of moss in between rocks, of beasts ruminating on wet grass, of fresh cow dung, of oranges just squeezed. That fragrance made its way to Alicia's bed and into her nostrils, caught her skin and made her hair curl. She felt an urge to go out in the open air, to the open country, to be going up and down the surrounding hills on her own—letting her stubborn mule lead the way.

"Where are you going? Have you lost your mind?" shouted her mother, seeing her on her way out with her hair undone.

She did not know where. Anywhere. She ran barefoot, like the Indian girls, through open yards full of chickens, past clotheslines with newly washed clothes, and by poor people's homes with their red gladioli.

"Miss Alicia, buy some peaches!" "Here, get some tortillas!" "Let me sell you this turkey!" She dropped by Santa Gertrudis to see the burlap factory, the latest novelty in Orizaba. For hours she observed the four hundred laborers milling around like ants. Amazed, she tried to understand how the falling water could move the looms and the machines to spin the fibers, to sew the sacks, to roll the fabric.

"The water falls with the power of eight hundred horses," said the foreman, who explained everything all over again each time she came.

"Of eight hundred horses," echoed Alicia, and she asked him again about the dynamos, about the Pelton system, about the copper strips that distributed the electricity.

There were days when her mule's easy trot would take her far, up to the cotton textile factory in Rio Blanco. It was the largest and most modern in the world. Six thousand men, women, and children worked there. As she was getting closer, her heart beat faster, her mouth became dry. She and Ramón had been there once. She liked to stay there for a while, looking at the big clock the owners had placed on top of a tower facing the buildings, with its four transparent quadrants lit by night, and the loud bells and whistles to strike every hour on the hour. There was nothing like it in Orizaba.

"Let's get out of here," Ramón had said.

"Let's wait a little bit more, the clock is just about to strike," she pleaded.

"Let's go now, this place has the smell of blood."

On the way back Ramón told her what nobody in Orizaba ever mentioned. He made her swear, kissing a cross, never to repeat it. If anybody found out he had told her that, he would be thrown out of the army.

"A few years ago there was a strike here and workers were killed. I do not know how many of them, probably hundreds. A friend of mine who worked for the local sheriff's office saw their corpses. They were piled on the two railroad platforms, so many he could not even count them. There were women and children, and also loose parts, arms, legs. My friend told me that the train left for Veracruz, where the dead were thrown to the sharks."

Orizaba grew chilly in the afternoons, the fragrances in the air died out, and smells from the kitchen invaded the house, particularly that of hot chocolate with cinnamon and vanilla. There was often a persistent light rain the townspeople called *chipichipi*. Her mother and her aunts turned wistful. Sitting at the long dining room table, Alicia listened to their talk, while dunking bits of Mexican *pan dulce* into her hot chocolate. Doña Petra and her sisters waxed nostalgic about many things, but above all about the day they saw Emperor Maximilian passing by at close range, his golden beard parted in two, accompanied by the demented empress in her mauve silks.

After the chocolate they usually joined the religious procession. Alicia tried to protect her head from the drizzle with a black lace mantilla and accompanied all the women in her family, including the maids, to take Our Lady of Sorrows for an outing. They would rescue her image from its niche in the Temple of the Twelve Virgins, where she had been agonizing since colonial times, her face haggard, and take her on their shoulders to parade her in the streets, decked in her black velvet mantle all embroidered in baroque pearls.

The evenings belonged to the ghosts. At the Rovira home, the family retired early to hear them pass by. At the stroke of midnight, in a vertiginous horse carriage, death would take the legendary figure of la Monja Alférez (the Ensign Nun) to receive her nightly punishment for the unmentionable sins she had committed in life. Then, through all the underground tunnels beneath the city, Mexican soldiers marched, trying to escape from the invading French, and one could hear the trampling of their feet and their laments. And through small openings in the draperies, dead orphaned children, called *chaneques* by the locals, would peer in from the darkness in order to spy on the lit interiors of the town houses. These giggling chaneques, with their lighted candles, were small, infantile, wicked.

But neither the nun's cries nor the taunts of the chaneques got the best of Alicia because her father, Don Félix Rovira, kept a small bed next to his in the master bedroom where she could come running at midnight if she woke up in a panic.

"Father, the chaneques are trying to pull my hair," she would tell Don Félix, and he would keep her company until she fell asleep again. But in fact, those who appeared in her nightmares were Our Lady of Sorrows and the dismembered arms and legs of the Río Blanco workers.

Yarn over twice, insert hook, draw up a loop, and close the row with a double stitch; Alicia spent many hours with her two sisters making feather stitches for the roses and nightingales of her lace wedding dress. The three of them would sit on Turkish-style stools in an intimate, closed circle. They would make fun of the large bedsheet with the big eyelet in the center that Alicia was going to use on her wedding night so Ramón would not see her naked. They giggled, whispered to each other, and one would stick her finger through the eyelet and touch the other's cheek.

"Peekaboo, guess who's inside you!"

Huddling close together like clandestine accomplices, they covered their mouths to contain their laughter, repeating as if it were a tongue twister the words that were taught to future brides being prepared for marriage: "We do this, O Holy of Holies, not because of our evil ways, nor for fornication, but to bring forth a child in your holy service"—and they competed to see who could say it fastest—"Do this, Holy O, to serve in your holy fornication, the holy vice of your holy son, Fornitio, venicio, holy servitio."

Her mother, Doña Petra, would cross herself at such heresies. But then, moving closer to them, she would get into the conversation and break the gap, risking an argument.

"If ever, God forbid, a man is about to rape you and there is a gun within your reach, kill yourself before you are dishonored!"

The girls would laugh.

"You're crazy, Mother, it would be better to shoot the man."

They doubled and redoubled a strand of thread and tacked it to the arch. The three of them took turns in their needlework, but Sarita had a tighter stitch than Alicia, and Esther's was looser, and so the nightingales in the wedding dress were large and angular in some places, and smaller with fat wings in others. Their mother made them undo their work and start all over again. One day while embroidering they were eating cherry chocolate cordials and stained the lace. Hiding from Doña Petra, they washed it with hydrogen peroxide and salt.

They would again bring the yarn over twice, insert the hook, and draw up a loop to make a double stitch while listening to their mother's domestic advice.

"For stomach pain, remember this. When you are in Clipperton, if you run out of your paregoric elixir, boil an avocado seed for fifteen minutes: that tea makes a good substitute."

The girls just laughed.

"But the avocados will be gone before the elixir!"

Yarn over twice, insert hook, draw up a loop, and the wedding date was approaching. One day a messenger arrived in Orizaba with a long necklace of gray pearls for the bride to be that her fiancé had sent her from Japan. The whole neighborhood found out about it and came over to admire the pearls. Alicia delighted in wearing them around her neck and went outside to the patio to do acrobatics and cartwheels with the servants' children.

That is how her life went. She would embroider her white dress and learn to cook rice on the big coal stove so it would not come out too salty or lumpy. When nobody noticed, she would lock herself up to read and reread alone her fiancé's love letters and to answer them on small notepaper from her stationery set, taking great care in penning her round lowercase letters and large, elaborate capitals.

Before writing to him she would review the latest news, the important happenings in Orizaba during his absence. A pregnant Indian who used to sell tortillas and tortillas chips in the market was gored in the belly by a cow. The woman was still alive, bleeding and screaming, and Alicia helped to take her to the Women's Hospital, where they saved her and her baby. Another day, the satyr in the Santa Anita neighborhood was finally caught and hanged. He had raped fifteen girls, giving them the French venereal disease and getting all of them pregnant.

In the end, Alicia would reject these stories because Ramón would not be interested, and she wrote only about her love for him, such as the card written in English that, years after the tragedy, appeared in a book about Clipperton by General Francisco L. Urquizo, which says exactly this on one side:

Señor
Ramón Arnaud
Acapulco

And on the other,

I never forget you
and I love you with
all my soul, Alice.
Orizaba, June 14, 1908

A line in violet-colored ink springs up from the letter *e* in "Alice," turns back and curls around the last *a* in "Orizaba." Yarn over twice, insert hook, draw up a loop, close the row, and end off.

Mexico City, Today

"NO, IT ISN'T TRUE, she didn't embroider her wedding gown," Alicia's granddaughter, Mrs. Guzmán (née María Teresa Arnaud) tells me, then going on to quote from the book she wrote on family memories: "Alicia's wedding gown has arrived from Europe; it is very elegant, and for several weeks now it has been on display in the shop window at Las Fábricas de Francia. The wedding is to be held shortly," she says, reading from *La tragedia de Clipperton*, published in Mexico in 1982.

"Of course I know this very well. I know my grandmother's life to the minute, I see it all through her eyes. Do you want more details about that dress? It was ordered through the Chabrands, the owners of the best clothing store in Orizaba, Las Fábricas de Francia, which had sent for it by telegram to France. Many years later, for my own wedding—my husband is a water management engineer—I said I wanted to get married in my grandmother Alicia's wedding gown. I was told I was crazy, that it would not fit me, since she was almost a child when she got married. But I was bent on wearing it, and it smelled of mothballs when I took it out of the chest. Up to the last minute, people were telling me not to be so stubborn, I couldn't possibly get into it. However, it fit me marvelously: I could button it easily. We were exactly the same size; we resembled each other, and had the same body shape, the two of us!" says her proud granddaughter, sitting on a heavy wood rocking chair, Mexican colonial style, in the living room of her San Angel home in Mexico City. Her snow-white hair, clear proof of a recent visit to a beauty salon, frames her doll face: perfect features, slightly dimpled chin, and luminous complexion in spite of her being fifty already.

"My whole family tells me now that I look exactly like my grandmother. You don't know me, you know nothing about us, but you have called me Alicia a couple of times, though my name is María Teresa. Even though she died long before I was born, there is a deep bond between us that goes beyond logic. I can never put her memory down to rest. Her intense suffering and courage were remarkable. No one recognizes that today."

Through the large windows we can see the meticulously manicured garden. In the center of the living room there is a table, and a Talavera ceramic vase with five black feathers in it. There are several seashells in a little box.

"Those are feathers from Clipperton birds; the shells are from Clipperton beaches. Does that surprise you? My home is truly a sanctuary for the island. For years I have saved all the newspaper and magazine articles written about it from around the world. I still have letters from my grandfather, and clothing that belonged to my grandmother. I have soil samples and water samples from Clipperton—I am a chemist by profession, you know. These things were brought to me because I have never been there. When I wrote my book about the isle, I met my destiny. I knew that my mission on earth was to tell that story, which is also my own story. I am selling the book from home and from my husband's office. He is, as I already told you, an engineer in water management.

Every week I make a presentation on Clipperton. The navy invites me, I have friends there. For me, each conference is psychologically and emotionally exhausting, because as I talk, I revive the tragedy, I relive it again. I come back home two to five pounds thinner, and I have to stay in bed for a couple of days in order to recuperate."

At that moment her husband comes down the stairs. He is a short man, wears glasses, and is carrying his raincoat over his arm. On his way to work, he greets us politely and looks at her tenderly, with admiration even, and then leaves.

"Did you see how he looks at me? He shares my mission and has worked tirelessly to make my book widely known, but sometimes it worries him to think that I go too far. 'Come down to earth, María Teresa,' he tells me, 'come back to reality.' And I tell him that my reality is not here but in Clipperton, because that isle is my life."

María Teresa goes to the kitchen to make coffee. On the dining room wall there is a large portrait of her, hands on her lap, her white muslin strapless dress baring her equally white shoulders. She is looking straight ahead, unsmiling. In a silver frame propped on a mahogany sideboard is a photo of her grandmother Alicia. They really resemble each other.

María Teresa brings the coffee on a tray. Unlike her dress in the portrait, the one she is wearing now is severe, with a collar up to her neck and sleeves down to her wrists, in a dark shade of purple, a color of mourning. She wears no rings on her fingers, just a pair of showy gold earrings and a cross, also in gold, on her chest.

"People say that I am a *porfirista* like my grandfather, who fought in Porfirio Díaz's federal army. It is true that I feel nostalgia for the past and have no interest in present-day politics. But I am not a throwback. We all have our idiosyncracies. Look, my grandfather was really a Frenchman, his parents were French, and he sacrificed his life so that Mexico would not lose a piece of land, which today, after many a turn and tumble, is precisely in the hands of the French. That is why, because of his spilled blood, my family finds no peace and cannot rest until Clipperton is again under the Mexican flag."

The big entrance door to the house has amber glass panels on both sides. The light comes through them and falls on María Teresa while she says good-bye with an admonition.

"So you are taking on Clipperton? Do you really want to trace its tragic history? Do you honestly want to understand all the love and all the forgiving that occurred on that inhospitable rock in the midst of the Pacific Ocean? You better watch out then and mind my words. Clipperton was not always its name. Its original name was Isle of Passion, and whoever gave it that name understood it very well. Whoever enters its world pays dearly for it. What you'll find there is a sea of sorrows."

Señora María Teresa Arnaud (Mrs. Guzmán), the granddaughter of the Arnauds from Orizaba, has come to see me off at the door of her San Angel home. She stands next to the glazed door. The light coming through gives her complexion a strange tone, alabaster-like. She has something else to say.

"Let me make one more thing clear: my grandmother and her sisters did indeed spend time embroidering together a few months before the wedding. They spent hours and hours doing that. Not making a lace dress, no. They embroidered all the linens for the home on the isle— sheets, towels, tablecloths, napkins. They even embroidered the famous saintly bedsheet, with its keyhole opening and all, which was used in those days on the wedding night to consummate the marriage. They did a beautiful job embroidering the bride's initials, A.R.A. That is why you became confused. It is because of such things that my father and I do not want anyone outside of us two to tell our story. People talk of things they know nothing about, they spread versions that are not accurate."

Orizaba, Today

SITTING IN THE KITCHEN AT PENSIÓN LOYO, Alicia Arnaud remembers the gray pearl necklace that her father sent her mother from Japan.

"I remember my mother wearing that necklace. She liked to finger it, caress it, while she spoke about Dad, while she told us all that happened. I do not know who might have it now. When Mother died, Aunt Adela Arnaud, my father's sister, took us in. Had it not been for her, we would have ended up in an orphanage. We never found out what happened to Mother's things, the ones that were left after her death. I do not know who might have that necklace now, but I remember it as if I were looking at it."

In the whole Clipperton story, the gray pearl necklace takes on a political significance, apart from its emotional value: it is the only evidence left of Ramón Arnaud's trip to Japan. As far as it's known, he didn't tell anybody the reason for his trip, and didn't leave any written record either.

"We never found out why he took it. I think he didn't even tell my mother," Alicia Arnaud says.

Porfirio Díaz himself commissioned him and took the trouble of interviewing him personally for it. The trip took place in 1907, immediately after Arnaud was named governor of Clipperton Island. By then, relations between Japan and Mexico were becoming stronger. Japanese imports became fashionable in Mexico City, judo was the rage, poets wrote odes to bamboo trees, and the ladies bought parasols and silk fans.

Then there were persistent rumors of a secret treaty between Mexico and Japan. People said that Japan would declare war on the United States to secure its control over the Pacific, and that Mexico would be its ally. In accordance with such an agreement, it is possible that Clipperton would have been considered of strategic importance due to its location. On the other hand, it is also possible that this often-mentioned secret treaty between Mexico and Japan was just a rumor. That is, nothing but a distracting strategy on the part of the German government, which, in an attempt to kill two birds with one stone, wanted to set the United States and Japan, its two principal enemies, against each other. To spread the tale of a sinister plan to gain control over the Pacific region would foster the paranoia of the "yellow peril" that was affecting the United States.

That leaves another possible explanation: that Arnaud did not say much about his trip, leaving no records, not because of its secret and transcendental historical import, but just the opposite, because of its mere triviality. For instance, Ramón might have been sent to Tokyo as a translator for formal diplomatic affairs. Or to take to the emperor of Japan a piece of Sèvres porcelain as a gift from the president. And perhaps Clipperton never had any strategic importance for anyone, except for birds as a convenient place to leave their droppings.

Whether it was decisive or trivial, this piece of the puzzle has been hopelessly lost. Nothing is known about why Lieutenant Ramón Arnaud went to Japan. There is only one known fact: that from Japan he sent his fiancée a necklace of gray pearls.

Orizaba, 1968

THE MORNING OF JUNE 24 was a bit warm. The stones at the portico of the parish church, still wet from a midnight downpour, were quickly being dried out by the brand-new sun. Steam was rising from the ground. The early morning mists and the incense that from time to time escaped from the interior gave the facade of the old church on the plaza a blurred, milky appearance, a nervous silhouette.

At five minutes after six Alicia appeared as if floating on the white ocean spray of her wedding dress and trailing a cloud of tulle after her. She walked holding on to her father's arm from the wrought-iron fence up to the entrance and then, one step at a time, up the stairs and inside the church, all the way to the main altar. Ramón in his dress uniform was waiting for her. By his side, the voluminous, solid figure of his mother, Doña Carlota, all draped in black.

Alicia was bedazzled by the thousands of lit candles, by the tiny flames that multiplied in the reflection on the gold leaf that covered the carved cedar of the altars. She felt overwhelmed by the quantity of flowers. The saints, niches, naves, corners, both sides of the aisles, the pulpit: the whole church was bursting with blooms. They combined in a full range of colors and scents, dominating all the available oxygen inside. She felt asphyxiated and a little dizzy, and, closing her eyes, she slowly let some air into her lungs and tried to focus only on the smells. In spite of the incense, she was able to distinguish floral scents—the sweet jasmines, the slightly acrid daisies, the steamy gardenias, the familiar roses, and the almost imperceptible yet treacherous charm of orchids. The overloaded breath of air wrapped around her and numbed her senses, isolating her from reality.

She opened her eyes, inhaling deeply, and was able, little by little, to focus on the blurred images. Particularly one of them, a stranger who stood stiffly by her side. She looked at him in amazement, as if seeing for the first time his thin mustache, his doll-like eyelashes, his round, introspective eyes, his hair, disciplined with brilliantine and sharply parted in the middle. He, Ramón, the stranger with whom she was to live for the rest of her days, turned to look at her and smiled. Though it came from that strange face, his smile was warm and familiar, and brought Alicia back down to earth.

I know him little, but I love him, Alicia thought, after catching her breath, and she busied herself arranging her tulle veil around her feet. Actually, they had known each other since childhood and had been engaged since adolescence, but during their courtship they never had the opportunity of being alone, of talking freely until they ran out of topics to talk about, of being close, of being in physical contact, of scrutinizing the nooks and crannies of each other's soul. In the last seven years, Ramón had been away on military duty. Once or twice a year he had been granted a furlough to return to Orizaba, and on those visits, which would last a few days or a few weeks, he alternated between sleeping all his postponed siestas, letting himself be fed and pampered by his mother, and courting his fiancée.

An engagement in Orizaba—a twisted, fearful, and overly pious town, teeming with gossip—consisted of no more than after-dinner family gatherings, bouquets of roses, croquet games, kissing of hands, and walks on the alameda. There is testimony, for instance, that after their engagement was formalized and made public, the two lovers began to stroll arm in arm. This is stated in an unpublished manuscript by a local friend of Alicia's family, Don Antonio Díaz Meléndez, entitled "Orizaba de mis recuerdos" (The Orizaba I remember).

There is no mention in it, however, of the piles of garbage on the streets where the pigs snooped around, of the dark vestries where priests used to exorcise epileptics by beating them, nor of the street corners, right in the center of town, where the poor used to relieve themselves. But the lost graces of Orizaba do get nostalgic mention: the well-trimmed lawn and shade trees in the alameda, the fountain of playful waters, the aristocratic family gatherings listening to the strains of the Municipal Military Band playing Juventino Rosas's "Over the Waves" waltz in the gazebo of the central plaza after the eleven o'clock mass. Don Antonio tells how one Sunday in the middle of an open-air concert and the pleasant strolling of the townspeople, he saw a beautiful girl "wearing an elegant hat and a dress with a discreet neckline, reaching down to the tips of her shiny patent leather booties, as the fashion in those days demanded. She was Miss Alicia Rovira, on the arm of a handsome officer, whom she introduced to me as her fiancé. It was Captain Arnaud. This was the first and last time I saw him, and he made an excellent impression on me with his pleasant conversation and loving behavior toward his fiancée, charming Alicia."

One day, dressed up and serene, they were walking a few steps ahead of her parents, siblings, and cousins when Alicia stopped suddenly and told Ramón, "Besides being in love and getting married, I would like us to be friends, you and me."

Ramón looked at her in surprise. He kept silent for a while.

"I would like that, too. But that will have to be when we live together, alone. For now, with so many people around us, it's even difficult to be romantically in love like in the novels."

The time came to set the wedding date and begin the preparations. Ramón was no longer a decent, pennyless adolescent, nor a dishonored military man labeled as a deserter. Now he had a career and a future—risky and unpredictable, but still promising—to offer his beloved, so he asked for her hand in marriage. On a windy night, accompanied by his mother, Doña Carlota, he arrived at the home of Félix Rovira and his wife, Petra, Alicia's parents, who served them glasses of sherry and some olives, while Don Félix overdid himself, being gallant and making pretentious jokes. He was courteously pompous when he offered a toast for the future couple. Nobody suspected that his eyes were swollen and his nose red because for hours before the visit, he had locked himself up in the library in a rage and he had cried and had thrown on the floor, tome after tome, most of his *Encyclopedia Britannica* in an attack of paternal jealousy.

The announcements and the invitations to the wedding were ordered to be printed in an ocher shade. There was a breakfast planned for after the ceremony with French-style hot chocolate, link sausages, the blood pudding that Don Félix, who was from Galicia, prepared himself, and the assorted hors d'oeuvres with Doña Carlota's famous mayonnaise.

The day had come, and now the wedding ceremony was coming to an end without a hitch, apart from the collectively experienced lack of air. Alicia followed every detail and imprinted them all in her memory, where they would be etched forever: Doña Carlota's large diamond, which Ramón had set in an engagement ring that reflected tiny rainbows from her little girl's hand; the weight of the earrings, which matched the ring; the Holy Sacrament of the Communion held on high by the priest's fat fingers; the nostalgia on her father's face, which everybody except Alicia simply interpreted as pure emotion; the extremely sharp timbre, practically superhuman, of the solo voice from the choir singing the "Ave María"; Ramón's beatific smile as he thought of breaking his fast with the sausages and the chocolate. And above all, overpowering everything, the dense, compact scent emanating from the flowers.

At the climax of the ceremony, the final benediction, Alicia looked at the black feathers of her mother-in-law's outrageous hat. They annoyed her, they seemed to her like a bad omen, and, involuntarily, she made a face. As if he had heard what she was thinking, Ramón bent down toward her and whispered in her ear: "I told my mother not to wear that ugly bird hat because it was going to scare you."

Orizaba, Today

✦

I COME TO ORIZABA looking for traces of that wedding. It is a small city, dull and graceless. In the Pensión Loyo—where Alicia Arnaud Loyo lives alone since she became a widow—I find one of the marriage announcements, printed in ocher on heavy paper and folded in four. The message is written twice, according to custom.

Mr. Félix Rovira and Mrs. Petra G. Rovira
are pleased to inform you of the forthcoming
marriage of their daughter Alicia
and Mr. Ramón Arnaud

Mrs. Carlota Vignon Arnaud
is pleased to inform you of the forthcoming
marriage of her son Ramón
and Miss Alicia Rovira

According to the Arnauds' biographers (their granddaughter, María Teresa Arnaud Guzmán, and General Francisco Urquizo), the wedding took place on June 24. However, the wedding invitation contradicts this fact because it says ". . . has the pleasure of inviting you to the ecclesiastical ceremony, which will take place on the twenty-fourth of the present month," and it is dated "Orizaba, July 1908." They were married then in July, not June. This is not the first time that the calendar of their lives gets muddled, and it will not be the last in which time plays tricks on them.

In his manuscript "The Orizaba I Remember," Don Antonio Díaz Meléndez writes that after the religious ceremony "they headed for the Hotel de Francia, where the customary wedding hot chocolate was served."

I have come to learn more about this hotel, which still exists. At that time, I am told, it was the most prestigious social center of the city. Today it is in ruins. The sign that presents it as the Grand Hotel de France has several letters missing, the tiles that cover the walls are falling off, and its fifty-nine rooms are indefinitely closed "for repairs." From its times of splendor, as a memento, there is one guest remaining who suffers from all sorts of minor ailments. A Spaniard who came to Mexico fleeing from the war, he has stayed here ever since, and when the hotel was closed, the management could not get rid of him. He still walks around its balconies, now without railings, and its fountains, dry for some time, while he curses the humidity and his arthritis.

However, in spite of the passing of time and the extensive dilapidation of the Grand Hotel de France, one can still perceive traces of Ramón and Alicia's wedding. They remain imprinted in the spacious hall that was once the dining room, in the midst of the scaffolding that holds the now worm-eaten beams, in the green spots that are taking over the walls, and in whatever remains of the Art Nouveau stained-glass windows, badly in need of restoration. Whenever the wind blows in, the ghosts of that wedding reception seem to be floating around again: white dust clouds come up from the rubble that very well could have been rice showers, icing from the cake, or the bride's veil.

But no. It seems there is some error here, too. In spite of Don Antonio's assertion, it is improbable that their wedding breakfast was held at the hotel. Their granddaughter, for example, says otherwise in her book. She insists that it was held at the home of Alicia's parents.

Seeing Orizaba the way it is now, not as it was then, Ramón and Alicia's bucolic romance seems inconceivable, unreal. I try to visualize them crossing these streets, now riddled with pollution and congested with cars, and stopping on the same sidewalks—narrow, devoid of trees, with open sewers—to greet friends, pay their respects to acquaintances, and smile at strangers. I attempt, but without success, to picture them having tea, solemn and a little smug, in the resounding mediocrity of the two-star Hotel Alvear, recently restored, with its beveled-mirrored lobby, its synthetic plush furniture, and the sign that reads "We accept Diner's Club and American Express."

Pale and old-fashioned Alicia and Ramón, in the mild attempt at a city that is Orizaba today. . . . I don't even want to imagine them—with the Avenida Oriente buses roaring past—discovering in front of TE-CA, the "First Tools Boutique," the modest monument donated five years ago by the Lions Club.

The top part of the monument has the bronze bust of a Mexican officer wearing a Prussian helmet, and on its side is a pathetic little plaque in which the same officer is represented, now at full length, holding by the hand a woman with three children. The five of them are on a wild ocean shore under stormy clouds, all barefoot, their clothes in rags. Below this, on a smaller plaque, they would be aghast to read their own names and to learn about their fatal destiny, just as it appears on the inscription:

Captain Ramón Arnaud Vignon, who,
accompanied by his heroic wife, Alicia Rovira,
a good model of the virtues of Mexican women,
maintained Mexico's sovereignty on the Isle of Passion
until his death on October 7, 1914.

Clipperton, 1917

❦

H. P. PERRIL, CAPTAIN of the American gunboat *Yorktown*, had never ever had anything to do with Clipperton. The place did not intrigue him. Quite the contrary, it inspired in him a deep lack of interest and even an uneasy feeling. Against his will, however, that isle was fated to acquire great importance for him. En route from his naval base in California, and due to a whim of fate, he not only arrived there but did so at the right time. Not a moment too soon, not a moment too late.

He wished to leave a record in his own words of that story, which he considered unique in his long experience at sea and, as he commented to his family after returning to California, he had the impression of "carrying Robinson Crusoe tied to the mast." He meant that the misfortunes of this shipwrecked legendary figure seemed like only the first chapter of those suffered by the Clipperton castaways, which he had been able to see with his own eyes.

When the captain finished writing, he had spent the whole night of July 18, 1917, telling the recent events in exact detail. It had been his lot to become witness and actor, both judge and participant. He stayed awake in his cabin until dawn, writing a long letter to his wife, Charlotte. Once in a while he would pause, absorbed in the metallic coldness of the moon reflecting on the waters. He felt he had to control the turmoil of the day's memories so that he would not allow them to trample his measured and precise prose. "Tonight," he wrote to his wife, "I have something really interesting to tell you."

Twenty-four hours before, he had been sure that on his tedious voyage through Mexican waters only a few routine entries would be made in the ship's log. However, strange things happened. So strange that they touched the heart of the unflappable Captain Perril, and made his hand tremble as he wrote to Charlotte: "It is something I will remember as long as I live. I hope to be able to tell you about it in a way that you and the children can also appreciate."

He wanted to tell his wife the story in every minute detail, but begged her not to read it in haste, because: "In order to develop it in the proper chronological order, I am going to begin with its less important aspects." He did not wish to render chaotic a story already confusing in itself, so he at first avoided broaching the heart of the matter. That would have to wait until later, and he was counting on her patience to last.

Pacific Ocean, 1908

ALICIA GLANCED AT her reflection in the porthole and did not like what she saw. Two days before, when she came on board, her long brown hair was piled high on her head, a hairpiece inside a horizontal curl that framed her face. It was an old-fashioned coiffure, rather too adult for her, that clashed with her girlish face, though she thought otherwise and lamented that the wind had undone it. Her hair fell on her shoulders, disorderly and sticky with sea spray. Dark shadows under her eyes, like the ones she had when she was sick with German measles, darkened her luminous complexion. And her small, perfect features appeared enlarged and distorted in the concave glass of the porthole.

On August 27, a month after the wedding, she and Ramón had boarded for Clipperton on the *Corrigan II*, a large gunboat of the Mexican Navy. In the compartments below deck they had all the paraphernalia necessary to turn that barren isle into a livable place: bags of black topsoil to make a garden and seeds to grow lettuce and other greens; an enormous supply of grain and fruit, including several hundred citrus; tools, rolls of fabric, and a sewing machine; carbines, machetes, and other weapons; a silk Mexican flag, green, white, and red and with the coat of arms embroidered in silver thread by nuns; pigs and chickens; pounds of dried beef from Oaxaca; medications and first-aid manuals; potted plants; coal and other fuels; family portraits and photographs; an Austrian formal sitting room set; wicker rocking chairs from Acapulco; a mandolin; a phonograph and some popular recordings; a set of silver horsehair brushes for Alicia's hair; a pair of canaries in their cage; some delicacies to eat; books and newspapers; and in a leather trunk, carefully packed in mothballs, her wedding dress and its twenty yards of lace train.

Traveling on board with the couple were eleven soldiers, together with their children and camp followers, that would make up the garrison commanded by Arnaud. For all of them, a small, suffocating corner next to the engines had been assigned, where their pallets could fit only when placed one against the other. Before they were stricken by seasickness, they had enclosed themselves in the semidarkness to gamble their last pay on the whims of dice and playing cards.

The camp followers fluttered about the soldiers like anxious hens. Loud-mouthed, sweaty, rough and with unruly manes, they smelled of smoke and female musk. All of them, young and old, seemed to be of the same indecipherable age. With their raspy voices, which sounded like cornets, comic sopranos, or geese, they mingled prayers with blasphemy, and sweet, tender words with cursing and crude language. They elbowed their way and fought over a place to stow the few belongings they had on this earth: some rags and serapes tied up, a metate to grind corn, and a pot to cook beans. They had followed their men—their johns—on board without knowing where they were headed. As usual, they boiled some gunpowder in water and then drank it. This was how they tried to find the courage and the resignation to run around battlefields without thinking of anything else but having their men's food ready as soon as the shooting stopped.

Compared to the hole where the underlings were quartered, the small cabin occupied by the Arnauds was luxurious. It had two bunks, a ewer with its dish and mirror for their personal cleanliness, and they even had some comforts that in a warship are usually the captain's exclusive privilege, such as a coatrack and a desk. At first Alicia was very happy to spend her time there, fixing everything as if it were a dollhouse. Since it was her first ocean voyage, Ramón advised her to take precautions against seasickness, like having only whitefish with no condiments, and drinking *atole* and lemon water. In spite of that, on the third day she overslept and woke up restless, overwhelmed by being locked up in her cabin. Ramón had not been there for hours. She got up quickly and went up to the deck. While climbing the ladder, she was startled to see her distorted reflection in a porthole. She looked awful.

With the early morning light, the sky was so overcast and the horizon seemed so close that she felt she could almost touch it with her hand. Between the sea and the sky, only a narrow strip was left for humans, and there the temperature was that of a steel furnace. All of a sudden the breeze had died, and a few small but viciously choppy waves were rocking the ship mercilessly. An unmistakable smell attacked her nostrils. Acrid and organic. It was vomit. Seasickness had spread like an implacable ritual baptism for the people who had, for the first time, ventured out to sea. Alicia saw soldiers, camp followers, and children wandering about, transparent and ghostly, and in the midst of this sorry spectacle, she heard again, for the hundredth time during that voyage, a childish voice repeating a silly ditty: "Day star of gold, don't let me get cold, during the night, when there is no light, day star of gold . . ."

The hellish heat threatened to crack skulls, as well as the woodwork, making people's heads hum with fever, and making the deck hot enough to fry johnnycakes. However, that child kept singing his ditty all throughout the voyage, "Day star of gold, don't let me get cold," sitting on a bench, his large eyes looking at nowhere in particular, his white piqué sailor hat down to his ears, while he bobbed in the air his little chocolate-colored boots with preposterously long shoelaces.

In the stillness of that sweltering heat, his piercing little songbird voice reached every corner. It was a minimal torture, but sustained like incessant drops of water on a prisoner's head. Alicia wanted to distance herself, but she sat near him as if impelled by a small fatal fascination, and started to review in her mind ways of silencing him. As if it were all-important, as if in that child with his boots and bonnet, exactly in his voice, precisely in the particular timbre of that voice, lay the epicenter of the heat wave, of the collective seasickness, of the suffocating sensation of ill-being. Who were his parents? Where was his father, to pull his ears? Alicia's nerves were raw, her humor prickly, and her thoughts turned to cruel ways in which to silence him. She remembered the nuns at school, Sister Carola and Sister Asunta, who, unexpectedly materializing from the shadows, used to pinch her, and then she felt that pain in her arm, brief like a hen's peck but sharp. She would never do that to this child, but it calmed her nerves to entertain the thought.

Sensing that her system had reached its limits of endurance, Alicia leaned over the guardrail, hoping for an improbable breeze that would take away that nauseous feeling in the pit of her stomach. She then looked at the Pacific Ocean. It was churning, dense and gray, and on her face she felt the warm, soupy vapor. "If I keep looking at it, I will also be undone," she told herself, and turned around so as not to see the spray and the bubbling dark waters. Then she noticed that her husband was only a few feet away.

Captain* Ramón Arnaud of the Mexican Army was bending pitifully overboard, jolted by retching, throwing up the very last yellow remnants in his stomach. He was not a seaman but an army man, a landlubber. Those rough years in a mad rush from one barracks to the other had seasoned him to overcome terrestrial calamities, but he was not prepared to confront the pounding of the ocean. He kept throwing up, though it seemed there was nothing else left, and in each spasm he got to know another dark corner of hell, trying to hold his entrails in but afraid he would be turned inside out like a glove. His drill uniform was soiled and unbuttoned, and his face wet with a cold sweat. His hair, however, held by brilliantine and oblivious to the violent jolts the rest of his body was experiencing, remained in place, perfectly parted in the middle, neat and martial-looking. To her he seemed tidy and elegant in spite of his disheveled appearance, and solemn even in his desolation. His hair is not even ruffled when he throws up, Alicia thought, and her miserable mood dissipated.

At that moment, wondrous gusts of cool wind began sweeping across the deck, brushing against the faces of the bedraggled passengers. That clean air renewed the condition of their lungs and sedated their digestive systems, soothing their death wishes. A seagull flew leisurely over the ship, announcing the proximity of land. As if by magic, the waters became calm, and the ocean, recovering its liquid state, became golden and smooth. The collective intestinal nightmare abated, and the child who sang like a bird became silent.

Men and women lifted their heads and saw it in the distance: before their eyes, white and radiantly barren, was the silhouette of Clipperton Island. It was August 30, 1908.

---

*Actually, Lieutenant Arnaud was not promoted to captain until August 26, 1913 *(Author's note)*.

Clipperton, 1917

ON THE MORNING OF JULY 18, 1917, U.S. Navy captain H. P. Perril saw Clipperton Island for the first and last times. He never came ashore, but he took a very careful look at it from his ship, the *Yorktown*, through his spyglass. He circumnavigated the isle—outside the barrier reef, and at a safe distance from it—exactly in an hour, and confirmed that it was about five miles around. "Clipperton Island," he wrote, "is a dangerous low atoll, approximately 2 miles in diameter."

An atoll is an astonishing formation in the shape of a doughnut, with water in its center and around its perimeter. A ring of land with a lagoon in the center, floating in the middle of the ocean. At some moment in its prehistoric past, Clipperton had been a volcanic mountain surrounded by a powerful crown of coral reefs. The mountain in time sank slowly, and disappeared under the water, and the reef wall was the only thing left above sea level. What had been the crater of a volcano was now a lagoon of brackish waters, effervescent with sulfur coming from the belly of the earth.

The captain goes on: "[The isle] has a promontory 62 feet high on its southwest coast, which at first sight looks like a ship's sail, and on approaching it, like a gigantic castle. This promontory can be seen from a distance of 12 to 15 miles provided there is no fog: then, the promontory and the isle itself can only be seen when it is already at very close range.

"The breakers on its eastern shore do not provide early enough warning for a ship to change course in order to avoid running aground. The isle is surrounded by an uninterrupted coral reef on which the ocean pounds heavily and ceaselessly, sometimes covering the isle. There are sharks swimming around. During the rainy season, waterfalls cascade on its southwestern coast.

"While we were circumnavigating the isle, I saw more seagulls, flying fish, and butterflies than I had ever seen on a similar stretch of coastline," Perril comments, amazed at this place which, lacking any vegetation, no blade of grass to soften the hostility of those rocks, nonetheless abounds in an unusual and alarming proliferation of animal life. "Thousands of birds fly around the island, and the guano deposits are being exploited commercially. A colony was established to operate a phosphate plant some years ago. [. . .] A layer of guano several feet deep covers the isle. There is no doubt that birds have inhabited it for years."

Nine years earlier, and from the deck of another ship, the *Corrigan II*, the Arnauds had viewed, full of expectation, what for them was a promised land. Though that happened long before and they were seeing the isle through glasses of a different color, what they saw could not have been much dissimilar to what the American captain, H. P. Perril, saw when he accidentally approached its shores.

Clipperton, 1968

THERE WAS A BUNCH OF CHILDREN and women watching them from shore. Alicia looked at them from the barge, and they seemed dejected and lonesome in that hot weather. Their tanned skin, dark and dry, withstood the rigors of the sun while the white sun glare bleached out all the colors, already faded, of the scant garments they wore. Boobies, the shore birds, fluttered around them and walked over their feet, and people shooed them away with either strong arm gestures or lazy kicks.

The small, faded universe in front of her eyes reverberated and consumed itself in a slow combustion. Alicia saw how the ocean seemed to explode over the reefs, pounding the rocks, the few sickly coconut palms, and the human beings, then coming to rest on every crevice, hollow, and cranny. The sun lost no time in evaporating the water, and everything was soon covered with a mirrorlike layer of salt, refulgent, blinding. The ocean spray would fall slowly on the people, transforming them into salt statues. It was only in their eyes, in the feverish eagerness in their gaze, that Alicia discovered the great expectations, repressed but fierce, for the boat's arrival.

A few yards ahead of the women, a half-dozen soldiers stood firmly, their heads covered with big straw hats, their drill uniforms battered, their feet in huarache sandals. They also appeared sleepy and blurred, like tin soldiers melting in the sun. They all look like castaways, Alicia thought uneasily. Someday I myself will be watching for the arrival of a boat and will also have an expression on my face like Juan Diego's when the Virgin of Guadalupe appeared to him.

Two masculine figures stood out in the group. One was a youthful man of medium height in uniform and the only one who seemed vital, miraculously fresh in his clean shirt, and the other was a big strong man, radically blond, with a single thick eyebrow extending from one temple to the other without a break in the middle. On a big pole set in a cement base in the midst of everything, a very faded national flag was waving rather reluctantly, as if it were laundry hung out to dry in the wind.

The *Corrigan II* was anchored at a prudent distance from the dangerous reefs surrounding the isle, and passengers and crew were disembarking from flat-bottomed barges. Alicia's first sensation on setting foot on Clipperton was one of annoyance: the land was not firm enough, and her shoes sank into the black-green, sticky guano.

More conscious now of the nauseating vapors coming from the lagoon than of the prophetic vibrations that had jolted her a few moments before, she wrinkled her fine little nose and observed, "The whole thing smells like rotten cabbages."

Suddenly Ramón came out of his mesmerizing seasickness, as if the penetrating smell of cabbages had the same effect on him as did the smelling salts on those who had fainted. Keeping in mind the role he had to play, he regained his natural color, composure, and energy and, with a commanding air, greeted one by one all the members of the reception committee, including the children, with an accompanying firm hand-

shake. He immediately called his men and ordered an improvised ceremony for saluting the flag. His first act as governor would be to replace
the existing flag with the brand-new one embroidered by nuns.

While the soldiers were delayed searching for it among the dozens of
wooden crates they had brought ashore, the Arnauds pulled aside the
young-looking officer and the strong blond man. The first was Lieutenant Secundino Angel Cardona, stationed in Clipperton for over six
months and assigned as Ramón's assistant. With six men under his command, he had come to the island before his superior in order to ready
the necessary installations for the arrival of Alicia and the incoming
troops.

Cardona was a good-looking guy, his hair arranged in the fashion of a
neighborhood bully. His impeccable white teeth produced an open,
frank smile, and not even his slightly prominent ears nor a few pock-
marks managed to detract from his handsome presence.

The blond one was a twenty-eight-year-old German fellow, Gustav
Schultz, who represented the English company exploiting the guano,
the Pacific Phosphate Company Ltd. He had been established in Clipperton for four years, in charge of processing and exporting the product,
and of a number of workers that fluctuated from fifteen, at best, to only
two or three when business was not so good. Beneath his bushy, gruff
eyebrows, his eyes looked gentle. He smiled softly, balancing on his
enormous feet like on a platform, and seemed to expect the newcomer
to make a speech.

Arnaud knew that one of the reasons he had been assigned to Clipperton was his knowledge of several languages. More than for interna-
tional litigation—that was the province of diplomats in Europe—he
would need them for communicating with the representatives of the
guano company and the supervision of their activities in the name of
the Mexican government. He greeted Schultz in strained English, taking
extreme care in his pronunciation.

Schultz's loud laughter interrupted him. Then in an incomprehensible pastiche of German, English, Italian, and Spanish, he mentioned something about palm trees and laughed again with great relish. Disconcerted, Ramón grew silent, and Lieutenant Cardona rushed to explain.

"Do not worry, Captain, nobody understands the blond guy—none of the workers, not even his wife. He lives here surrounded by foreigners. His men are all Italians who have not learned Spanish. He has in his head such a jumble of languages that he is the Tower of Babel personified. But he works hard and keeps good company records. At least we can understand his numbers, and that way we find out what is going on. Every time you see him, he tells the story of those palm trees. He brought them himself, it seems, and then planted them over there." Cardona pointed his index finger at a group of ten or twelve coconut palms, the only trees on the island. Schultz was looking at Cardona and nodding, either in approval of or stunned by what he heard, as if he, too, did not understand anything other people were saying.

The troops finally came up with the flag. Those who had just landed stood in formation next to the soldiers already assembled. One of the new arrivals, no older than fourteen, who had made his living as a mariachi player before signing up, was now the army bugler and made the call to attention.

"Platoon! Fix . . . bayonets!" ordered Arnaud, trying to instill some life into those present.

With dissonant metallic clatter, the bayonets were attached to the muzzles of their rifles. The flag was hoisted, green, white, and red, with the eagle at its center seemingly pecking at the serpent, all shining brightly in the sun. The adolescent bugle boy played the national anthem with surprising elan. In a timid voice, as if breathed in, the others sang, "Think, O dear homeland, that Heaven has sent you a soldier in every son . . ."

Arnaud would have liked to feel moved, but only succeeded in feeling worried. Are these the sons of our homeland? he wondered. They look like a sorry lot. He took a good look around him: about thirty half-naked people, a lot of crabs, a depository of bird droppings, and a large rock. That was all.

This is Mexican land, and I am its governor, he thought, with a creeping feeling between ridicule and pride. It's slim pickings, but still Mexican pickings, as long as I live. Let them send the whole French army if they wish, but nobody will get me out of here. They can torture me, but they will not get me out.

Now he was moved. His eyes welling, he stumbled over the words of a speech appropriate for the occasion, then shouted, "Viva México!" three times. And thus he closed the ceremony of taking territorial possession of Clipperton Island, formerly known as the Isle of Passion. It was over, and after leaving orders for unloading the cargo, Arnaud, together with Cardona, started on a reconnaissance tour. First, they were to take Alicia to her new home, then to inspect the constructions, and, finally, to get together with Schultz at his cabin. He had said good-bye still dwelling on the palm trees story and uttering, from the depths of his throat, the word "drinks" several times.

"He means that he is inviting us for a toast," explained the lieutenant.

They started walking toward the southwest of the island, where the Arnauds were going to reside. On their way, they passed by the sheds used to store the guano, by the workers' quarters, and by the soldiers' barracks. These were flimsy rudimentary structures, barely able to stand and offering scant protection from the elements. All around there were large earthenware jars to collect rainwater, besides garbage, dogs, and a few skinny pigs running after the crabs for a meal.

An air of poverty permeated everything. Alicia was then amazed to see, solitary in the distance, the house that would be her home. It was a wonderful one-story structure in fine varnished pine, with a pitched roof. It faced an open stretch of beach and rested on stilts about five feet above the sands, safe from tides and crabs. There was an ample veranda all around, and, inside, the sunny and airy rooms were interconnected, each with its own access to the veranda. They were all spacious except one, which later became Alicia's favorite refuge. It was a small study next to the master bedroom, with large stained-glass windows in various colors, all facing the ocean.

It was not precisely a mansion, but in the midst of everything else it seemed like a sample of Oriental splendor. There was nothing in the house that was not functional and in good order, nothing left to improvisation: everything had been made with care, to perfection. It had belonged to the preceding representative of the guano company, an Englishman who returned to Europe when the German Gustav Schultz came to replace him. The former owner, Arthur James Brander, was persnickety and a lover of luxury. He had accepted the position from the other side of the planet on condition that he be allowed to take with him a ready-to-assemble house of the best quality, and that the company would also pay for his Filipino servant's fare. The man was a devoted servant who allowed his master to win at chess and who, even in Clipperton, served him his tea with just-baked muffins, promptly at five o'clock.

The Englishman had set the house in the only place on the island where the opaque, gray Pacific Ocean became translucent with underwater glimmerings, and where the unhealthy, suffocating smells from the lagoon were blown away by the breeze from the trade winds. An expert carpenter himself, Brander had complemented the basic structure with details of refinement: built-in bookcases and shelves, carved shutters for the windows. For the veranda facing east, he had brought from Nicaragua a hammock where he would lie, a shot of authentic Scotch whiskey in hand, to watch the sunrise. On the other side, on the corridor facing west, he enjoyed another hammock, another Scotch, and sunsets.

Within an hour, boxes and trunks filled with the Arnauds' paraphernalia invaded the corridors of the Brander house. In the following days Ramón watched, crestfallen, as Alicia toiled with the eagerness of a worker ant and the nimbleness of a squirrel, moving things around and locating them almost anywhere but the places he had so meticulously planned.

She ordered the pots of geraniums to be unloaded where he had thought of constructing a chicken coop; she placed beds and mattresses where he wanted to have the dining room; kept her embroidery and sewing fabrics in the drawers of a desk he had thought his; housed chickens and ducks where he had the toolshed in mind; and stored preserves and marmalades on the shelves he had reserved for medications.

"Please stop for just a minute, honey," he begged her, "and let's have some lime blossom tea, which will soothe us while we put some sense into this pandemonium."

She sat beside him, perspiring, listened to him uneasily, and five minutes later was again on her feet emptying trunks, hanging curtains, planting lettuce. She ordered her Pianola unloaded and placed in one corner, then in another; then she changed her mind and ordered it taken out again.

"You are running around like a chicken without a head, without thinking," Ramón said to her on the third day of seeing her incessant rushing around, not even allowing time to eat or sleep.

"And you think and talk, give opinions and give orders, but you do not *do* anything," she responded, and in this way they opened a discussion that they were to repeat hundreds of times, give or take a few words, during the years they lived together on the isle.

When practically everything was unpacked and they were close to having the house ready, she discovered, together with other pieces of linen in the bottom of the trunk, the saintly bedsheet, the one with the matrimonial keyhole in the center. Far from Orizaba, from Doña Carlota, from the Ten Commandments and the Seven Sacraments, Alicia had completely forgotten about it. Seeing it again made her feel guilty, but at this point, she thought it absurd to start using it, after so many nights without it.

For a moment she thought of giving it to the camp followers, but changed her mind, considering its fine embroidery. In the end she decided to use it in the dining room as a tablecloth for big occasions, placing a heavy pheasant centerpiece to cover the hole.

Clipperton, 1908

AFTER BEING ANCHORED for three days outside the reef barrier and passively allowing the breakers to jolt her at will, the *Corrigan II*, relieved of her cargo, set sail for the return to Acapulco. From the dock, Ramón Arnaud saw her depart. The gentleman's agreement he had made with his superior and advisor, Colonel Avalos, was that every two months, three at the most, without fail or delay, either that ship or *El Demócrata*, also from the Mexican Navy, would bring to Clipperton all the supplies necessary for survival.

It was well established that from such an isle, a lazy, barren piece of rock, they could not get much more than crabs, salt, and polluted water. The arrival of the ship would be like the umbilical cord that would keep them alive. As the *Corrigan II* sailed away, Ramón felt that his only connection with the outside world was drifting farther and farther out of reach, lost behind an ocean wall.

When the ship could no longer be seen, Ramón realized that he felt offended, hurt, abandoned like a dog. His nomination as governor, the promotion to the rank of captain, the interview with Porfirio Díaz, all seemed now like fancy decoys covering up the stark reality: he had been totally forsaken in the last place he would have chosen to be, had he the freedom to choose.

The old feeling that he had been made to pay too dearly for his mistakes returned, and he ran, over and over in his mind like a rat in a maze, through all the twists and turns. That old resentment knew very well all the labyrinths in his gray matter because he himself had trained it each and every day and night during his incarceration in Santiago Tlatelolco. And during every hour of his training as an army private. It was a resentment so close to him, so domestic and familiar, Ramón thought now, that he had not ceased nurturing it for a second. And this truth surprised him.

Since he was a child he had entertained the suspicion that someone, some powerful and abstract being, was cruelly punishing him. And now, at the Clipperton dock, this punishment acquired the shape of an old and lost meaning in the English language, derived from the Spanish. It was a combination of just a few letters, unknown to him until a few days ago and which, notwithstanding—it was very clear now—had been his destiny from the beginning. This word, which sounded cabalistic to him, was "marooned," derived from "cimaroon"—in turn derived from the Spanish *"cimarrón,"* or runaway slave. And by some logical play of association, "to maroon" also referred to the capital punishment meted out to traitors by English pirates in the Caribbean: they abandoned them on a deserted island in the middle of the ocean, with nothing but a few sips of water in a bottle and a gun loaded with only one bullet, to use when the torture and the agony became unbearable.

"Marooned," Arnaud repeated to himself, fascinated by its sound. *"Marooned,"* and a sticky malaise took hold of him. Standing there facing the Pacific Ocean alone, he offered no resistance. A hot wind ruffled his eyelashes, buzzed over his ears, kept flapping on the nape of his neck

the kerchief he was wearing to protect himself from the sun. An endless series of waves, resigned and identical, crashed against the boards under his feet, and he observed them, mesmerized, and let them lull him with their monotonous murmur: *marooned*, they whispered, *marooned*.

He was comfortably installed in his melancholy and without any intention of getting out of it, when he saw Alicia in the distance trying to carry a barrel heavier than she was up the steep steps leading to the house. She would advance two steps and the force of gravity made her go backward three, just to start again, unflaggingly. Ramón thought that the diligence his wife applied to the task at hand was an irrational defiance of the sweltering heat, that her useless doggedness disrupted the relaxing inertia that the heat imposed on everything else. He saw her as being obsessed with her futile endeavor, her porcelain complexion beaded with pearls of sweat, and completely oblivious of the departing ship, of the resentments and premonitions that were asphyxiating him, of the cruelty of the Caribbean pirates and of the human race in general. Why does she persist in not letting the soldiers take care of those tasks? How can she possibly not understand that on a disastrous day like today such things as barrels don't deserve our attention? Ramón wondered anxiously, and ran to help her.

By the time he reached her, she had already succeeded in carrying her load up to the porch.

The days began to go a little faster. Not only had the ship departed, leaving them in God's hands, but two or three hundred yards away from the place where it had been anchored, there still arose, now and forever, the silhouette of the *Kinkora*. Or her ghost. Or whatever was left of her. On a pitch-black night a few years ago, the Japanese ship did not see the isle and fell into its trap, lunging against it as if it wasn't there. Clipperton had lain in wait for her, crouching and invisible, then ensnared her in its reefs and tore into her hull with the sharp fierceness of its corals.

Haunted by the somber, unavoidable presence of the *Kinkora*, through whose dilapidated timbers the wind whistled sad tunes of ship-wrecks, Arnaud decided to dismantle her board by board. He could no longer stand the ominous energy that he perceived as coming from the wreck, which made his head burst and even gave him a toothache. He would remove that grim monument to failure from the coastline and neutralize its influence, and would use whatever he could recover to construct decent living quarters for his soldiers.

As usual, Ramón had suddenly shifted without any warning from a state of depression to one of euphoria, and during the following days he and his men were earnestly dedicated to their task. And from the worm-eaten timbers of the *Kinkora*—once cleaned and sanded—they built a small house for each soldier, with its oil lamp, its coal burner, and its cistern to store rainwater.

While Lieutenant Cardona and the others were in charge of the masonry work and the carpentry, Arnaud tried to solve the problem now annoying him: the crabs, which crawled around everywhere without any respect—not even for the soup pots, the clothes chests, or the babies' cradles—and also fell inside to die in the rainwater tanks, their small corpses polluting the pure waters. Ramón designed traps and fortresses, and after several failed attempts at creating barriers to the thousands of persistent crabs, finally one morning he left the toolshed carrying some ingenious wooden covers with double gratings that attained their purpose.

In spite of the hellish oppressive heat and the ill-tempered breezes, Arnaud and his Clipperton men persisted in their construction frenzy. After the soldiers' houses, they continued with a Decauville track brought from Acapulco. They labored hand in hand with Schultz and his workers, and they managed to make a toylike train, which hauled its row of small, uncovered wagons on a track that extended from the soft mounds of guano on the north of the isle and followed the eastern shore down to the storehouse, where the cargo was dried and processed, next to the dock.

Then came the reconstruction of the lighthouse on top of the big rock on the southern coast. The old one had an obsolete mechanism, already in total disrepair. Arnaud restored it by installing new prisms and burners on the old base. He ordered the construction of six sections of stairs, ten steps each, to civilize the steep ascent to the lighthouse, which had been a suicidal enterprise due to the slippery rock. He filled the tank with oil, and one starry and moonless night, he lit the burners.

Down below, men, women, and children were sitting on the beach in mystical silence around a fire they had built to drive away the mosquitoes. Behind them they had made pavilions with their rifles, leaning them against one another in threes and fours. They saw the big beacon light up and remained there for several hours, staring as if hypnotized at the pallid light as it turned. This was an important occasion. They no longer were a speck lost in the big nothingness. Now they were offering to the world an assertive testimonial: the Clipperton lighthouse, a little candle flickering in the midst of the infinite darkness where ocean and sky merged.

That night, at the foot of the lighted beacon, Lieutenant Arnaud commanded peremptorily that the light never be allowed to grow dark, and right then named one of his trusted men as the lighthouse keeper. He was a black soldier from the state of Colima named Victoriano Alvarez. So that he could attend to his duties with the necessary zeal, Arnaud assigned as his living quarters a small sheltered cabin at the base of the big rock. It was, in fact, a cave inside the rock, and he adapted its interior and added a log-cabin facade. The soldiers called it "the lighthouse lair."

For Victoriano Alvarez, living there meant being isolated from his comrades, but in compensation, the appointment invested him with a special importance, an almost priestly aura. He became the man of the light, the guide to lost ships, the point of contact between Clipperton and what lay beyond.

The following weeks were also filled with hard work. The dock was reinforced, and a saltworks was constructed on the low cliffs so as to keep a permanent source of salt. Pig stalls and chicken coops were built so that the animals would not be running around free. Strict regulations were decreed so that human beings, no matter what their ages, had to use latrines for their physiological needs, unlike before, when people relieved themselves wherever the need arose.

As for feeding the troops, Ramón put an end to the anarchy of each one on his own and established a food store. There, under his strict control and according to family size, proportional rations of corn, beans, chiles, rice, coffee, flour, cereals, and dried beef were distributed. On Saturday mornings the soldiers were paid, and since there were no cantinas for them to get drunk, they had the luxury of buying in the store even items that, given the conditions, could be considered nonessential, such as soap, condiments, and beer. The stealing of supplies, common at the beginning, was curtailed by means of severe punishments imposed by Arnaud, ranging from whipping in the worst cases, to digging ditches under the noonday sun.

Next to the store, Ramón set up a pharmacy with surgical supplies, disinfectants, and remedies. Guided by the medical dictionaries he had brought from the continent, he personally turned apothecary first, then medic after gaining some confidence, and finally, when circumstances demanded it, surgeon. Clipperton offered him the opportunity to act in the profession he had wanted to follow but could not.

During the first months he limited himself to prescribing methylene blue gargles for sore throats, gentian violet for scrapes, magnesium sulfate enemas for stomachaches, ipecacuanha powder as a laxative. He learned that *arandula vertiginosa*, better known as *agua zafia*, was incomparable, if properly administered, to combat heartburn, lack of appetite, and lack of sexual drive as well. However, if the patient ingested more drops than prescribed, he would die in a matter of hours, his lips purple and blistering. Agua zafia came in small blue flasks that Ramón carefully kept under lock and key, given its lethal properties.

If a case presented crab bites or Portuguese man-of-war burns, he ordered that a child be brought to pee on the affected skin. For the common cold, he rubbed hot glycerine on the torso and wrapped it in paper strips. As the glycerine grew cold, it hardened under the paper and the grippe victim had to remain stiff and wrapped up like a mummy for hours. Later he also took care of serious wounds: knife fights among the men who became irascible and desperate in the island prison, or severe blows among the camp followers because of jealousy. In this way, Ramón learned to dispense first aid and got his training for what he had to deal with months later: childbirth, epidemics, and death.

Taking care of the vegetable garden became a ritual. In the middle of the bone-dry Clipperton terrain, the thousand square feet of black, moist soil speckled with green was a mirage. It was weeded and sprinkled with the tenderness granted to a firstborn child, and in the afternoons everybody, even those dedicated to other tasks, stopped by for a while before dusk to watch its progress. They stood in groups, next to the furrows, and voiced their alarm if they saw a worm among the cabbage leaves, or else clapped for the green carrot tops beginning to come out. This daily habit turned the garden into a meeting place serving all the functions of a town's main plaza.

The soldiers spent all their time growing greens, carving chairs, taking care of the pigs, counting bales of guano, while military discipline was reduced to a minimum: close order and salute to the flag at dawn, cleaning of weapons and uniforms, and exercises within the limited space available. The practice of trotting around the isle was discontinued because the broken coral was destroying their boots and huaraches, and there were no replacements. Defense was limited to the rotating guard duty, day and night, at the lighthouse and the brigades of two or three men who made the rounds to patrol the order of the community. All of this troubled Ramón, and he told his assistant, Secundino Angel Cardona.

"Rather than a military outpost, this seems like an artisans' commune."

"Don't worry about it, Captain," Lieutenant Cardona responded, "here the coral reefs are in charge of the true defense. If an enemy ship approaches with intentions of invading, it will soon become firewood against the reefs. If the ship passes that barrier, then we fire at it from the lighthouse until we run out of ammunition, because there isn't very much. If, in spite of all that, the enemy disembarks, we'll engage them in hand-to-hand combat. And if they are too many for us, then the Faceless One will take us out."

"That might sound absurd, but it's really the only possible strategy," Arnaud agreed. "You are right, it's no use fretting any more about it."

And life went on, full and bearable enough, within that penny-sized universe. The tremendous amount of work rendered results, and the people's measure of well-being lay in simple things. The inhabited part of the isle did not look either like a slum or like a mound of bird droppings, and the first harvest of the vegetable garden was celebrated with a large salad shared by all. It consisted of lettuce, onions, radishes, and turnips, and Arnaud himself prepared a dressing of mayonnaise, the recipe for which he had inherited from Doña Carlota.

They carried on a routine in imitation of the civilized world, and the resulting peaceful monotony mimicked happiness. Only one expectation, one faith, united all the inhabitants: the arrival of the ship. Two months had gone by since their ship had weighed anchor, and there were no signs of its return. There was still no real cause for alarm because the schedule allowed for another month's leeway.

One afternoon, while they were straightening accounts in Gustav Schultz's cabin, he made one of his indecipherable statements, in the middle of which Arnaud picked up with total clarity a name that gave him goose pimples: that of Robinson Crusoe.

"Tell the German gentleman we do not welcome idle comparisons," he told Lieutenant Cardona, so that he, making faces and gestures, would explain it to Schultz. "The only things that man had when he came to his island were a knife, a pipe, and a tin of tobacco, while we have more comforts here than the Queen of Sheba."

"And that is not all," he added without an iota of conviction but with an evident aggressiveness that altered his voice. "Tell him also not to forget that, unlike Crusoe, we are here of our own free will."

Secundino Cardona did not understand why his superior had taken Schultz's comments so much to heart.

Clipperton, 1908

OCTOBER CAME BUT the ship did not. Instead, devastating rains threatened to erase Clipperton's precarious existence. During the heaviest storms, the ocean waters flooded the lowlands on the island for hours or days at a time, while the highlands became isolated promontories.

Because of the rain, all military operations and most communal tasks were suspended, and everybody retreated home to hibernate. Water was closing in on them from the sky and from the sea. The lagoon was overflowing and smelled like rotting skunks. The moth larvae were fat and even nested in people's hair. The remedy was to sleep between damp sheets, but the humidity made one's skin wrinkly like raisins.

During the time of forced seclusion, Ramón divided his working hours between the feverish reading of a series of books on the pirate Clipperton that he had found in the library abandoned by Brander, and writing his long, detailed reports, which no one was ever likely to read, about the production of guano and about how he was carrying out his mission on the isle.

Meanwhile, Alicia embroidered dozens of beautiful bedsheets and tablecloths that would never be used, since they had enough to last them till the end of their days. She used to sit on a wicker rocking chair by the stained-glass window in the studio next to her bedroom. While her expert fingers moved fast by themselves, time flitted by as she looked at the stormy waters turned icy through the blue-colored glass: frenzied through yellow; slow, almost dead calm, through green; nocturnal and not of this world through violet.

Ramón became obsessed with the notion that their isolation and the lack of any news from Orizaba was dampening his wife's spirits. His own, though he would not admit it, were lost in the deep. It tortured him to remember the good life they had left behind, and he was beginning to think of it with heavy nostalgia as a thing of the past. Not the big things but the smaller ones tormented him the most: things he had considered insignificant before that now seemed unattainable dreams and gnawed at his heart like persistent little rodents. Such as the smell of clothes just washed clean and hung out to dry in the sun or the pleasure of smoking a good Havana cigar, the precise, cold sensation of the Solingen blade on his cheek when shaving, the fresh coolness of drinking in the shade a glass of tamarind water; the sound of his mother's voice telling stories about Emperor Maximilian's marital infidelities and about Empress Carlota's fridgity.

One day Captain Arnaud, unable to contain himself any longer, burst into a rage in Alicia's presence, nonstop until all his bitter litany came out.

"We cannot keep thinking that life is somewhere else, or that we have already lived and the only thing we have left is to reminisce. There must be more to life than watching the rain fall. I'll be dammed if I have to continue watching water and more water come down, and keep waiting for a boat that never comes, and counting every last grain of rice that everybody gets to eat. Or fighting an enemy that never shows up, and writing reports about bird shit. It's one thing to fulfill one's military duty and another one to be expected to do without like a Mormon. Or like an idiot. A man has the right to do well for himself, damn it. He has the right to have fun, to be doing something he really likes once in a while: to eat his fill, to get rowdy, get drunk. . . . Just to talk to friends already seems like a luxury! I want to be able to talk to people again, even to that German S.O.B., though I can't understand him at all!"

Then, as if it were his only possible escape valve, Ramón created and established the Friday soirées. In these weekly evening gatherings held at his home, he attempted to recover, even though artificially and for only a while every week, some of his lost sense of well-being. His guests were Lieutenant Cardona and his wife, Tirsa Rendón, a gorgeous brunette with almond eyes and uncompromising character. And Gustav Schultz and his adopted family, a full-figured mulatto woman called Daria Pinzón—whom the German, in need of a woman after spending a year alone in Clipperton, had brought from the island of Socorro—and Daria's daughter, a twelve-year-old girl, taciturn and strangely sexless, whose given name was Jesusa and her last name, inherited from someone nobody knew, was Lacursa.

Counter to their Franciscan restraint during the rest of the week, on Fridays they would prepare mole in tremendous quantities, tacos *huitlacoche*, refried black beans, sausages, dried beef, and dark coffee. While the others savored every bite as if it were their last, Schultz gobbled everything up, his eyes closed: according to what they believed to have understood, he had said that one had to be Mexican to be able to eat so much food that was black. Ramón Arnaud could never forgive him for this.

After dinner on those evenings, Arnaud took out his mandolin. Alicia would have preferred he played the guitar instead, or any other instrument. The mandolin seemed rather feminine, with its mother-of-pearl inlays and its high pitch, and with so many tuning pegs and fancy curlicues that it seemed ridiculous to her. But Ramón paid no attention and played with the verve of a Cossack taming a wild horse and the absorption of a virtuoso violinist on his first Stradivarius.

Lieutenant Cardona sang afterward and pleased Alicia with songs that had been popular in the dance halls of the capital, such as "White Kitten" and the one about picking violets at twilight.

Cardona produced a velvet tone, enchanting and seductive, going from bass to tenor as he warmed himself up with alcohol. Drinking gave his eyes a strange glimmer and his voice the mature, ladies' man timbre of a veritable Don Juan, or a life-of-the-party professional. He set aside the trills and tricks, the white kittens, violets, and dance halls in the capital, and brought forth a full-throated deluge of totally plebeian, coarse tunes. Such as the one about the unhappy Empress of Mexico, who returned to Europe after losing her crown and her wits: "The rabble with the crosses scream and get excited, while the gale winds blow, and make your boat capsize: Mama Carlota, sweet darling, good-bye, good-bye."

Accompanied by the strings of the Pianola, they danced polkas, waltzes, *danzones* and *jarabes*, and by dawn they started playing Parcheesi, dominoes, or cards, all of which ended in screams after it became clear that Daria Pinzón had been cheating.

The Friday festivities became a ritual, religiously observed even on the day a hurricane plucked the Pianola from its corner and smacked it against the rocks, and made the mandolin spin together with the coconuts, the chickens, and some chunks of wood, finally leaving it floating on the ocean.

But that was later. Now, and contrary to Ramón's fears, his wife looked happier every day. Not because of the evening gatherings. What had happened, thanks to the rains, was that Alicia found herself in a world of ideal solitude, meticulously shared with Ramón within the complicity of the four walls of their home. In the midst of all their deprivations, Clipperton allowed something Orizaba would surely have denied them: the opportunity of becoming great friends and lovers.

In Clipperton they had the time and intimacy necessary to master the art of making love to each other, and after many failures and misunderstandings, they deciphered the exact science of mutual pleasure. They managed together to temper the chaos of their impulses to the rhythm of their hearts, softened their granite morals, got used to their nakedness, became more skilled and less timid, prayed less and laughed more. "Oh Lord, don't allow me to enjoy this! Oh Lord, please, don't allow me to enjoy this," Alicia uselessly prayed when she felt an electric, inevitable wave of happiness that jolted her body.

Protected by the thick curtains of rainfall, they celebrated the daily lovemaking ritual in a postcard atmosphere, in the hammock of the western balcony, bathed in the golden reflections of many sunsets.

The lack of supplies—due to the delay in the arrival of the ship—imposed on their bodies physical transformations that exerted a favorable influence on this burst of passion. One of the first items that ran out in Clipperton was brilliantine, which forced Ramón to forgo the rigid coif that made him look like a ventriloquist's doll and set free his thin, stiff mustache, which became thick and sensual. Besides, far away from the imperial banquets Doña Carlota had served him, his double chin disappeared as well as the incipient belly that was starting to give him a rounded figure.

For her part, Alicia ran out of rice talcum powder, and once she stopped using it, her translucent doll-like complexion took on a more human texture. She abandoned the mannequin stiffness, the rigidity of the corset and the crinolines, and her dainty silhouette recovered the childlike elasticity she had left behind in the hills of Orizaba. She lost one by one all of her hairpins until she had to renounce her old-fashioned tight buns and let her hair loose and free like a lion's mane.

The hot sun of the preceding months had changed the ghostly paleness of their bodies into a healthier-looking tan. And once they used up the last drop of milk of magnesia, which applied to their underarms sweetened the humors of their armpits, they discovered the attraction of their natural animal odors.

This was also the time that Alicia remembered later as the happiest of her life, when she and Ramón engaged day after day in an interminable conversation, continued compulsively for many years. Not even Ramón's death interrupted it, since Alicia would repeat it afterward all by herself, saying her part of the dialogue and repeating the answers that he had given her, which she knew by heart.

In this infinite dialogue that coiled upon itself like a snake, or a figure eight, they used to recite with all the inflections, all the intense feelings, all the upsets, the reasons and demands of their love, in counterpoint or in a duet. They made an inventory of all the good and all the bad traits of each and every person they knew; they would draw and erase future projects; they reviewed the commonplace and probed the transcendental; they evaluated past and present moments of their lives in this world and confessed to each other their fears and expectations about the one beyond.

Sometimes, in the middle of the lull brought by an afternoon downpour, any careless remark could trigger a conjugal fight. As when Alicia commented that Doña Carlota had wasted the Arnaud fortune, or when Ramón suggested that Don Félix Rovira was a domineering, possessive father. Then they stopped holding hands, and heatedly released an angry stream of words that would take them, without their knowing exactly when, to a point at which, viciously trying to hurt, they screamed their imperfections at each other, showing the animosity of two fighting cocks. Invariably, it all ended with an explosion of accumulated and festering pockets of jealousy that each of them had stored, without ever admitting it, in some corner of their livers.

Ramón accused her of swooning over Lieutenant Cardona's singing on Friday evenings.

"Do you think I don't notice that you prefer to dance the polkas with him?" he asked her with an indignation befitting someone who is demanding an explanation from his aged mother's murderer.

Alicia swore to God that it wasn't true, saying she recognized that Cardona did indeed sing and dance like an angel, but that did not mean anything. Ramón was the only man in her life, she purred, cuddling next to him, soft and loving like a cat, and suddenly, if Ramón was still offended and indifferent, the kitten became a tigress. Her eyes shone with rage, and she practically spit her words through clenched teeth.

"And what about you and that good-for-nothing Pinzón woman?"—she was referring to Schultz's lover—"Why can't you take your eyes off her bottom when she stops by the infirmary to meet with you alone, on the ridiculous pretext of asking you for a remedy for her headaches?"

"It is no pretext, the poor woman suffers from terrible migraines, and besides, her ass does not interest me," Ramón countered. He was playing kitten now, and Alicia was the one showing indifference.

And in this way the perfect harmony they had achieved before their argument was crushed to smithereens, and their eternal love was scattered on the floor, their lives destroyed, riddled with discontent. Alicia ran to the bedroom to cry her eyes out, and Ramón locked himself up in his office. When they grew tired of ruminating in spite and of flagellating themselves with jealousy, when their anger came down like the foam of boiling milk after it is removed from the fire, they found some excuse to meet again, to embrace with the absolute happiness of reconciliation, and without more ado, without transitions or logical reasoning, order was restored, and their hurt feelings disappeared somewhere as if they had never existed, and everything returned to the way it was before.

As a reminder of their tragic moments, there were Alicia's swollen eyelids, which Ramón tended to by applying tea compresses. Life went on until another placid afternoon, a few weeks later, when a loose comment would again trigger a conjugal fight, copious like the rain, and thus fulfill its decisive and definite function of restoring their faded emotions and sparkling their dialogue, which was so endless that otherwise it would have to repeat itself like the piano roll of "White Kitten" in her Pianola.

The effect of so much isolation was soon felt. The calendar became a useless object in the unchanging Clipperton time, and for Alicia the notion of dates had dissipated. Monday was the same as Thursday or Sunday, and there was no difference between September and October or November. At the beginning of December, however, she realized that for a long time she had not needed to wash the linen used for her menstrual flow, and when she looked at herself in the mirror, she saw that her waist was gone.

News of the pregnancy made Ramón unreasonably anxious about the delay, already incomprehensible by then, in the arrival of the ship. December marked the fourth month since they had been forsaken on the isle, and there was no excuse for this. It was in blatant disagreement with any arrangement made. The rains had eroded the garden soil, and the shortage of greens and citrus fruit began to be felt. He was afraid they would all soon be suffering from a terrible disease, the one that attacked seamen and shipwrecked sailors, and about which he had informed himself in the medical books: scurvy. He did not want to cause panic needlessly, and he did not say a word about it, but while he spoke with anyone, he surreptitiously tried to take a look at their gums to see if they were blackened, which would be the first signal.

But above all, Ramón was tormented by the idea that his wife could have complications at the time of delivery and that they might not be able to resolve them due to the isolation from the continent. In the delirium of his frequent sleepless nights, he obsessed about being marooned on the island and about having a wild creature born to them. The only things that assuaged his throbbing anguish were their sessions of lovemaking, which had not been interrupted, and the certainty, grow-ing in him as he kept reading and rereading all the documents about Clipperton, that a fabulous treasure had been abandoned by the pirate somewhere on the atoll, which had to be, Arnaud concluded, in the la-goon or in the big rock to the south.

In spite of these reassuring ideas, people noticed his lost serenity when he developed a nervous tic that curled his lips on the left side, which became progressively more obvious and frequent, and eventually accompanied by a quick blinking of his eye on the same side.

"Stop making so many faces, things are not yet a matter of life and death," Alicia kept telling him. "The stupid ship will come."

Finally while they were talking in the studio one afternoon, through the yellow, red, and violet stained-glass windows, they saw Cardona's wife, Tirsa Rendón, coming by. She was dripping wet and screaming that a ship was approaching. They all ran to the dock, where they stood un-der bursts of rain, their palpitating hearts in their throats, and waited until the approaching blurred silhouette took shape among the raging waves.

It was neither *El Demócrata* nor the *Corrigan II*, but the ship from the American guano company, coming for its annual visit to pick up the product. It brought exquisite gifts from Brander to Schultz, his succes-sor in the post: bottles of French champagne, Amaretto di Saronno, boxes of dates, olive oil from Seville, jars of maraschino cherries, and canned Danish ham.

But it also brought them news that dealt a heavy blow to their thin hopes: the Pacific Phosphate Company Ltd. was no longer much inter-ested in Clipperton. They had found unexploited and abundant guano deposits on islands that were closer and presented a less risky approach. Therefore, they announced that they were cutting down the frequency of their trips to the atoll but were asking Schultz to stay there a few more months as holder of their concession, until the definite closing of the plant and his transfer to another one.

From Schultz's throat surged a long series of incomprehensible obscenities, and Ramón's facial tic increased in frequency to two or three incidents per second.

Clipperton Island, 1705

◆

THIS WAS NOT its name yet. At the beginning of the eighteenth century, people believed this island had no name because it did not deserve to have one. Only those well versed in maritime routes and cartography knew that Magellan had sailed close to it and given it the sonorous but desolate name of Isle of Passion.

In 1705 the English corsair John Clipperton landed on it for the first time. Some say that his vessel, the *Five Ports*, did not fly the usual pirate's black flag with skull and crossbones, but always proudly flew a vermilion flag with a winged wild boar. Whether the boar was alate or rampant, or both, nobody knows for sure.

Miraculously, he managed to dodge the isle's surrounding reefs, which had destroyed—and will destroy for centuries to come—so many other vessels. Some people say it was because the isle recognized the flag of the man who was to become its master and bowed down, allowing him safe passage. Others say that the explanation lies in the shape of his vessel, sleek and swift, narrow in the beam, and with low draft and freeboards.

One fact is undisputed: the name of his vessel, the *Five Ports*, honored the ancient brotherhood of buccaneers to which he belonged: the Cinque Ports (Hastings, Romney, Hythe, Dover, and Sandwich, old bastions on England's southern shores). The rebirth of piracy in America, now at the expense of the Spanish galleons, had also revived the confederation and its ilk—the Shore Brotherhood, or the Beggars of the Sea—in order to protect the Turtle Island corsairs.

Captain John Clipperton sighted the atoll that today bears his name one good day while navigating through uncharted waters far from the common sailing routes. The story is told that he was looking for a place, a sandbank or rock out of the water, in order to abandon and punish with death a member of his crew considered a traitor because he had violated the oath of strict obedience. "Maroon!" was the unanimous demand of the *Five Ports* crew in punishment for his guilt, and marooned he would be: the law of the sea would be carried out.

Clipperton, cruel and notorious for his drastic sanctions, spotted the silhouette of the atoll, which he had never explored, and gave out orders to approach it and to prepare the condemned man. It is rumored that showing a slave trader's mercy and a murderer's humor, Clipperton said a few sarcastic words of consolation to the wretched man and handed him—as prescribed by maroon law—a bottle of drinking water and a gun with a single bullet.

But in crossing over the reefs and looking closely at the coastline, Clipperton found much more than he was looking for. He discovered the ideal place, not to cast out a traitor but to find refuge for himself. It was the perfect hideout.

Treatises on the pirate world indicate that a buccaneer feels no attachment to his ship. He can bare it of all wood carvings, of luxurious furnishings, of anything that increases weight and decreases speed, since what he needs is a swift and seaworthy vessel, efficient in the assault of his victims. A buccaneer is willing to get rid of his ship without any sentimentality, and to replace it any time he captures a better one.

It's not the same with his lair. On inhabited and regulated lands the pirate is merely a fugitive, a criminal who ends up losing his freedom and his life. So when he finds a piece of land belonging to no one, where he can establish the same dominion he enjoys on the high seas, he keeps it to himself, and loves it fiercely. He feels a very vital connection to his hiding place.

Henri Keppel, a shrewd pirate hunter, knew what he was talking about when he said that the lawless men of the sea, just like spiders, are found in the nooks and crannies. And Clipperton Island was full of them: it was an isolated corner of the world providing the right protection for spiders and pirates.

John Clipperton made a quick decision as soon as he saw the atoll: it would be his hideout. Remote and hostile, it was surrounded by sharp coral reefs like fangs that would make a breach in the hull of any other vessel that dared come close enough, while he and his men could camouflage their presence along its many bays.

Nobody would find him there, nobody would even look for him there. So he established his shadowy domain and called it Clipperton Island. Not to give it his name, but to declare his act of possession. The island belonging to John Clipperton, buccaneer and rebel, solitary prowler with lots of raw courage, very few loves, and no faith. Perhaps he never learned that the place had already been named the Isle of Passion, or if he did, he probably thought it sounded too romantically Iberian and disregarded the fact.

Another characteristic made this atoll the right place for him: its location. It is well documented that for years John Clipperton had centered his efforts on a desirable target: the Chinese fleet also known as the La Plata Fleet. Its galleons were loaded with three hundred tons of precious merchandise being transported from Manila to Acapulco. And then another three hundred tons on the return crossing from Acapulco to Manila, following the route Friar Andrés de Urdaneta had discovered, which, unbeknownst to him, passed within a few miles of the Isle of Passion.

On their outbound voyage, the China Fleet carried damask, woven fabrics, muslin, stockings, and Spanish shawls, dishes of fine Ching dynasty porcelain, tea, cinnamon, clover, pepper, nutmeg, saffron, lacquer, and folding screens. On the return voyage—when the ocean currents brought the ships closer to the isle—they carried gold bars and silver and gold ornaments as well as coffee, cacao and vanilla beans, sugar, cochineal, tobacco, aniline blue, sisal, flannel, and straw hats. Sometimes there were kidnappable passengers—high officials, friars, noble ladies, military officers—whose ransom could be a negotiated from Turtle Island.

To attack a Chinese *nao* was a dangerous adventure. For protection against corsair raids, each fleet was composed of four ships—two galleons and two tenders—all with dual capabilities as freighters or warships, armed to the teeth, including an assigned artilleryman for each copper cannon and an arsenal for the crew. To board such ships was an endeavor for suicides. Or for experts, like Captain John Clipperton.

Holed up in his lookout, chewing American tobacco and hawking up bitter spittle, Clipperton would wait tensely for days and nights. When he smelled the right moment—it was said he could whiff the air and detect the presence of precious metals several leagues away—he rushed to intercept the convoy and board the ships.

His island always welcomed him on his return from an assault, and he sometimes sought refuge on its black sand beaches, overwhelmed and physically wounded, his ship badly battered and his crew decimated. At other times, his return was accompanied by howls of victory, with the *Five Ports* lumbering in, overburdened by the weight of his booty. Once the cargo was unloaded, the orgy of apportioning the treasure floated down rivers of alcohol. Meticulously fair in this, Clipperton distributed the gold pieces equally among all his men, himself included, and reserved as the captain's due only the best piece of gold jewelry in the lot. He used to favor heavy Baroque chalices encrusted with precious stones. More than for their value, he chose them to enhance his pleasure as he committed the sacrilege of using them to drink his favorite mixture of coconut milk and rum from the Antilles.

Over their tatters eaten away by the surf and salt spray that also roughened their skins, these sea wolves from Clipperton donned the silk blousons and the damask jackets they had peeled off their victims. They wore too many periwigs and too much perfume, too much jewelry and lace, and thus bedecked, resembling Easter Sunday altars, they started their celebrations.

Only rarely did they bring women from the continent, kidnapped from prisons, orphanages, or brothels. These were mostly beastly whores, covered with lice, who ministered to them without any tenderness, but after all the frolicking was over—by dawn the next day they had mellowed with homesickness—they gave off a tepid maternal warmth that lulled and consoled the men.

Most often the feasts were for men only. They played a pistol game, first covering all windows and sealing any cracks in a room to create total darkness. A man would then sit in the center of the floor and place two pistols in front of him. The others would trample one another blindly, seeking a space to crouch in a protected corner. Someone gave the signal and the man in the middle took the pistols, crossed his arms, and shot. Not until the next light of day did they find out who had died.

Enough victuals were laid out, and the men gobbled up pork, fowl, turtle. They drank until they burst, and in the nebulae of their savage, childish bouts with alcohol, they threw food and poured wine on one another, laughed, pulled each other's ears, pinched and pricked with their daggers, vomited, sobbed, fell into pools of their own urine and slept there. The next day, Clipperton Island would see them wake up battered and foul-smelling, their throats dry, and walk around on the beaches, overcome by the lasting melancholy that usually follows such brutal excesses of merriment.

Of all the loot they had hauled, there is now only the memory. Of all the gold that John Clipperton and his pirates took to their island hideout, nothing remains. Nobody left buried treasure, because to save money and increase one's fortune is of no concern to men who are amazed each day to find themselves alive.

None of them was patient enough or eager enough to accumulate wealth, least of all John Clipperton, a show-off, gambler, and spendthrift who prided himself on having wasted, coin by coin and without any regrets, an immense fortune.

The inhabitants of Tortuga would attest to that, since one morning they saw him land his *Five Ports* loaded with gold ingots, hostages, and sacks of goods; they saw him negotiate everything that same day for fabulous sums of money; they saw him that evening strutting in the local taverns and bawdy houses, where he threw money away right and left, boasted of being a cardsharp, and bragged about money spent on reveling and on alms. And at dawn they saw him lying in a dark corner, in a happy drunken stupor, while a badly mutilated beggar removed from his purse the last few coins, final vestiges of his prodigious loot.

Clipperton, 1908–1969

THAT CHRISTMAS WAS a silent one in Clipperton. After dusk on New Year's Eve, torrents seemed to break the sky open, and when the waters fell on the isle, the people, already taciturn, went early to bed and covered their heads in order to keep from being blinded by the glare of the relentless lightning flashes. At the Arnauds' home the usual Friday guests had gathered, feasting on the delicacies and spirits Brander had sent them. But the midnight toasts were laconic and the embraces tearful: the ship that was not coming and the feeling of abandonment weighed too heavily on their souls.

The true celebration was on the second day of January, the day *El Demócrata* finally arrived with supplies, relief personnel, bags of topsoil for their green garden, letters from relatives, and news from Mexico. The forty-four adults and children who at that moment were the entire Clipperton population joined the captain, nineteen sailors, and six passengers of *El Demócrata* to eat, dance, and drink all night, gathered in an empty guano storehouse.

Ramón, eager to have news from Mexico, pulled aside the ship's captain, Diógenes Mayorga, and the man reeled off a long string of bureaucratic excuses for his delay in arriving at the isle. Then his expression acquired a pained, sad look.

"Things in the country are turning ugly," he said.

He told how Don Porfirio Díaz—eighty years old and thirty years in power—was getting ready for his sixth reelection, and how his enemies were suddenly coming forth out of nowhere. They called themselves "anti-reelectionists" and the name of their leader was Madero. Francisco Madero.

"This Madero is a short man with a goatee, the heir of one of the five largest fortunes in the country. The Porfirio followers call him "the loony man" because he is devoted to spiritualism and astrology. He believes himself to be a medium and speaks with spirits. What I am telling you is that he might be crazy, but he is still dangerous, because he has the Indians all excited with the slogan that we have had enough of Porfirio and his tyranny."

"And he talks to spirits?" asked Ramón in disbelief, his eyes round and wide open.

"That's what they say, Governor. That he communicates daily with his kid brother, Raúl is his name, a little angel that burned himself to death with a kerosene lamp. People who know say that little Raúl's spirit has possessed his brother Francisco and that he dictates what Francisco is to do; that in spite of being an innocent soul, he knows a lot about politics; and that because he died with so much suffering, he must have become a visionary in his other life. They say that Madero does exactly whatever his dear brother's spirit demands. And what do you think he's asking for? Well, he wants his brother to give up drinking and smoking, to distribute his fortune among the poor, to cure the sick, to observe carnal abstinence. . . . And Francisco Madero is doing all that."

"Instead of a troublemaker, that Madero sounds more like a saint to me," commented Arnaud. "How could a man like that cause any harm?"

"Well, so far so good. The trouble is that the spirit of the little dead one became revolutionary: the word is that he ordered his brother to devote himself to the campaign against Porfirio's reelection. Madero, who does not dare to disobey the child because of his supernatural powers, followed his instructions and wrote an incendiary book that is selling like hotcakes."

Arnaud was listening in silence and the captain of *El Demócrata* continued without taking a breath, scrambling his words one on top of the other. He said that Madero's book called for sabotaging the reelection the following year, and he was sure of this because he had read it himself. And that the book urged the founding of a party to oppose the president.

"I assure you, Governor, that this damned party has many members already. The disgruntled, those with a chip on their shoulder, the ungrateful ones, all follow him. Francisco Madero has turned into the leader of those who believe that thirty years in power is enough, and that at eighty Don Porfirio is ready to wear the wooden suit rather than the presidential sash."

Distressed about the amazing news but unable to wholly believe it, Ramón left the celebration, which had just begun, and walked in darkness all the way to his office.

On the way he met a group of his men, all huddled under the light of a candle to read the letters their relatives had sent.

"What news did you get from home, soldier?"

"Nothing but bad news, Captain. My mother is sick, and she is all alone now because my brothers decided to join the insurgents."

"And what about you, Corporal?"

"About the same, sir. My uncle says the peons in the hacienda where he works also want to leave and join the rebels. And maybe he will also join them."

Arnaud locked himself up in his office and lighted the kerosene lamp. He wanted to read the newspapers and magazines that his superior, Colonel Avalos, had selected and sent on *El Demócrata*. He devoured every issue of *El Imparcial,* page by page, looking for clues of the discontent, for indicators of the national commotion, traces of the opponents of the "reelectionists" or of Madero and his little brother. He found not a word. Not even a hint of their existence. All the news was about the inauguration of another new bridge or another new segment of railroad track, or the receptions honoring this or that foreign ambassador, or about the decoration bestowed upon Don Porfirio by the Emperor of Japan.

Arnaud had to double-check the dates to make sure he had not been sent newspapers from a year or two ago. No, they were all recent, not even two months old. However, it seemed to him he had read those exact words many times before. The only novelties he found, and he clipped them for his archives, were an extensive article about the influence of cold weather on the Russian character, another one on anthills, and, lastly, an article about botanical science in Manchuria.

He walked back, with long strides, to the party in the storehouse, mixed with the people, played his mandolin with more zest than ever, and danced out of step as usual. When Alicia approached him to inquire why he was so euphoric, he surprised her with an answer that sounded rather like a harangue.

"There is nothing going on in Mexico. Everything is fine and dandy. If Captain Mayorga says otherwise, then he must be the one who is raving, the one who is loony. That old Porfirio will not be toppled from his throne, not even with dynamite. And as long as he keeps his post, I will keep mine. The old fox might be very old, but he's still very foxy, and he can swallow all of them whole. He can withstand six, ten, twelve reelections. This Francisco Madero is plain humbug!"

The last storm had come on New Year's Eve. Then, after the electricity dissipated and the hysterical rains subsided, the winter skies, which had hung over Clipperton asphyxiating it like a cardboard ceiling, lifted and the azure reappeared, rising higher and higher.

After the arrival of the ship, and under the vibrant January sun, Clipperton came back to life, and its residents emerged as if roused from a heavy, humid siesta. There was again a flurry of activity in every corner of the isle.

Gustav Schultz made his employees double their workload, while he tripled his own. He repaired all the damage the rains had caused to the Decauville train tracks, filled the empty storehouses with tons of guano, and made a clean copy of his accounting records. In two weeks he had everything working again like a Swiss watch. He behaved as if he had never received orders from his company to start dismantling all installations, or as if he had misinterpreted them to mean just the opposite: that Clipperton was their future key location. Nobody questioned his actions since, as a given, no one expected to understand his reply. Alicia, however, thought she understood.

"Schultz, in his way, is reacting in the same way as all of us," she told Ramón. "He simply does not want to recognize that everything he has accomplished here is a complete waste."

The obsession with finding the Clipperton treasure took hold of Arnaud's body and soul, and he, in turn, infused his delirium into Cardona and the rest of the men in the garrison. They decided to begin their search in the lagoon, and for that purpose they improvised a diver's suit and fixed, as best they could, a damaged deep-sea diver's headgear given them by the captain of *El Demócrata*. Cutting through the timeless waters, they descended into a dark, elusive world where they experienced the sensation of burying themselves alive. They had always thought there were no fish in the lagoon: nobody had ever fished there. However, in the deepest zone they could see ancient, timid creatures, the size of seals and armor-plated with thick scales, lying in wait in the grottoes or seeking protection behind clouds of volcanic lime. The men were convinced that the monsters, the only inhabitants familiar with these depths, could lead the divers to the place where the treasure was hidden, and more than once trying to follow them, they got stuck in the underwater rock labyrinths.

After a couple of months, they had to knock off their project. They had found nothing more than crumbling old detritus, and even though they obstinately persisted in their search, they could not continue because the strong salt and sulfurous acid concentration was burning their eyes and eating away their skin. Neither the deep-sea diving headgear nor the improvised diver's suit had given them enough protection against these malodorous waters, powerful enough to corrode anything that touched them.

They abandoned the lagoon but continued the exploration of the big rock on the southern shore of the isle. They climbed to the top, holding on to the sharp-edged ridges along its sides, and explored all its caves and crevices. They discovered that the big rock was hollow the day they found a hole near the top. At first they thought it was a lair, but it proved to be the entrance to its great interior space. With the help of ropes, they dropped down inside the cave, convinced they had at last found the place where Clipperton the pirate had hidden his treasure.

From the top opening, a cone of sunlight penetrated the interior, interrupted from every direction by thousands of bats in blind flight. In all the surrounding darkness there was a bitter, sticky smell like the musk

of a caged animal, secreted by the glands of the bats or by the amor-
phous mass of fat toads huddled on top of one another in the background. In this exceedingly compressed kingdom of small black
animals, the silence was so overpowering that it produced a ringing in
the ears. In this spot, neither a puff of wind nor the sound of the sea
could reach them.

While gold fever made the men search for jewels and ancient coins
even in the toad's bellies, the women, brandishing brooms, mops,
feather dusters, brushes, bottles of lye, and pieces of soap, were busy
cleaning up the tidal debris brought in by the storms. In spite of being
pregnant, Alicia was at the head of the cleaning brigades and more energetic than ever.

She did not suffer from morning sickness, nor was she sleepy or de-
pressed. The whims of her pregnancy took into account the prevailing
limitations of their isle: she could feel compelled to drink coconut milk
at any hour, and she enjoyed being alone for long periods of time in the
least hostile cove of the beach, sitting at the shore and feeling the tame
waves caressing her belly after crashing against the rocks and turning
into white foam.

Doña Juana, the midwife, had already performed the needle test, the
tape measure test, and the cup of coffee test, and, according to all of
them, the baby was a girl. Ramón was saying the same thing, based on
what his medical books stated as to the size and height of her pregnant
belly.

Against all evidence, Alicia was convinced otherwise. As if she could
see inside herself, she knew it was a boy. She knew even more: the exact
color of his eyes and hair, and the perfectly round shape of his head. She
was sure that his name would be Ramón, that he would be a short,
sweet boy, and that by an uncanny communion, his joys and sorrows
would fluctuate—just as was happening already—in perfect harmony
with hers, for years after he was born.

According to Ramón's calculations, the ship should be back in May, which would give them enough time for a trip to Orizaba. In that way, the June delivery and the baby's first month could be properly attended by doctors and relatives.

"This baby is going to be born in Clipperton," Alicia assured him.

"I have told you a thousand times not to say that," he answered. "Colonel Avalos gave me his word of honor that this time there will be no delay. He knows about the impending birth, and he is not going to fail us."

"Then I don't know what is going to happen," she insisted, "but I know that this baby is going to be born in Clipperton."

Thoughts of her own child, whose presence was becoming more and more tangible, made Alicia aware for the first time of the existence of other children on the isle. She had looked at them before without seeing them, and suddenly, like creatures coming out of the sea, they were there, all of different ages and races, running around among the crabs and the booby birds. That was when she decided to take care of the school and to dedicate most of her time to it. On the beach, next to Brander's house, they built a small open shelter with a thatched roof, and there they sat the children—nine in all—around a long table. The oldest one, twelve years old, was Jesusa Lacursa, Daría Pinzón's daughter. Soon, the youngest one was to be a small, sweet child, always clinging to his mother's skirts, Ramón Arnaud Jr.

By then the women began to put aside their private jealousies and gossiping, and to weave a tight solidarity circle, a secret feminine group that was not ever going to dissolve and that, years later, would allow them to survive during the ominous times in which they were to go through hell.

It was not their domestic chores that united them, or the school, or the sewing and embroidery workshops. It was the collective care of their hair, which became a weekly ritual. All of them, without exception—Alicia, Tirsa, Doña Juana the midwife, and the camp followers—had, reaching to their waists, splendid long tresses that had not been cut since their infancy. Except of course for the trimming ritual on Saint John's feast day, when the moon's influence pulled the hair sap in toward the roots and the tips could be trimmed without major damage.

Every Wednesday at dawn they would gather around the washing sinks to rinse their hair with rainwater in clay vessels left exposed to the stars overnight. To counteract the lightening effect of the sun's rays, they applied chiles mixed with aromatic herbs. To neutralize the drying effect of the salt spray, they applied a poultice of booby eggs. To strengthen their hair, they massaged it with Barry's Trichoferus or snake oil; to perfume it, they sprinkled a few drops of vanilla. They rinsed it again and wrapped a shawl around their heads, pulled some chairs out in the sun and sat there to let it dry. Then the women brushed one another's hair for hours and later, with wooden or bone combs, pulled it back so hard that their eyes seemed slanted. After braiding their hair in strands of three or four, they tied it with colored ribbons. On Saint John's feast day, they trimmed their hair and carefully collected the cut-off tufts into little bags to be placed under their own pillows.*

During these long sessions of hair care there was more than enough time to talk. They chatted about births and miscarriages, about love and deceit; whole family sagas were told, and stories of past battles and of other battalions were remembered.

By the end of March or beginning of April when dozens of black fins began to appear in the waters around the reefs, the topic of sharks displaced all others, becoming obsessively frequent. The women tried to outdo one another with stories about isle inhabitants who had died in the jaws of sharks. Like the one about the nine fishermen who left at dawn on a barge, and only a big splash of blood in the water returned, dragging itself onto the sandy beach and staying there, forever indelible.

*As in Adela Fernández's *El Indio Fernández*, Panorama Editorial, 3rd ed., Mexico, 1986.

Or about the effeminate gringo working for the guano company who, while getting a suntan close to shore one day, lost both his buttocks in one shark's bite.

"That was God's punishment, taking away his sinful body part," Doña Juana used to say, crossing herself.

While they talked, they looked into the distance at the metallic gleams of the sharks' backs, listened to the noise they made with their fins, cutting through the water like razor blades. The women believed they could detect fetid breath coming out of their jaws. At night they had nightmares of fangs and mutilations, of spooks that took the children away, of sharks that forced themselves sexually upon the women or came out of the ocean in human form in order to commit some atrocity.

On Wednesday mornings, brushing their hair together, the women exorcised their fears by telling these stories, which up to then were only dubious memories and horrible dreams, impossible in the real world.

Clipperton, 1909

ALICIA WAS SWIMMING, gliding through the warm-water currents, which seemed to open like transparent blue curtains in her path. Her contact with these liquid barriers was unrushed and pleasurable, and it made her feel good. Many feet above her head she could see a sheet of silver, the sleek, shimmering surface. The sun hitting on the water from above made it appear metallic, like warm light beaming on a mirror.

She perceived a ceaseless, soothing gurgling sound, like a pot bubbling on the stove. She felt bubbles tickling her throat, an effervescence coming up to her ears and caressing her timpani. The peaceful rhythm of the ocean lulled her and kept her company like the heartbeat of an enormous creature, an invisible protector, a powerful but docile beast. Alicia dived down, and looking up into the distance above, she saw the brilliant surface and knew she did not need to come up to reach it. She walked slowly underwater, without fear, without shortness of breath. Her breathing was deep and serene, her lungs expanding with the warm breath of the big animal. Her heart and that of the beast beat together. Everything was all right, translucent. Everything was peaceful and safe.

Everything was fine, except for a gnawing suspicion. Alicia had the intuition that out of nowhere there were harmful shadows lying in wait for her. Dark, cold shadows like rocks, like heavy, living rocks that were evading the sun rays and were circling around her. Damaged and causing damage, they crouched, marauding, lying in wait for an opportunity.

But she also knew that now they could not touch her. They would not come after her as long as she was underwater, as long as she did not pop her head up on the other side of the silvery sheet. They would not touch her as long as she was protected and watched over by the creature, by the underwater recesses of warm light, by the complicity of the powerful but quiet waters.

She could have stayed forever in the effortless, timeless pleasure of this great aquatic bed, but she started slowly if reluctantly to wake up. She saw herself in her bed, practically sitting, propped up by the necessary pillows that, because of her enormous belly, helped her to breathe. It took her a few seconds to understand that the warm, wet sensation she felt on her skin was due to her own waters that had broken a while ago, announcing the impending delivery of her baby. She began to feel the pain a few minutes later.

Up to a few weeks before, Ramón still had confidence that the ship would arrive in time to take them to Mexico. But frantically searching for treasure, he had been too busy to get into a frenzy about the ship's delay.

All the men's efforts to find the mythical treasure of Clipperton the pirate had been useless. After their search in the lagoon had failed so miserably, they also failed at the big rock on the southern coast. During two weeks of exploring it inch by inch, inside and out, they had gleaned only a few fossils and some lichens, ancient seashells, giant mushrooms, and lava rocks. The men cursed, fashioned amulets for themselves from some fossil or mother-of-pearl conch, and began, one by one, to abandon the project.

The first ones to desert Ramón were those who had been skeptical about the story of the treasure all along and collaborated only out of discipline. Next were those who had their doubts. A few days later, the enthusiastically confident ones, and finally the truly confirmed fanatics. The last one was Arnaud, for whom it had become a matter of honor. They were all exhausted, with the taste of failure in their mouths, and with their hands full of warts and their eyes boiling with sties, after getting so permeated with bat urine and toad milk.

By June the outlook was critical: they had lost a lot of time searching for the treasure, Alicia was beginning the ninth month of her pregnancy, and the ship had already been delayed five months. Ramón saw with rancor in his heart that the old anxiety, the tachycardia, the sleepless nights making and discarding hypotheses, praying to Heaven and cursing Colonel Avalos, were all coming back in an identical and useless repetition, and he refused to fall into that trap again. If the ship arrived, fine; if not, they would make do. At least as long as they could. As long as they didn't die. He applied some leeches to suck up his bad blood and poisoned bile, exchanged the treatises on pirates for books on medicine, and devoted his time to preparations for personally taking care of the birth of his son. Doña Juana, the wife of the oldest of his soldiers, Jesús Neri, was experienced as a folk healer and midwife, and she could help him.

Early in the morning the day Alicia woke up all wet with amniotic fluid, Ramón took out from the closet the objects he had already prepared and disinfected for the occasion, and ordered them neatly on the table at the foot of the bed. There were white rags boiled for hours, antiseptic soap, alcohol, scissors and pincers, clean ribbons to tie the umbilical cord, two large basins, needles and surgical gut twine in case sewing a tear was needed. Feeling with his hands and listening through

the fetus-scope, Ramón helped Alicia lie down on clean sheets, re-
arranged her pillows, brought her a big pitcher of fresh water, opened all
the windows to the breeze, lowered the jalousies to keep the room in
semidarkness, and sat next to his wife, waiting for the birth of his son.
Doña Juana was also waiting to be called in to help.

It was a long wait, more than ten hours. Her pains were intermittent,
suddenly surging like thunderbolts. Then they went away like the tide,
leaving her body in a relaxed rest and her mind lost in limbo, where all
references to the concrete world were obliterated. Until the pain
brought her again to reality and, tensing all the fibers in her body, jolted
her in hot waves shooting from her innermost center up to her two eyelids and each one of her twenty nails, then gradually folded into itself in
reverse, easing the tension, and dissolving into peace.

Between one contraction and the next, Ramón refreshed the water in
the pitcher, caressed her hair, cooled her off with a fan in his hand.
Sometimes they killed time playing checkers or card games, until interrupted by a returning stab of pain. When these became so close that
they seemed to be only one with minor interruptions, and the pain
came with triple intensity, they both knew the moment had arrived.

Alicia let go freely in an impulse that was more telluric than human
and that exploded inside her and reached all of her senses. Her pain,
though it had reached its maximum point, became secondary, turning
into a weak, unimportant sensation, compared with the power in her
effort. The fear and the uncertainty of the previous hours vanished in
the face of a glorious willpower, a blind faith in her own strength, which
surged overwhelmingly. After her last push, big and definitive, Alicia
Rovira lost herself in the same drunkenness that makes a god dizzy after exercising his greatest gift, that of creating life.

Ramón was watching in wonderment mixed with terror. His guts
twisted and turned, and his heart levitated at this very violent and
bloody last act of procreation. He saw the head beginning to come out,

and immediately receding again. In the third attempt it was fully out, wet and gelatinous, and Ramón was able to hold it with both hands. He saw the little face in an ugly adult frown, and without having to pull, he felt how the rest of its body was sliding out, swift and elusive like a lizard. He counted five fingers on each hand, five toes on each foot, and checked that its facial features, though contorted by the effort of crying, were perfect.

It was male, just as Alicia had foretold.

"It's a boy," he announced, "a beautiful baby boy."

With skill and a sure hand, as if he had done it many times, and with the help of the midwife, who toiled back and forth with the cotton rags and the boiled water, Ramón cut and sewed, extracted residues, and cleaned the rest. Before handing the baby to Doña Juana to be checked and cleaned, he stopped for a few seconds to look at him.

A little Martian, he thought, a little frightened Martian who has just arrived from an exhausting trip.

Then he lay down to rest next to Alicia on her bed, and Doña Juana returned the newborn to them. All cleaned, wrapped in a white linen gown, less shaken and less purple, he looked more like a creature of this world. From the depth of her exhaustion, Alicia looked at him with love and anguish, actually with too much love and too much anguish, like all women, female bears, tigresses, and cats right after giving birth.

"I was only mistaken in one thing," she said. "His head is not round but pointed, like a gnome's cap."

She had not been mistaken in that either. After being out of the womb for a while and once it recovered from the struggle of going through the narrow tract, the baby's head, still malleable, lost its sharp point and became rounder than a ball of wool.

Ramón opened one of the jalousies. Through the open window they saw the magnificent blue of the skies, high and limpid. Alicia remembered her dream. An image flashed through her brain, again showing her the paradise of the underwater world, and she was happy to be awake.

At this moment, life is also wonderfully perfect, she thought.

She looked at Ramón and the baby, who were both asleep, listened to their peaceful breathing and allowed herself to doze also.

It was hours later, or maybe minutes, that shouts from outside startled and woke them up. People were crying, calling out, running aimlessly. Ramón and Alicia opened their eyes and noticed that the piece of blue sky they had seen as bright and static had turned dark and was quickly changing from rose-colored to violet, and from violet to a voracious purple that swallowed everything. It was almost nightfall. The shouting was in crescendo and closing in.

Ramón hurried to the door still half asleep and, clumsily leaping over the porch steps, made his way through the circle of people, which opened for him. He saw in the center, lying on the pavement and covered with his own blood, the remains of a man. The dead man was Jesús Neri, the husband of Juana the midwife. He was an old soldier who had spent more time in Clipperton than the rest. They were all shouting at Arnaud about what had happened. There were different and contradictory versions, each one reflecting a particular vision.

The old man had been in the ocean up to his waist; no, up to his neck. He was next to the dock; no, not so close, ten yards from the dock. He was unloading from his barge some barrels he had brought from somewhere else on the isle. Five barrels that contained kerosene. No, not kerosene, fresh water. The old man wanted to carry drinking water from the dock to his home. Suddenly, they saw him flail his arms wildly. Victoriano saw him first; Faustino's wife was the one who saw him first; no, it was some kids who started to scream.

The old man sank into the water and reappeared; one could see his head, his back, his arms, and then, he was gone. "He is being attacked by a manta ray," shouted Victoriano. "It must be a jellyfish," screamed Faustino's wife. The children were shouting. Five men, no, they were four, six—three men and two women—came running to the dock. They saw him defending himself from the dark shadows attacking him, with his teeth, with his feet. They saw him helpless, overcome, with a plea for mercy on his face, with an expression that showed great pain, beseeched. Smacking the water with heavy sticks, the men scared off a school of sharks. There were three sharks; there were two sharks and a barracuda; it was only one enormous shark; there were six: five were black and one was white. The waters were red with blood by the time the men drove them away. Pedro managed to harpoon one of them; Pedro almost harpooned one. They rescued whatever was left of Jesús. When they got him out, he was already dead. When they got him out, he was still alive. Lying on the dock, he breathed with difficulty for a while, prayed to the Virgin of Guadalupe, and called out to his wife, Juana. Lying on the dock, he did not say anything, he just died without saying anything. He tried to sit up with whatever was left of his body, a spurt of blood came out from his mouth, and he died. Right after he died, blood came pouring out of his wounds, his nose, his mouth. Then they placed him on a large blanket, carried him to the entrance of the big house, and called out for Captain Arnaud.

Ramón was perplexed at so much damage, so much misery for this mangled old soldier, so much sadness at seeing this man reduced to a bloody rag. He was stunned, just standing there looking at him. His skill as a doctor's apprentice was gone, his authority as governor had vanished, he had lost his capacity to react. He could only stand there, watching. The impact of the delivery was still too fresh, and the two images were juxtaposed, melded, confusing. Crouching next to the dead man was Doña Juana, sobbing quietly, evenly, with no overblown gestures or even tears, resigned to death since long ago, since forever.

The voice of Lieutenant Cardona broke the collective hypnosis of watching the corpse.

"We must bury him," he said.

"We must bury him," Ramón repeated mechanically. "We must find an appropriate place for a cemetery."

The layer of soil in Clipperton was so thin that to bury a man was almost impossible. To cover the body with shovelfuls of guano would be unsanitary and sacrilegious, and to dig a grave in the rock would be too arduous an enterprise. "Throw him into the sea," someone suggested, but the idea of letting the sharks finish the job horrified Ramón. If the man had been a sailor and had died on the high seas, maybe they could have done that, but the old man was a soldier, and he had died right there, close to land.

The women drove away the pigs, which had gone crazy sniffing around, and the flies swirling over the dried blood. One could begin to feel in the air the quick decomposition of the cadaver in the heat of a twilight without any breeze. A rapid decision was needed. After inspecting several sites, Arnaud decided on a secluded high area at the beach, near the lighthouse tower, where the water never reached. The accumulation of hard sand in that place made it possible to dig a deep enough grave. That would be the inauguration of their cemetery.

They wrapped Jesús Neri or whatever was left of him in shrouds and placed him in a square pine box, one of those in which the ship had brought them foodstuffs, and they buried him under a wooden cross. Lacking flowers, they arranged palm fronds over his tomb. Doña Juana had stopped crying and only whimpered softly, rhythmically. Arnaud said a few words.

"On this day, the second of June, 1909, life and death visited Clipperton for the first time since we arrived," he said.

Mexico City, Today

❦

I AM LOOKING FOR traces of Lieutenant Secundino Angel Cardona Mayorga. Of the life he led that finally brought him to Clipperton. I have found a photo of him, which I have on my desk. I found also an invaluable document for following his tracks, the complete dossier of his military record, from the time he entered the service until he died.

The photo, taken at a local studio, offers some faded brocade curtains in the background and a little round table in the foreground. Resting on the table, a nunchaku and the lieutenant's right hand, the tips of his fingers barely touching the surface. With his left hand he is holding his sword by the handle, its point resting on the floor. In his military uniform, with its long army jacket, double row of golden buttons, and wide belt, he is a good-looking man, self-assured, and holding a martial stance without rigidity. Almost seductive, perhaps, but with a detectable tinge of sarcasm.

He appears to be about twenty years old. Behind the charming smile and the dress uniform, something reveals his Indian ancestry. He seems a little too cocky for his young age and humble origin.

His healthy head of dark hair has been combed back. He has a tanned complexion, straight nose, square jaw, Indian-looking eyes that don't gaze at the camera but a little off to the left. His facial features are pleasant, chiseled, with the exception of his ears, two prominent half circles. In spite of the careful neatness of his attire, his boots are dusty. Those boots have traveled many roads and are well planted on solid ground.

His military record consists of a hundred or so handwritten reports in different styles of calligraphy, signed by Cardona's diverse superior officers. They do not contradict the low-class dandyism that the lieutenant demonstrates in the photo. Just the opposite.

Secundino Angel was born on July 1, 1877, in Chiapas, Mexico, in the gutters of the city of San Cristóbal, a colonial enclave that exerted its domain over extensive indigenous territories. Its houses, all painted blue in honor of the Virgin Mary, were inhabited by white lawyers and clerics. In its stone-paved streets the Indians offered their wares, waited to be hired for jobs, and got drunk on alcohol or ether until they fell to the ground asleep, unconscious, or dead.

In the midst of the many Chamula Indians sitting in the dirt and filth of the plaza, Secundino was one more child, sickly, inveterately unclean, invisible, clinging to the dark woolen skirts of his mother, Gregoria Mayorga.

He was only one more child with adult resignation and burdens as he went up and down mountains carrying firewood behind his father, whose name was Rodolfo Cardona, and who was a Chamula Indian like any other: heavyset, hairy, with docile eyes. His only clothing was a short tunic that left his legs bare, a sheepskin over his shoulders, and a rolled white kerchief on his head. This was styled after the patron saint of the

Chamulas, Saint John the Baptist, according to the biblical custom of these mountains, where tribal fashion was dictated by specific patron saints. The Chamulas were not the only ones in the world dressed in the style of a saint; the Pedranos wore capes, haversacks, and tunics in the style of Saint Peter; and the Huistecos had the mantles and the baggy pants of old, like the archangel Saint Michael.

Like his father, Rodolfo, and his mother, Gregoria, Secundino as a child was illiterate and did not even speak Spanish. However, by the age of twelve he could deal with hunger, withstand loneliness, and overcome fear, so he decided to abandon the land in which the life of an adult was worth nothing, and that of a child even less. It was not a willful decision, but the path he was following took him farther and farther away. He gradually left behind the mud huts, the sheep and the pigs, the land of the red earth. He went through the thick pine forests, and when he got to the blue mountains on the horizon, the ones he had seen from his home, he found himself at the barracks entrance. It was a National Guard battalion. The child dared to go in, and he stood in a corner at the horse stables, but since he spoke only Tzeltal, his Indian language, he did not say a word to anyone. He simply waited for hours, until somebody noticed him and signed him up as a volunteer.

He did his growing up at the barracks and learned Spanish, reading, and writing. He also learned to play reveille, taps, and tattoo, and by the age of thirteen was made bugler. Perhaps because he grew up in a town that manufactured mandolins and drums, music and singing were easy for him. Everything else was more difficult. According to the reports of his superior officers, he was "refractory" to learning and a rebel in matters of discipline. But music was his gift. In his spare time he went from the bugle to the guitar, and from military calls to love songs. When he sang, he acquired poise, looked taller, lost his shyness. He distinguished himself.

Besides, he was handsome, and learned to control his hair in a decorous way, to trim his mustache, and to look half smiling, half sleepy-eyed, as if he actually did not see what he was looking at. He freed himself from misery and sadness, and discovered the advantages of his good voice and good looks. Those were the means he found to create a niche for himself. He became an adventurer and a ladies' man, a smart aleck who played dumb, a carouser and a troublemaker.

At seventeen he was transferred to the Public Security Battalion in the city of Tuxtla Guitiérrez. He was almost a man, not an adolescent anymore, and he was not an illiterate Indian, but he was not white either. He had exchanged his John the Baptist's tunic for a soldier's uniform, he was bilingual, and he knew how to court Indian girls as well as mestizo señoritas. Besides, he knew how to spell, and had a firm handwriting and pompous style that allowed him to work as an amanuensis at the political headquarters in the same town where he served. He had become the Indian who spoke Spanish, who acted as intermediary between the local authorities and the indigenous ones. Secundino Angel Cardona did not belong with his own, and neither with the others. But he counted on his voice, his looks, the shrewdness of an outcast, and a practical intelligence sharpened by misfortune, which he hid from others in order to go through life without being committed to anything or anybody, expecting no reward and avoiding any punishment.

For better or for worse, he managed to make a military career. Private first class, sergeant second class, sergeant first class, and second lieutenant in the auxiliary infantry. He left afterward for the war in Yucatán against the Maya Indians, who had taken up arms against white domination. There he discovered that the days he had lived in poverty with his parents and later in the filthy military barracks were not, as he had believed, the ultimate rung on the poverty scale, and actually not even the next to last. It was in the First Battalion, in the army campaign through the jungles of Yucatán, that Secundino Angel and his comrades in arms reached the bottom rung of the human condition.

They had buried themselves in a labyrinth of swamps with no exit, defeated beforehand not only by their confusion but also by malaria, mountain leprosy, extreme heat, and snakes, while the enemy knew the jungle inside out and lay in wait, immune to venom and miasmas.

They were moving with the pachydermic heaviness of the regular army while their adversaries, using guerrilla tactics, attacked them from all sides. War for them was an accursed mission, a detestable duty, while the Mayas were fighting for themselves in a holy war, and they fought with the conviction of cornered beasts acutely aware that the question was to kill or be killed.

Sometimes the soldiers' guts would burst after drinking from a well poisoned by the Indians. Sometimes they fell into traps full of spines that had been kept for a while inside the decomposing body of a fox, and which, upon sinking into the flesh, produced ulcers that would not heal. Other times their bodies were exploded by prehistoric grenades, made with raw bullhide and tied together with sisal fibers. It could also happen that they would be gunned down by the luminous blasts from modern Lee-Enfield rifles that the rebels had obtained from the English in Belize.

These soldiers of the Mexican Army were immersed in the last circle of hell, subject to bureaucratic orders from an absentee general, while the enemy, descendants of the Mayas, had gone to war by divine design and received their combat orders from the so-called Saint Talking Cross, whom they were fiercely guarding in a fortress-sanctuary. There was no way to defeat them.

Whether it was for some act of bravery not specified in his military records or perhaps simply for having survived his Yucatán ordeal, Lieutenant Second Class Cardona received from the governor of the state a medal of valor and merit. It was the only decoration he ever received.

Punishments, on the other hand, seemed to rain on him. After his return from Yucatán with the First Battalion, while stationed in Puebla, he suffered a bout of rebelliousness and defiance of discipline, and his stays in the army prison became a matter of routine. His record is specific in this, overloaded with warnings and sanctions: he spent fifteen days in the military prison at Santiago Tlatelolco for failing to report for duty for two days; he was arrested in the flag hall for marching in a parade without his pistol; later, another fifteen days for showing disrespect to an officer. Then he was jailed for fifteen days for insulting an officer and "forcing him into a fight." For this incident he received a reprimand equivalent to the step previous to being discharged by the army. Cardona did not pay much attention.

He turned to alcohol. He got apocalyptically drunk, and he would then do everything he had not dared to do sober. He would hit his friends, embrace his enemies, disrespect his superiors, rape the wives of his inferiors, reduce his guitar to smithereens, vomit on his uniform, and curse his fate.

He would not allow anyone to tell him not to drink because as a child he had been nurtured with firewater. When his mother suffered from convulsions that made her body stiff, the medicine man made her drink to drive the sickness away. When his father made straw hats and sold them in the market, he would go afterward to a cantina in San Cristóbal and fill his belly with firewater. Soaked in drivel, oblivious of his body, he would go into an autistic and astral trip to faraway and better worlds. Four or five days later, he would be found, in a ditch alongside the road, wearing the ragged costume and beatific expression of a saint that has been knocked down from his niche.

Secundino himself, as a child, learned the bittersweet happiness of being drunk when the firewater gourd was passed around during the fiestas and a cap of monkey fur was placed on his head.

"Be happy, my child," he was told, "enjoy the fiesta. Be happy and dance and jump like a monkey."

At twenty-eight he was dishonorably discharged from the army. He was an adult but not mature; he was neither an Indian nor a white man; neither a country peon nor an urban weasel; an alien among civilians and a reject among the soldiers. There was no place for Cardona in this world.

The following year he applied to the Ministry of the Army and Navy, asking to be reassigned on probation. The answer was unequivocal: "Not apt," for being abusive with those of lower rank and considering himself equal to his superiors; because "coming from the troops, he adopted their ways and cannot change." And in case this was not clear enough, the reporting officer wrote at the bottom of the page: "Tell the person concerned not to insist."

But Cardona did insist. For three years he tried his hand at various jobs: as an employee for Mr. Enrique Perret, owner of a printing press at 3 Espíritu Santo, Mexico D.F.; as a clerk for Mr. Steffan, owner of a stationery store at 14 Coliseo Viejo in the same city; as a collector for Roger Heymans; as a construction worker for Mr. Enrique Schultz. He asked for letters of reference from all of them, and attached them to a new application for rehitching with the army. The answer was again no.

Among Cardona's gifts were the patience of a saint, the tenacity of a beggar, and the ability to jump rank in order to reach the top authorities directly. He devoted a whole year to collecting his references, but this time he exceeded himself. He obtained letters from the head of Cavalry, Guillermo Pontones; from the head of Infantry, Félix Manjarrez; from the inspector of Police, E. Castillo Corzo, who professed to know him as an honorable person. And a last letter, which must have been the decisive one, signed by General Enrique Mondragón, stating that "this gentleman has improved his behavior considerably and, therefore, deserves to be admitted again in the military."

Finally, the Ministry of the Army and Navy, having run out of patience, or because of pressure from above, repealed the previous resolutions and authorized Cardona's readmission to the army, to the

Twenty-seventh Battalion operating in the Sonora campaign. He was sent to fight the Yaqui Indians and later he was assigned to the mines in Cananea. His old tricks made a comeback, and he was arrested again repeatedly: nine days at the flag hall for failing to pay attention to his superior; nine more days for going to a cantina in his uniform; fifteen for absenteeism; another twelve days for the same reason; ten days with no specified motive; ten for not working on the firewood-gathering detail and not responding to the calls at six, reveille, and retreat; a month in the military prison at Tokin for serious misdeeds against the bugler's wife; another month because, being under arrest, he asked permission to pee and bolted; eight days for not being present at reveille; eight days for not attending instruction meetings; eight days for errors committed in the performance of duty; eight more for the same; thirty days for wounding a comrade; a month for manhandling another soldier's wife; a month for public disturbances.

His superiors decided to stop arresting him, because it didn't solve anything, and opted to send him on dangerous missions, like the campaign against the rebels in the state of Guerrero. Later he was promoted to lieutenant for his daring behavior during several shooting incidents, but as he continued drinking, he was relegated to undesirable assignments. First he ended up with a group of handicapped and ragtag men and lost souls who called themselves the "Irregulars" Battalion, and then he was literally put away, like fourth-class material, in the Officers and Chiefs Depot.

From this depot he was rescued to be sent to Clipperton Island. There he was promoted to captain second class. But Secundino Angel Cardona never got to know it.

Mexico City, 1913

❦

IN DECEMBER OF 1911 *El Demócrata* arrived again at Clipperton. People had been waiting for seven months under extremely hard conditions, but somehow during the previous two years the inhabitants of the isle came to the conclusion that the real periodical arrival of the ships was actually not every three months, but every six, approximately.

During this period a second child had been born to Ramón and Alicia. Since the firstborn had been a boy, he had been given his father's name; this was a girl, and she received her mother's name. She was growing up a happy and healthy child, as if beyond Clipperton there were nothing else, as if there were no better meal than a shark fillet, and no more enjoyable toys than seashells and crabs.

If Ramoncito was very close to his parents and overwhelmed with adult worries, Alicia, the younger one, was his total opposite. From the moment she learned to use her legs, at eleven months, she started running and organized her own world among the coral reefs, in the sand, in the mud puddles. It was an ordeal to put her to bed or to keep her contented inside the house.

As the years went by—a lot of them—this little girl became Alicia Arnaud, Mr. Loyo's widow, the charming old lady in the Pensión Loyo, Orizaba, who, sitting at her kitchen table, pours milk into jars and enjoys her happy memories.

When *El Demócrata* arrived at last, there was a letter for Ramón from his mother, Doña Carlota. It was dated Orizaba, December 1910, so it had been delayed for a whole year. Before attending to anything else, Ramón locked himself up to read it.

It was unusually long and detailed, full of optimism and good humor. The mother was telling her son about the Centenary of Independence holidays, held in the capital in September 1910. Her invitation had come through some friends she still had in government. The centenary had coincided with General Porfirio Díaz's birthday, and the old president, already in his eighties, decided on a grand celebration for the double occasion. The festivities were going to be the most lavish his poor country had ever seen. For a whole month there would be bread for everybody, and circus performances everywhere.

She wrote that there were people who tried to oust him through uprisings and revolts, but that he would take charge and demonstrate to all that he was still holding the reins, and quite securely. That some people said he was old and cracking, that anything made him cry like a babe in arms, that he was as deaf as a doorknob and had whims like a pregnant woman. That he was unbearable because he was such a sourpuss, and that his mind was gone and he could not even remember his second family name. Of course Porfirio Díaz would show them that his balls were still in the right place, whole and hale. All phonies and amateurs at taking over would learn who was the authentic "Patriot Nonpareil," the

"Prince of Peace," the "World's Statesman," the "Creator of Wealth," the "Father of His People." They would find out.

Doña Carlota was dazzled by his presence when he showed himself in the balcony at El Zócalo, his breast glittering like a Christmas tree, or the starry heavens, with the hundreds of medals that he wore pinned to his uniform.

"You had to see it to believe it," she commented in the letter to her son. "The older he gets, the more handsome, and even whiter, the old man becomes. I remember him when he was young, when he looked like what he really is, a Mixtec Indian. Now he looks like a true gentleman. Power and money whiten people."

Doña Carlota proudly wore her high feather hat to attend the great allegorical parade during which all the characters in Mexican history, ancient as well as recent, marched down the Paseo de la Reforma. To open the parade there was a half-naked Moctezuma, with even more feathers than Mr. Arnaud's widow, and to close it, a stylized, rejuvenated version of Don Porfirio himself.

Behind the parade came the retinue of invited guests, first those from foreign countries, then the ones from the provinces. Among these, proud and rotund, was the matron from Orizaba, Doña Carlota. Agape, she watched a capital city bedecked with arches of flowers, artificial lights, flags, brocade hangings. Only handsome faces and fine garments everywhere, and she noticed that the guards were keeping out of the paved zone its natural inhabitants: the lepers, the syphilitics, the harlots, the cripples.

The grand Gala Ball, which she also had the opportunity to attend, was more fantastic and magnificent than she could ever have dared dream. She had stood there—still handsome, candid, and dazzled like an aging, plump Cinderella—in that princely palace, impressed by the hundred and fifty musicians in the orchestra, by the five hundred lackeys serving twenty whole boxcars of French champagne, by the thirty thousand lights garlanding the ceiling, the countless dozens of roses crowding the halls.

"What a pity that you were not here to enjoy all the greatness of these moments," she wrote to Ramón. "This is the right place for a young officer like you. A brilliant future would await you here, in the service of General Díaz. Even though people might think that I am interfering, I repeat again that my blood boils when I think that you are throwing your life away on that isolated island."

Doña Carlota hit the bull's-eye with this argument as she always did when it was a matter of manipulating complex guilt mechanisms, regrets, and resentments that Ramón sheltered inside his heart. But this time it lasted only for a few minutes.

Folding the letter carefully, Arnaud kissed it and put it inside his pocket. He immediately walked to the dock to receive the captain of *El Demócrata*, Diógenes Mayorga, who had seemed nervous before and truly upset on account of the last news he had brought from Mexico. This time, Mayorga looked serene, sure of himself. He seemed even to have an air of petulance or superiority. Not in a rush at all, he began to render his news report to Arnaud, while at the same time painstakingly picking his teeth. He opened his mouth, interrupting his phrases halfway to look—with curiosity, almost with pride—at the small particles on the tip of his toothpick.

"You people must be the only Mexicans who do not yet know," he said. "Porfirio Díaz is out . . . out already."

"What?" shouted Arnaud, his round eyes wide open.

"You heard right. Old Porfirio is out. He escaped on a boat to Paris, and there he must be, nursing his prostate."

"It's not possible, I do not understand it, how can you say that?" Arnaud's tongue tripped over itself, his voice dissonant. "You are misinformed, look at this letter, it says here that General Díaz is stronger than ever, that he made a show of all his power at his birthday celebration, which was a great event—"

"Oh, yes," interrupted Mayorga. "That big party. It was the last kick of a hanged man."

"And who could have ousted General Díaz?"

"What do you mean 'who'? Francisco Indalecio Madero, of course."

"Madero? The little man with a goatee? The madman who invoked spirits?"

"Well, not so little and not so mad," said Mayorga, digging his toothpick between his canine tooth and the first molar. "He is now the constitutional president of Mexico. Didn't I tell you last time that there was a war? Well, Madero won. We are all on his side."

"I don't understand anything. How can you be on his side? Didn't he defeat Porfirio Díaz and our army? At least that is what you are saying. Don't you see how you are contradicting yourself? That President Madero you are talking about, who is he, finally? Friend or foe?"

"Just try a little harder, Captain Arnaud, to see if you can understand," said Mayorga calmly, looking at Ramón with a defiant, sideways smile. "He was an enemy before, but now that he has won, he's a friend. He promised not to dismantle the federal army, and you can see he is not a man who carries grudges, because he is going to keep us officers in our posts."

"What a strange war," commented Arnaud softly, practically to himself.

That night Ramón and Alicia could not sleep at all. They talked for hours on end, discussed, juggled and rejected possibilities, fought, made up, and by dawn they had agreed that the whole family would leave that same day for Mexico on *El Demócrata*'s return trip. They needed to have firsthand knowledge of the situation. To find out what designs this new government had for Clipperton.

"I don't believe we're going to find anything good for us," Ramón whispered to Alicia during their long time awake. "I'm more and more convinced that this little island was only a personal whim for Don Porfirio. The new president probably has no idea where the heck we are."

A few hours later they departed with their two children on the way to Acapulco, after packing just a few things in a suitcase and leaving instructions with Cardona to take charge until Arnaud's return.

During the voyage, Captain Mayorga gave them a warning.

"Do you want to visit your families in Orizaba? You better forget that. You cannot travel with children on Mexican roads now. If the cattle rustlers do not hold you up, the revolutionaries ambush you, and that is worse. You would get killed, and they would entice the young orphans and take them away."

Arnaud did not believe a word. He did not want to rely on, nor could he contradict, what Mayorga was telling him. It was as if Mayorga had come from a different time, from the future, and was speaking about a planet no longer familiar to Ramón.

Three days later, after they arrived in Mexico, they discovered all of a sudden that Colonel Avalos, Ramón's friend and protector, was no longer in charge of Clipperton and no longer in Acapulco; that Doña Petra, Alicia's mother, had died; and that her father, Don Félix Rovira, had left Orizaba and was now living in the port city of Salina Cruz, where he held a high position at the Moctezuma Brewery.

The last was the only good news, because from Acapulco it was easy to sail to Salina Cruz, where they indeed met with Don Félix. They were amazed to find him looking younger, full of enthusiasm, spring-like, wearing a white suit and white shoes with a mariner's cap. With a grandchild on each knee, smoking his pipe with one hand while caressing Alicia's hair with the other, he spoke fervently about democracy and Francisco Madero, whom he had met in Orizaba during a gigantic support rally.

"I don't want to offend you, Ramón. I know that you favored Porfirio Díaz," Don Félix told him. "But honestly, he was a real bandit. I do think that now we are in good hands."

"I'm not a politician, Don Félix, I'm a career military man," answered Ramón. "I am with whoever commands the federal army."

Alicia and the children stayed with Don Félix in Salina Cruz, while Ramón started out on his exhausting peregrination to the capital to find out about his future and the future of his isle. But that was an old concern of the past administration. Nobody in the capital remembered that issue, and nobody cared. So, for months he was forced to fall asleep in interminable waiting rooms, explain the whole thing to a hundred government officials, pen hundreds of applications, fight hundreds of bureaucrats.

In the meantime, the country, which had gone wild, was suddenly reined in, then overflowed, found the right way, lost it, found it again, and lost it again, in the vertiginous rhythm of Pancho Villa and his Golden Warriors in the North, the cautious advance of Emiliano Zapata and his dispossessed peasants in the South, and the silent steps of Victoriano Huerta and his enclave of traitors in the capital.

Ramón, a man prone to obsessions and fixed ideas, was too much involved in his own problems to be fully aware of the whirlwind around him. After a lot of struggle, he finally managed to locate, covered with dust and lost in the last archive, some papers of importance to him. It was a document signed by Porfirio Díaz a few years before he fled from Mexico, according to which the French and Mexican governments—at the latter's initiative—asked for Victor Emmanuel III, the king of Italy, to be the arbiter as to the sovereignty of Clipperton Island, vowing to accept his ruling.

With this document in hand, Arnaud finally managed an interview with the Madero administration's Minister of the Army and Navy, who

signed all the necessary authorizations for him to continue in his post
and to keep the logistic support coming from Acapulco by ship.

In the meantime, Alicia, pregnant for the third time and getting close
to her delivery date, went to Mexico City with Don Félix and her two
children in order to be reunited with Ramón there. They moved into
three large, comfortable rooms in a hotel located right in the center of
the city, the San Agustín. They hired for their private service one of the
hotel maids, named Altagracia Quiroz. She was a girl of fourteen from
Yautepec, state of Morelos, who had been forced to flee to the capital
during the disruptions caused by the revolution. She continued to dress
like the other hotel maids, with a white percale apron and a red kerchief
tied around her neck. In spite of her name, she was altogether lacking in
grace. Her body was strong like a tree trunk and just as cylindrical. She
was short and flat-nosed. But to counter her plain features, nature had
endowed her with a glorious head of velvety black, silky hair reaching
down to her ankles. "Your hair is like the Virgin of Guadalupe's," her
mother had been telling her since she was a little girl. But she did not
like her hair and always wore it tied up or braided. Given the choice, she
would much prefer to have the Virgin of Guadalupe's upturned little
nose, her pink feet, or her generous miracle eyes.

Mrs. Arnaud asked her to take care of her two older children while
she attended to delivering and nurturing her third child, and offered her
a salary of ten pesos a month, which was double her hotel salary. Altagracia accepted, and from then on her life was inseparably tied to that
family, strangers to her until the day before. Without knowing it, she had
made a tragic pact with destiny in exchange for ten pesos a month.

A few days later, Olga made her entrance into the world. She was the
only one of the four Arnaud children not to be born in Clipperton.
Maybe because of this, the isle did not mark her the way it marked her
siblings, in spite of the years she had to live there. Perhaps for the same

reason, in her adult life Mrs. Olga Arnaud Rovira, Ramón and Alicia's third child, born in the Hotel San Agustín in Mexico City, always refused to talk about Clipperton or to reminisce about that part of her life, either with relatives or outsiders.

On a February afternoon in 1913, Ramón was walking down the street on the way to his hotel when he could not pass through. There were free-shooters posted on the roofs, stray bullets whistling in every direction, corpses piled up at the corners, big fires blocking the streets, houses being tumbled down by cannonades, barricades of soldiers preventing crossings. He managed to find out what was going on. General Victoriano Huerta had initiated a coup to oust President Madero, and the city was at war.

For the first time since his return to the continent, Arnaud met with reality head-on. He had stumbled into a dilemma: the army was divided, and soldiers in the same army uniforms were killing one another. Which side should he take? Should he defend the government or the insurgents? He could not find an answer but realized that he did not care. It was too late for either.

For ten days and ten nights he stampeded with the masses. He roamed about, keeping close to the walls to save his neck, helping the wounded, who hung from his shoulder as if they were drunk, while attempting to draw some conclusions out of the contradictory reports. Most of all, he tried to get back to his hotel to find out how his family was.

Finally he succeeded. He stormed into the family's rooms looking distraught, his clothes filthy and ragged, his hair wild like a madman's. His wife and his father-in-law embraced him long and tight. He began to pace the bedroom in long strides like a caged beast, his words gushing forth. Without concern for order or logic, he began telling them what he had seen and heard.

"The president of the United States sent a message that there had been enough revolution already, and that if Mexico did not establish a better government, he was going to send warships and four thousand marines to invade. President Madero's brother had both of his eyes gouged out, the good one and the glass one, with the tip of a sword. Madero's loyal men were executed. The president fell prisoner, was obliged to resign, and was then assassinated. The American ambassador, Henry Lane Wilson, was behind everything. They say that the only thing he did not get to do was to pull the trigger of the gun that killed Madero. General Huerta, a friend of the gringos, is now in power—"

Arnaud suddenly stopped his tirade and remained motionless in the center of the room, observing the members of his family. Once the commotion of his return was over and the anguish caused by his disappearance had subsided, they were now listening to him in silence. His family was evidently upset and alarmed by the news, but remained static as if immobilized by a serene stillness. Lying down wrapped in the white linen bedsheets, Alicia was breast-feeding her new baby. Don Félix was slowly drawing on his pipe. The two children were silently building towers of wooden blocks.

"It's funny," said Arnaud, now in a low voice. "On the other side of that window the whole world has just crumbled down. But here, the equilibrium continues to be perfect."

He dropped like a piece of lead onto the bed next to his wife, fully dressed and with his shoes on, completely filthy and with blood, not his own, smeared all over. He fell asleep instantly.

A few days later Don Félix returned to Salina Cruz to oversee his business, which he had left adrift in the middle of the national commotion. The departure of her father, the postpartum blues, the series of violent events that the family had experienced, and even the smell of damp carpets in the halls of the hotel had sunk Alicia into deep melancholy.

One afternoon she finally spoke to Ramón.

"I want you to tell me honestly, from the bottom of your heart, what you think of all this."

"Of all what?"

"Of all that is happening in this country."

"I don't know," Ramón answered, without any hesitation. "I don't think anything of it. I don't believe this is my war."

"Then, let's go," she pleaded in a tone that he had never heard. "Please, let's go back home. Clipperton is paradise compared with the rest of Mexico."

Ramón did not answer her right away. He took out of his shirt pocket the orders he had recently obtained from the Ministry of the Army and the Navy, and with the edge of the paper he stroked his wife's nose.

"We must wait, darling," he said. "This piece of paper was signed by a government no longer in power. Now we have to see if Huerta's will ratify it."

Marooned

Clipperton, 1914

THE OCEAN SURROUNDING CLIPPERTON is dense and dark, muddled and entangled with an overload of plankton and other substances. Deep underwater currents determine its movements. When Ramón and Alicia managed to overcome all the red tape and returned from Mexico during the first months of 1914, they experienced such joy to be on their isle again that they devoted their time to finding unexplored nooks. They discovered then that bordering the barrier reef around the isle and under the opaque and seemingly hostile surface of the water, there was a diverse and luminous universe. It was impossible to explore it on the windward side: the enormous waves exploding against the reefs would overpower any human being who dared try. But it was possible on the leeward side, where the sea withdrew, its will already broken after crashing against the rocky shoreline of the isle.

Making use of the old diver's suit, Ramón and Alicia spied on the secrets of those monumental underwater palisades formed by billions of minute coral polyps piled on top of one another, making the reef come alive, breathe, move, and have a will of its own. They were always amazed at the whimsical, baroque structures that expanded in the shape of tree branches, mushrooms, umbrellas, cauliflowers, deer or moose antlers, deer horns, spines, lace, ruffles, and fringes.

On land, out of the water, the sun incinerated and bleached everything it touched. All except the crabs, with their bright red shells. Everything else was drab and brownish: the rocks, the sand, the sea, the seagulls. It was all a fading, monotonous body, in a camouflage of gray-brown tones with veins in paler shades. Like in an overexposed photo, the elements and the animals fused together, and it was impossible to distinguish one from the other, except for their silhouettes.

Underwater, in contrast, it was a bright, multicolored universe. Against the dark bottom, one could see dots of dazzling light and explosions in phosphorescent violet, methylene blue, neon shades of green, translucent mauve tones, and iridescent golds. The rigid and desiccated textures found out of the water would become softened and spongy, organic, sticky. Through the cracks and rocky galleries, hallucinatory guests would peek out: bunches of little pink fingers, swollen livers sporting electrified manes, transparent tubers with luminous eyes, creatures with flexible arms that delicately reached for their food and took it to their mouths.

Alicia and Ramón let themselves go with the timeless rhythm of the underwater world. Porfirio Díaz, Francisco Madero, Doña Carlota, even their own beings and all their history and everyday lives disappeared like fleeting ghosts when faced with the eternal reality of the squids' slow-motion dances of love and death; with the rocklike creatures that, waking up apparently hungry, surprised their victims, sardines as well as occupants of sunken galleons; or with the sleepy lumbering of the sea bass, that sweet giant of the deep.

This placid existence of the Arnauds would have continued slipping by, rocked only by the ebb tide, were it not for the dawn of February 28, when they were awakened by a strange, humid, asphyxiating heat, like a damp towel covering one's nose and mouth.

By five A.M., Ramón kicked off the sheet and began tossing about restlessly in bed.

"The problem with the ocean is that it's too noisy. All the time, day and night, it's making noise. I've already forgotten what silence is. I miss the silence," he whispered in the hush of night. He turned this way and that, rearranging his pillow and trying to go back to sleep, without success. "I must have slept on the wrong side of the bed and woken up angry. Even the sound of the waves, always so pleasant, is driving me wild today."

"You're not the one who is angry, it's the ocean. It's making more noise than ever," Alicia said, and got up to take a look out the window. In the sky, a sickly dawn was rising without any conviction. Under the scant light, the ocean itself was dead calm for miles. The motionless sea appeared gray, thick, and wrinkled, like the skin of an elephant.

"The strangest thing is how quiet it looks," commented Alicia in astonishment. "It roars like a wild beast, but it's still, as if it were dead."

For a long time they had gotten into the habit of making love at sunrise, almost without consciously wanting to, letting themselves be carried by the energies that awaken independently after a night of rest. That morning they tried, but failed. Something in the air made their bodies feel like rag dolls and paralyzed every impulse before it was born.

"I can't," said Ramón, sitting on the bed in order to fill his lungs. "I need air."

"I can't either," she said. "I need air, too."

The sticky weather made their clothes damp with perspiration even before they finished getting dressed. Ramón went into the hall to look at the barometer. He found it showed an extremely low reading and thought it was out of order. He looked at the time. It was already six twenty in the morning, but the amount of sunlight had not changed since five o'clock, as if the heavy air would not allow the light to filter through.

"What the hell is going on?" he said out loud, but he could not hear his own words because of the loud noise coming from the ocean. Walking on the beach toward the soldiers' barracks, he met Lieutenant Cardona, who was also looking for him.

"That gringo Schultz thinks that a hurricane is coming," Cardona announced. "He says we have to get ready, because it's a strong one."

"He is not a gringo. He is German."

"About the same, isn't it?"

"Anyway, what does this German fellow know about hurricanes?" growled Arnaud in disgust, just when a tenuous line, ruffled and nebulous, appeared on the horizon, scarcely visible above the water. Neither Captain Arnaud nor Lieutenant Cardona could actually see it.

Until noon they battled the weakness and heaviness that had come over them, in order to perform their usual chores. Wherever they went, they saw people lying down, children in silence, women inactive and distracted, soldiers sluggish and ill-tempered. Even the domestic animals were sprawled about carelessly, as if they had plopped down just anywhere.

Arnaud looked around and asked Cardona, "And what about the crabs? And the boobies? They are always all over us, and today I haven't seen even one since dawn."

"Heaven knows where they are," the lieutenant answered.

It was already noon, and yet, no daylight. A timid, unnatural light was filtering through, but it was not enough to dispel the darkness. Meanwhile, the sun seemed to have stopped in its position in the sky, swallowing timeless minutes.

Arnaud went to the supply store and set aside several bags of foodstuffs. In a flat, business-as-usual tone, he gave instructions to Cardona.

"Gather all the women and children at the vegetable patch, and have them wait there until we see what is going on. Ask the men to do a head count and make sure nobody is missing. Where do you think the people could be best protected? In the guano shed next to the dock?"

"That's correct, sir," Cardona answered in his most energetic military tone. "That is the sturdiest structure on the isle."

"Besides, it's on a higher ground and solidly built on pylons, so it will not be dragged away by floodwaters. Have someone take these food supplies there and a few barrels of drinking water. And make sure domestic animals are also sheltered."

"Two by two, just like Noah's ark," offered the lieutenant with a childish smile, seeming both excited and amused by the prospect of a great commotion.

While Cardona and the soldiers corralled the pigs, chickens, and dogs in an improvised pen at one corner of the shed, Arnaud went to the lighthouse to speak to the soldier in charge, Victoriano Alvarez.

"Turn on the beam, Victoriano," he ordered, "and keep it on at all costs. If things get rough, tie yourself to the rock, or do whatever you can, but don't let the light go out."

Arnaud joined Cardona and the other men in time to see how a sudden gust of wind whipped against the palm trees, folding their trunks almost at right angles and abruptly turning the fronds upside down as if it were pulling a bunch of reluctant young ladies by the hair.

"Look at that! It's the hurricane!" shouted Cardona, pointing toward it. "Here it comes already!"

"Well, let it come," said Arnaud. "Let it blow if it must but once and for all, because this dead calm is driving us nuts."

The unexpected gust of wind vanished and the palm trees recovered their composure, but the dark line that up to a minute before had seemed to rest on the horizon quickly covered in a few instants half the distance that separated it from Clipperton, showing its flying halo of leaves and other suspended objects being buffeted by the wind.

"It's time for the women and the children to get into the shed," shouted Arnaud. Don't let them leave until the storm is over."

At the mere mention of the word, as if it had been an invocation, the storm fiercely let loose all its force. As the jets of water hit them, the reality of the situation dawned, and the events, restrained up to then, came upon them in such rapid succession and with such violence that in spite of having been warned, they were taken by surprise.

Standing at the entrance of the guano shed—well constructed by Schultz during the company's golden age—Ramón helped the women in. With children hanging from their skirts, they came carrying baskets overflowing with serapes, pieces of cloth, scapularies, pictures of saints, kitchen pots, metates to grind corn: every imaginable thing that deserved to be saved from the deluge.

Ramón saw his wife and children coming in the middle of the group. As Ramoncito ran to him, eyes round identical to his, and eyelashes dripping water, he picked him up and tightly hugged his fragile frame, like a little bird's.

"Daddy," the child shouted in his ear, "the winged horses went mad and started to gallop in the skies."

"Who told you that?"

"Doña Juana told me, and it's true."

Alicia's hair was loose and wet, and it stuck to her face and body. She was carrying baby Olga on one arm, and with the other she was pulling a large trunk, helped by Altagracia Quiroz, who pushed it from behind.

Ramón quickly put his child down and lifted the trunk.

"You are always doing the wrong thing at the wrong moment," he told Alicia, but she did not understand at all.

"What are you saying?"

"What the heck do you have there?"

"My wedding dress, my best clothes, and my jewelry," Alicia shouted back.

"Why do you need them now?"

"The last thing I need is to lose these things to the wind," she said, now without straining her voice, more to herself than to Ramón.

He took the trunk inside and ran out again to help a woman whom another gust of wind had thrown into one of the rivers of rain running everywhere on the isle. He did not know how or where he caught her, a round, wet, soft, and difficult mass who held desperately to his legs, causing him to fall also. Finally he was able to drag her through the mud and bring her in. Through the existing confusion, Arnaud then looked at the back of the shed and in the semidarkness managed to see Alicia's silhouette, placing the baby on a wheelbarrow she had found in the shed.

Looking at her, he felt a tight lump in his throat. He had to refrain from going to help her, to dry her hair with a towel, to tell her, "Don't worry, everything will be all right," and to seek the shelter of her embrace, quietly hiding from the storm and from the unmanageable situation that had fallen on his shoulders.

What I have to do is go for my men, he thought as if waking up, and waved Alicia a good-bye that she didn't see.

He left the shed to fulfill his duty, clinging to the walls of neighboring houses and without knowing exactly in which direction to go. He was trying body and soul not to be dragged by the elements when an airborne sharp object hit him on the forehead and knocked him backward. He lay on the ground, his eyes blinded and his mind taken over by a burning pain that reached to every corner of his brain. After he had been lying there a while, stunned, the first thought that came to his mind was about Gustav Schultz.

Where could that German fellow be now? he wondered. Maybe he could tell me how long we can expect this to last.

He tried to get up, but the pain from his wound did not let him. Feeling the warm flow of blood collecting over his right eye, then dripping lazily to the ground, he managed to drag himself up against a wall

for some protection, and he lay there, looking at how the world was being transformed while darkness kept closing in around him.

He saw an intermittent point of light in the dark sky and knew that
the soldier in the lighthouse was doing his duty. Clouds in the sky were
dissolving as they flitted by in vertiginous succession. Next to him a
floor beam, still nailed down, vibrated incessantly, resisting the wind-
storm's attempt to pull it out. He saw zinc planks, chairs, and wooden
beams go by, surely on their way to crash down somewhere in the distance. Slowly turning his stunned head toward the sea, he saw instead
mountains of solid water rushing toward the isle and threatening to en-
gulf it. He noticed that the heat that had tormented him in the morning
had dissipated and that now freezing gusts of wind against his soaked
clothes were making him shiver.

I have to move away from here, he thought. Here I am going to
drown, or freeze. I am going to die, I must do something. We're not going to get out alive from this one. Where is everybody? Where is that
German fellow so I can ask him what to do?

He decided to give his wounded head a few more minutes of rest. It
was then that he saw a large, imprecise object rolling toward him and
making a loud, harsh noise.

"It's the Pianola," Ramón said to himself. "My whole house must have
flown out the window."

Revived by his premonition, he was able to stand. The first thing he
did was to move closer to the shed where the women and children were,
and he was relieved to see it resisting the pounding of the hurricane.
The effort of getting up made him nauseous but, in spite of that, he
tried to walk toward his home with the intention of securing doors and
windows.

He was digging his fingers into the rocks, into the palm tree trunks,
into whatever was closest by, in order to advance. His body felt heavy like
a sack of stones, the wound on his temple pulsated like a chronometer,

and the wind, which had torn his shirt, ended up taking away whatever was left of it. It seemed to cost him an eternity to advance every inch.

He managed to reach a point where he could have a glimpse of his house, and in that moment he realized the true dimensions of the catastrophe. He quickly abandoned his idea of trying to secure doors and windows. He even felt guilty for having such a naive intent when he realized that the hurricane winds were getting into his house through the gaping hole left by the roof, now completely gone.

All sorts of objects were flying out, as if a gaggle of madmen inside the house were throwing them up in the air. Ramón watched with resignation how his own dearest belongings and the ones that had accompanied them all these years were disappearing one by one. He allowed himself to feel bitter when he saw his reports and his books doing cabrioles in midair like pinwheels.

There is nothing to be done here, he thought. Let me find the rest of the people.

He looked in every direction without knowing where to head. There was only disaster around him, and then he saw, to the south, the beam of the lighthouse.

They must be there, he thought. Perhaps they took refuge in the cave.

He walked on, guided by the light, calling at the top of his voice, but nobody could hear him. The gusts threw sand in his eyes, and in the whirlwinds he was helplessly being pulled about like a puppet. The wound on his head hurt, his body was all bruised, and worst of all, he was alone, isolated by force from everybody. Ramón Arnaud felt personally aggravated and deeply humiliated.

Suddenly, when he was about to give up, he rebelled against so much humiliation. A wave of courage made his blood boil, and he regained control over his own body. He stood up, defiantly facing the wind, and in anger took off his belt and began whipping the air as if possessed. He brandished his belt right and left like a maniac while shouting at the hurricane at the top of his lungs. "Damn you, bastard, what do you have against me? Hey! What is it you want? Do you want me to finish you off with my whip? You've got five minutes, you shitty son of a bitch, I give you five minutes to get out of here!"

Giant angry waves, breaking into foam at their crests, were hitting Clipperton, running over it and coming out on the other shore undisturbed by this insignificant obstacle in their run across the ocean.

Ramón Arnaud kept shouting while holding on to his pants with one hand and whipping the air with the other, when one of those mountains of water reached him, lifted him, and hurled him a few yards away against one side of the big southern rock. Then it withdrew, leaving him stranded on one of the rocky recesses.

Arnaud coughed and vomited some of the water he had swallowed. When he was able to breathe again, he attempted to climb to a higher position, anticipating the next wave that would smash him against the rock. He had been lucky this time and miraculously made a soft landing, but in the next charge of the tide he could become imbedded there like the thousands of fossils that had found their eternal resting place.

In the meantime, in the shed next to the dock, the women and children, together with the animals, had spent several hours more or less protected from the elements gone beserk. At the beginning they had earnestly tried to cover, as best they could, all the cracks and holes where water and wind were coming in. Then they gathered in the center of the shed, huddling against one another in a tighter and tighter circle. They had been silent for a long while, stunned by the unbearable noise of the roof, which vibrated and screeched, threatening to fly off any minute, and by the wailing of the children, who competed all at once to see who could cry the loudest.

Some people had started to pray the litanies of the Holy Cross, and the rest slowly followed.

"If when I'm dying, / The devil wants to tempt me, / You will protect me, / Because at the feast of Santa Cruz, / A thousand times I repeated: / Jesus, Jesus, Jesus . . ."

Jesus, Jesus, Jesus, repeated without pause or respite a hundred times; Jesus, Jesus, Jesus, in an endless, dull murmur that through repetition became susje, susje, susje, susje, susje. Someone did the counting and when it reached a hundred times, interrupted with the prayer, "If when I'm dying, / The devil wants to tempt me," and the heavy torrent of voices repeated Jesus another hundred times, sounding like broken dishes rolling down, or rain falling, made almost inaudible by the roar of the storm.

It was not the feast of Santa Cruz that day—for a long time, dates had lost their significance for anybody in Clipperton—but there was every indication that the time of dying had come. "Because at the feast of Santa Cruz, / A thousand times I repeated: / Jesus, Jesus, Jesus . . ." echoed Alicia, but she was actually thinking of Ramón, and his absence made her feel anxious. They had lived together for a long time in close quarters on the isle, where, whether they wished it or not, they could seldom be more than five hundred yards apart from each other. Now that the danger of the situation was keeping them separated, Alicia let herself be overcome by an anxiety not experienced since her adolescence in Orizaba, when for months she had waited for her fiancé's return in the patio of her family home, besieged by doubts about ever seeing him again. Holding on her lap baby Olga, who was badly in need of a diaper change and kept crying with surprising strength for her age, Alicia whispered again, "Jesus, Jesus, Jesus." But instead, she was thinking, Ramón, Ramón, Ramón.

On the other side of the island, under a sinister sky, Ramón was clinging to the rocks like a housefly. He was nearing physical exhaustion and mental delirium, when he seemed to hear a voice other than his own. A lament, perhaps, or a scream. Weak and faltering, it came from the darkness below. He thought of going down to it, but he told himself that he would be then at the merciless whim of the rising tide. Anyway, he felt the need to respond. It was dangerous, and he had better warm up his rigid muscles before attempting it. After stretching his arms and legs, which barely responded, he managed to go down a couple of yards. He couldn't see anybody, but there was more urgency in the voice, which sometimes sounded human and at others it didn't.

Could it be someone calling for help? he wondered. Or is it only the wind whistling and trying to deceive me? Or maybe it's a mermaid. A wretched mermaid who wants me to die.

As if to settle the matter, the words were now pretty audible.

"It's me, Ramón. Help me."

It was the voice of Lieutenant Cardona.

"Is it you, Cardona?"

"It's me, Ramón, here, on your right."

"Are you there, Cardona?"

"Here, in the rubble."

"Can you see me?"

"Yes, I do see you, I'm on your right, Ramón."

"Where?"

"Under this beam."

"I don't see you, but I hear you fine."

"Because the wind has stopped."

Ramón then realized it was true, that the wind had unexpectedly stopped. A second before, it was all fury and chaos, and momentarily it all had become still, mysteriously quiet. The sea had gone back, ebbing quicky from the shore as if sucked into an enormous siphon. The wind was not calm, it seemed absent, leaving in its place a warm, thick substance that did not properly reach his lungs.

There was something phony and frightening in the abrupt stillness.

Ramón reached a deep recess at the base of the big rock perpendicular to the beach. Shaped like a cave, it had gathered whatever the hurricane had pulled out from various places. Blindly, feeling with his hands, Ramón began to dig, while listening to the lieutenant's heavy breathing, which came from underneath all the debris.

"Be careful," Cardona said, "my leg is trapped under something really heavy."

Ramón could distinguish the dark bulk of the lieutenant's head and trunk in the back, in a space bubble amid the debris. He could make out his left leg twisted into an impossible position and caught under a heavy beam with a pile of other things, unidentifiable in the dark, on top of it.

"You must have that leg completely smashed," said Ramón.

"Help me to get all this off me."

Ramón pulled with all his might, but the beam did not budge at all.

"I don't understand how you got trapped in here," he said.

"I don't either. But get me out of here, and I'll try to explain."

"Wait. Maybe if I can lean against something."

Ramón tried again, pivoting his own back against the big rock, to no avail. For a long while he jostled with the debris, which resulted only in increasing the pressure of the beam on Cardona's leg, almost driving him to the point of losing consciousness several times.

"Stop! Stop, Ramón, don't do this anymore, you're killing me. Look in my pouch for cigarettes, let's have a smoke before going on."

Ramón reached for the pouch and found them.

"This is unbelievable," he said, "they are dry!"

"Amazing."

There were matches, too, and Captain Arnaud lit one. The wind had calmed down so much that the little flame held steady without his needing to shelter it. When he drew the light closer to Cardona, he saw his face at last but could not recognize it. The expression of pain and helplessness had turned him into another man, like an older brother or a pitiful and older version of himself.

"Gee, my friend, you look pale," Arnaud told him.

"This might be the last cigarette we smoke together," whispered Cardona while he felt the smoke reaching in to his soul.

"No, there are three more, and luckily they are dry, too," Ramón answered.

"What I mean is that this is the eye of the storm. Don't you see? In a short while the wind will blow and the ruckus will start again. This cave will fill up with water, and you're going to be outside, and me inside."

"No, Secundino, never. Either we both live or we both die."

Arnaud tried again in the darkness, now more desperately than before. After a while he managed to remove many smaller pieces of rubble, but the beam was still stuck in the rocks, pinning Cardona's leg, and he moaned once in a while, more weakly each time.

Then the rumble began again. At first a faint dissonance like an irregular heartbeat, and then like obsessive but distant war drums. Pleasant gusts of wind began cooling their sweat-drenched foreheads.

"That's it," said Cardona, "here it comes again."

"We still have a little time, and this beam is starting to move, you'll see."

"Not at all. We'd better have another smoke. That will give you time to recover."

Ramón acquiesced because he had reached not only the point of exhaustion but also the conclusion that he could never get that beam to move.

"Did I ever tell you," Cardona asked, "that in San Cristóbal de las Casas the air is clean and light, and it always smells like freshly chopped wood?"

"Yes, you have told me many times."

"It's true. Now go, Ramón. There's nothing else to be done here. Not a thing."

"No, my friend, I'm not leaving. Keep telling me about the air in San Cristóbal while I take care of business here. Get ready for more pain, because I'm going to kick this beam to hell and you are going to see all the stars in the Milky Way."

Arnaud stretched his body over the lieutenant's, filling in the only free space left in that recess of the big rock. He pulled his legs up, then pushed against the beam with all the strength left in his battered body.

Cardona howled in pain, and Ramón stopped.

"No more," begged the lieutenant, "what you're kicking to hell is my leg, and the beam is not moving. If I'm going to die, let me die in peace, and not like a martyred saint."

"Bear with me, as I told you. I'm going to get you out of here, leg or no leg."

"Yeah," whispered Cardona, scarcely audible, "like a lizard dropping its tail to survive."

"You certainly have a knack for animal comparisons."

Ramón repeated his maneuver, and the effort was already making him dizzy when the first wave crashed into the cave, covering both of them, blocking their noses and lungs, almost bursting their hearts and ears, and leaving them flooded, almost drowned, for what seemed an eternity.

What a pity, we're going to die, Ramón thought.

But they did not die. The big wave receded with the same fierceness with which it had come in, yanking their bodies outward and carrying the rubble with it. And then it happened: it was only a fraction of an inch, but Secundino Angel Cardona sensed that the centrifugal force of the water was moving the beam, releasing some of the pressure.

"Now is the time!" he shouted, spitting salt spray, and with a merciless jolt, he liberated his leg and dragged himself to the opening of the cave.

Ramón Arnaud followed him.

Mexico City, Today

❦

TIRSA RENDÓN'S PHOTO was taken after all the events in Clipperton had ended; in it one can see clearly the ravages caused by the tragedy.

The focus is on the woman in the midst of a large group of people, and only her face can be seen. Her hair, not very professionally trimmed, is short and very straight, with a fringe in front that becomes rounded and longer on the sides, just covering her ears. This hairdo, plus the fact that her skin, naturally dark, has been tanned by the sun, gives her features, reminiscent of those of the Amazonian peoples, a slightly masculine air. This does not mean she is an ugly woman. Hers is an attractive face, handsome though not overly friendly, a face that stands out in a crowd.

It is her eyes that command attention. The high contrast between the whites of her eyes and her dark irises, the maturity of her gaze, the arrogance of the lifted right eyebrow. In this photo Tirsa presents herself as tough and primitive but not naive. She is not taken by surprise either by the camera or by life, not even when death menaces dangerously near. Though surrounded by others, she appears alone like an Amazon jungle native who has survived massacres and ravages, solitary, defiant, tough; a native who has seen it all, knows it all, who has managed to outwit all enemies through shrewdness, and who has returned from beyond life and death.

In the various existing documents about the Clipperton tragedy—those coming from María Teresa Arnaud Guzmán, General Francisco Urquizo, and Captain H. P. Perril—there are specific mentions of Tirsa. She is recognized as Mrs. Cardona, that is, Lieutenant Secundino Angel Cardona's wife.

In the lieutenant's military dossier is a letter signed by him in which he refers to his wife. He is asking that his weekly pay be reduced by fifteen pesos, which are to be given to her in the capital city. However, the name of his wife here is not, as expected, Tirsa Rendón. It is María Noriega. Either Tirsa Rendón was a name adopted by María Noriega, or Tirsa Rendón was not really Secundino Cardona's lawful wife.

This second possibility proved to be true according to a group of documents at the end of the lieutenant's dossier. Among them is a letter dated some years later (well after Cardona's death), in which "María Noriega, Cardona's widow," a nurse at Puerto Central in Socorros and mother of two children, claims from the president of Mexico her widow's pension. The confusion about the identity of the two women is evident in the answer the widow receives: "Please ask Mrs. María Noriega to send a copy of her marriage certificate to the deceased Captain Secundino Angel Cardona, due to the fact that in the investigation carried out by this ministry in reference to his last post on Clipperton Island, Teresa Rendón appears as that officer's wife and gives testimony to the events that occurred there."

María Noriega must have sent the requested marriage certificate, since the pension was granted to her, which corroborates the legitimacy of the relationship. This also proves that the woman who lived with Secundino Cardona until the end of his days was not his wife, but the above-mentioned "Teresa Rendón," a variant of the name Tirsa Rendón.

In the end, everything is clear. Secundino Angel Cardona married a nurse, María Noriega, and they had two children. The ordeals of military life induced him to abandon her, and at some point in his many adventures he got together with Tirsa, who followed him from then on, to Clipperton. So Tirsa Rendón must have been, like the other Clipperton soldiers' women, a camp follower.

Clipperton, 1914

UNDER THE PLANKS of the guano storehouse the roar of the storm was softer and more bearable, while outside, the isle was being pommeled by the tired, last battering. Men, women, and children were waiting, wide awake, for the coming dawn to clear the skies and finally quiet down the furies of wind and ocean.

Almost inaudible, a sort of piercing sound was resounding in their stunned eardrums. It was sharp and feminine, as if coming from a soprano, a ship siren, or a mermaid. A high C floating intermittently into the rarified air of the storehouse, sneaking into the intervals of silence when the roof planks stopped clattering. It was an urgent call, but so unexpected and unreal that the Clipperton survivors perceived it without hearing it, and nobody thought of asking where it came from. It was simply another incomprehensible and unmanageable phenomenon that the hurricane had brought along.

In a corner, Lieutenant Cardona lay on a straw mattress, a thick blanket over him. A bittersweet smile twisted his lips, allowing his white,

Chamula Indian teeth to show. The excruciating pain in his disjointed, splintered leg still produced a dull tingling under the effects of the morphine injections Captain Arnaud had given him. Kneeling by his side, Tirsa Rendón, his common-law wife, tried to wring dry the cloths drenched with his perspiration, since all the liquid element in his body seemed to be flowing out freely from his forehead, his underarms, his back. As if the man wanted to die of dehydration.

In the stupor of his weakness and his narcosis, lying at the borderline between this life and the other, Cardona also heard the surreal ringing and dreamed that women with friendly breasts and angelic voices relieved his suffering by singing lullabies in his ear.

A few hours before, when the hurricane still thundered in all its fury, both captain and lieutenant had made their ghostly appearance at the storehouse. They came after their terrifying night, nearly naked and exhausted, like Moses rescued from the waters, numb with horror. If they managed to move along the isle, upsetting the devastating designs of nature, it was by mustering hidden reserves of energy and postponing death, step by step, with the last lifesaving iota of adrenaline.

Between them, they had dragged Cardona's torn leg as if it were a third person, a dying man, heavy and swollen, whom they were trying to rescue from the storm. When they reached the refuge, Arnaud attempted to rearrange that mess of bone and blood, starting with the instruments in his first-aid kit and, when these proved insufficient, resorting to the work tools in the storehouse.

While Cardona howled and hallucinated about mermaids, Arnaud struggled with pincers and pulleys to reset his femur into the hip socket, to straighten his knee, which looked downward, to give some human form to this organic matter, so torn and disjointed.

He would not have accomplished much were it not for Tirsa Rendón's incredible level-headedness and almost virile stamina. Covered with blood like a butcher or a priestess, she helped consistently, without fainting or being repelled, helping him to unravel tendons, pull bones, and darn skin with needle and thread, like embroidering doilies with cross-stitch.

When Arnaud had reached his outer limits of alertness and of his modest resources as a surgeon, he made splints and bandages, and not until then did he embrace Alicia, kiss his children, take off whatever was left of his soaked clothes, and cover himself with the heavy tablecloth with bobbin lace from Bruges that his wife had saved in her trunk. Wrapped in white cloth, like a tragic hero, he did a roll call to make a count of those present: eleven men, ten women, and nine children. Miraculously, the Mexicans were all there, except Victoriano Alvarez, posted at the lighthouse. Some of the men had wounds and contusions, but with the exception of Cardona's leg wound, none was serious.

The only foreigner who had not left the isle, Gustav Schultz, was absent. Very early in the morning of the day before, Lieutenant Cardona had seen him observing the sky. He pointed his index finger up and predicted, "Hurricane."

The lieutenant now recalled that last impression of his voluminous figure silhouetted against the dim predawn light. He knew better than anybody.

"Maybe he's dead," someone said.

But Ramón Arnaud was convinced that wasn't so, and his face turned red with rage to think that instead of helping the community or contributing to its safety, Schultz had taken shelter on his own with his woman, inside the solid walls of his home. Arnaud imagined him to be at that moment dry, warm, and comfortably asleep in his bed, and felt something resembling hate.

The Arnaud family gathered in a tight group. Interrupted by the roars of the dying hurricane, the creaking of the roof, the cries of the children, and the nervous noise of the frightened animals, Ramón and Alicia almost didn't let each other finish a sentence, eagerly recounting all the events of the last hours, threading like telegraphic messages the fragments of the two stories into a single intermittent one. Every three words, Ramoncito, who wanted to know everything to the last detail, would interrupt to ask "What happened?" "How did you hurt yourself, Dad?" "Where did you fall down?" "Who was it?" "How was it?" "Why was it?"

"Someone is knocking at the door," a voice announced.

The storehouse door was opened, and a lot of water came in together with Daría Pinzón and her daughter, Jesusa Lacursa.

"Where is Schultz?" Arnaud asked them, no longer so sure about the answer.

"He's gone mad," Daría Pinzón answered.

"I'm not asking how he is, but where."

"He is around, mad as a hatter. While his house flew away, he spent the whole night outside, trying to salvage the train and all the machinery, and all those useless contraptions that the company abandoned. And he, also, he also was abandoned on this isle, but he doesn't care. And as for me, the wind might as well blow me away, he doesn't care about that either. He only cares for the interests of the company, as if they were his children," Daria said on the verge of a nervous breakdown, without being able to stop. "He has gone nuts, Captain, believe me, that gringo has gone crazy. He was brought to Clipperton to ship the guano, and he wants to ship guano even though there is no guano, no Clipperton, no company—"

"Calm down, Daría," Arnaud said softly. "Go and get some hot coffee and find a spot here for you and your daughter."

The women were throwing dough balls into the small fires they had made. Accompanied by a well-tuned guitar, someone was singing a strange *corrido* that told the story of a cockroach that couldn't walk. Several men were playing monte over a gray military serape, with total absorption, oblivious to everything. Every once in a while they shouted for everyone to hear, announcing the cards they had uncovered.

"Two, for your rheumatism and your flu."

"Four-ce off the covers to sleep with your lovers."

"Six days of battle, and they stole my cattle."

"Three things nice: chocolate and sugar 'n' spice."

In the meantime, the sharp whistle kept on unwittingly penetrating through every crack in the roof, subtle and distant but implacable, like a remote Judgment Day trumpet.

The tail of the hurricane dissipated when the sun came up, and people slowly left the storehouse with the caution of shy animals that leave their lairs blinded by the light after hibernating, dazed by so much sleep. Arnaud headed an impromptu procession that sleepwalked along the coastline in religious silence, without saying a word about the spectacle before their eyes. The vegetable patch and its black soil, the buildings, the dock, all traces of civilization, all human undertakings—which had taken years to bring to fruition—had all disappeared.

The fresh guano had also disappeared. The tons of excrement from hundreds of birds, deposited on land for years, had been dragged out to sea. Cleared and freed of the soft, greenish-black layer spread all over that appeared to be its second nature, Clipperton now displayed the cruel ancestral grayness of fossilized guano. There was a glorious stillness in the sky and in the ocean, a pristine calm. Clipperton lay in this half of the universe, clean and empty, virginal, like at the dawn of creation. The crabs and boobies had returned, by the dozens, by the hundreds, as if during their absence they had tripled in number. Now they were swarming around the bald rock, sure of themselves, arrogant lords of the reconquered realm.

The men walked to the south and found the lighthouse intact at the top of the rock.

"At least we have this left," said Ramón Arnaud in an old man's voice he did not recognize.

Victoriano Alvarez, the lighthouse keeper, came to meet them. The color of his skin had turned ashen, but his eyes sparkled with an unusual phosphorescence.

"Any news, soldier?" Arnaud asked, curling his mustache at the absurdity of his words under the circumstances.

"Yes, sir!" was his answer. "Come and see for yourself."

They all followed Victoriano to the entrance of the lighthouse lair. He pushed the door open, and Captain Arnaud went in. In a few seconds his eyes grew accustomed to the darkness inside. Then he saw them.

Lying on top of one another, asleep, their hair golden like that of the saints in colonial altars, there were nine men, one woman, and two children. Though they were lying down, it was easy to see how tall they were. The men had yellow beards, like prophets, and the skin of the woman was so transparent that one could follow, as on a map, the lilac veins of her arms and legs.

In disbelief, Arnaud looked at these mysterious beings come out of nowhere. Fallen from the sky, like the white gods the Aztec prophecies had announced. But their wet clothes and the tiredness of their unhinged bodies denied any such divine nature. On the contrary, their desolate, forlorn air was unmistakably human.

"Where did they come from?" Arnaud managed to ask after observing them for a while.

"They don't speak our language," Victoriano responded, "but they were shipwrecked out there."

The soldier pointed to the sea, and Arnaud saw, about a mile from the beach, practically underwater and lying on her side, a three-masted schooner. The Pacific Ocean was so placid that morning that the vessel seemed to be catching up on sleep, like her crew.

"All night long I heard their ship horn braving the storm," Victoriano said. "*Uuuuuuu uuuuuuu*, she cried, howling like a ghost. It made my hair stand on end. *Uuuuuuu*, so sad, so piercing, *uuuuuuu*. I thought it was the Weeping Woman, wailing for us."

Listening to Victoriano, Arnaud remembered hearing that anguished sound for hours, but his brain had refused to register it.

"It seems they got lost in the hurricane," Victoriano Alvarez continued, "and the Clipperton lighthouse attracted them. That's what I make of it, sir, though I couldn't understand a word they said. They thought they could find refuge here. That's it. And of course, their ship got smashed to hell against the reefs. When their boat sank, they kept afloat in the dark, holding on to the children so they wouldn't drown. Maybe that's what happened. They must have spent the night clinging like monkeys to floating pieces of wood, and at dawn they swam to shore. I saw them there and helped them. It would be better, Captain, when they wake up, for them to tell you their own story. You know so many languages, sir, you could understand them."

Ramón Arnaud felt compassion for this group of blond strangers lying at his feet. Perhaps they were not asleep but had fainted.

"Fate is a prankster," he finally said, too perplexed and exhausted to add a sense of drama to his voice. "In one blow it leaves us without food and brings bring us twelve extra mouths to feed."

Mexico City, Today

THINKING ABOUT TIRSA RENDÓN, I read old novels and documents from the beginning of the century to find out about camp followers. There is not much about them. They were the dogs of war. Half heroines and half whores, they marched behind the troops, following their johns; the men on horses, the women on foot.

They would sleep with a man for a couple of pesos and then leave him the next morning on a whim, unpredictable and slippery in their affairs. Or they could be loyal to him until death; get killed for just giving him a sip of water; steal or have knife fights over a chicken in order to have something they could give him to eat. They were the females in the troop, daughters of the hard life. Filthy, ragged, and drunk, like their johns. Tender and brave like them.

They knew how to do many things, and were indispensable to the men. Without them, the men would have died of hunger, of filth, of loneliness. Always agitated, always shouting, always carrying on their heads the water jugs, the luggage, and the cured meats. On the riverbanks they washed their petticoats and their men's uniforms. At night they went into the barracks or the military camps and in smoky bonfires they prepared fried chicken or turkey, made fatty salt pork soup, threw dough balls into the fire. They slept on the floor under their serapes, legs entangled with their soldiers. On very cold daybreaks, they sang *corridos* and *mañanitas* in their shrill voices, and warmed up the air with their steaming hot coffee. Then they picked up their rags and their things and left while the officers shouted at them.

"Out with these women!"

They were also in charge of the prayers: they prayed for the soldiers who were alive so they would not die, and for the dead ones so they would not have to suffer in hell. Rather than to Jesus Christ or to the spirits, they prayed to the Saint of Cabora, Teresita Urrea, a living virgin from Chihuahua who was catatonic and epileptic, and who performed miracles and blessed the carbines so that for each and every bullet, a dead man. The camp followers sought shelter under her great power and hung around their necks pieces of Teresita's poor garments, with tufts of her sacred hair. When a soldier died, they cried for him: with a lot of feeling or with a lot of wailing if he was someone they loved; and routinely just to fulfill their tradition if he was unknown.

They were also in charge of looting. After a battle, when victory was on their side, the camp followers sacked the conquered towns, the abandoned ranches. Stepping on the wounded, kicking aside the corpses, they stole, raided houses, set them on fire, and all bloody, black with soot, and intoxicated with victory, they returned dragging their booty.

As for smuggling, they were experts. In their bodices, in their babies' diapers, and in between the corn tortillas, they knew how to hide the marijuana leaves. To save them for their men, they knew how to escape the controls and the searches in the barracks. They were carriers of the *yerba santa*, the only true relief from their suffering and helplessness, the liberating weed among the soldiers at war.

The camp followers were also the news service for the troops. The men were confined, isolated, and got no news from outside. They knew only their officers' shouts, they saw nothing but their own misery, they wished nothing more than to do their time in order to leave the post. Whatever happened in the rest of the world did not penetrate the barrack walls. The camp followers, on the other hand, came and went, had a chat with the storekeeper who knew all the gossip in town, with the railroad man who brought news from distant places, with the general's mistress, who pricked up her ears to hear the plans of the high command. Through their women the troops found out if their battalion would take part in an attack or travel to another town. Thanks to the women they did not forget that there was still a world outside.

Given the opportunity, the women also participated in the fighting. At the death of her man, a woman inherited his horse, wore his cartridge belt, and shouldered his rifle.

Tirsa Rendón, Lieutenant Cardona's woman, was one of them. A camp follower.

They met one day, when military life united them on the paths of Yucatán, or on the roads of Cananea. Perhaps they celebrated an urgent wedding of love and convenience, such as the one told—with the same words but different characters—by General Urquizo in his book *Tropa vieja*. He knew all about such things from his years with the troops.

Young Tirsa and handsome Cardona had never met before. Perhaps they sat together on the train one day when the troops were being transfered. Fate squeezed one against the other in a car packed with soldiers, camp followers, and animals. The air was thick with sweat, dirty feet, rawhide, rifle oil, foods stored in pockets, farts, and burps.

The jolts of the train brought them closer until she was almost on his lap. They both liked their skin contacts. They found pleasure in each other's smell and body warmth. Perhaps he noticed her eyes, her very white whites and very dark irises, and perhaps she saw his smile.

After their flirting briefly and brusquely, came the ceremony, what General Urquizo called a "wedding in pure military style."

"What's your name, girl?"

"Tirsa Rendón, and yours?"

"Secundino Cardona."

"Are we hooked up?"

"Okay with me."

"Let's shake on it."

"Here."

Clipperton, 1914

"THEY ARE KILLING each other! They are killing each other!"

The women came running and cackling as noisily as barnyard fowl.

"They are killing each other!"

"Who? Who are killing each other?" Arnaud, who was trying to give his house a new roof, jumped down from the primitive scaffolding. "Will one of you stop shouting and tell me who's killing whom?"

But the women were already running to the north, and he had to run after them. Alicia followed him.

When they approached the Schultzes' home, they could hear the howls, the insults, the blows. Then they saw Schultz and his wife, Daría Pinzón, both in the buff, hitting each other hard and fighting like two rabid dogs. The man, growling and foaming at the mouth, held the woman by the hair and was spanking her with his enormous hand. She screeched and scratched at him, and bit his skin off. He seemed not to notice and kept on spanking her buttocks red. She gained some ground and with all the might of both her hands, grabbed the German by his

testicles, determined not to let go until Judgment Day. He howled like a
fox in heat, and after several useless attempts to free himself from
Daría, he finally pushed her away so hard, he sent her rolling like a ball
of flesh and hair among the coral reefs.

Standing in a circle around them, the women watched the scene, encouraging one or the other party.

"Cut his balls off, Daría! Cut his balls off, because he's a bastard!"

"Hit the bitch, gringo, teach her not to cheat on you!"

Arnaud, who had picked up a heavy stick, took advantage of a mo-
mentary pause, went up to Schultz and hit him hard on the head. Schultz
keeled over, melting like a wax mountain. Ramón, who had dropped to
his knees, was trying to get up when Daría Pinzón lunged on top of him,
crushing him against the ground with the weight of her mare's legs.

"Don't you meddle in this, Captain," she screamed. "This fight is between my man and me."

Arnaud managed to turn her over, and, climbing onto her back after
a scuffle, twisted her arm backward and immobilized her by pressing his
knees against her shoulders.

"I have to meddle," he gasped. "This is a matter of public order."

"This gringo is crazy, Captain. He tried to kill me."

"Shut up, you're no saint. Go get dressed! Aren't you ashamed? Bring
me a rope to tie Schultz up, now that he's out."

The women dispersed. Daría returned, half covered with a blanket,
bringing the rope. Arnaud tied Schultz, who was still unconscious,
pulling hard and winding the rope around many times until he had him
well wrapped, like a tamale. He dragged him to the entrance of the
house and tied him to a post. The man opened his eyes, looked around,
and tried to get up, but the ropes did not let him.

Alicia, who saw everything from a distance, brought Arnaud a gourd
with water. He drank from it first, and then offered it to Schultz, who
took a sip, and another, and spit the third one in Arnaud's face.

"Beast," he told him, and slapped him so hard his face turned.

"More water," Schultz begged.

"What?"

"More water."

"You better learn, damn it, to say please."

"Please."

"All right, but I'm warning you, if you spit at me again, I'll bust your mouth and your teeth will fly."

"I won't."

Arnaud put the gourd to his lips, and Schultz took several sips.

"Captain, the gringo is all yours," Daría said. "Do what you can with him. Get another woman to take care of him. I'm getting out of here."

"Oh really. Out of here? Can you tell me how? Walking on water, like Jesus Christ?"

"That's my business," the woman responded, and she left, walking fast as if she knew where she was going.

"Stop wiggling your ass, Daría Pinzón, with your lewd ways you're driving the men wild," Arnaud shouted.

"You see?" Alicia piped in. "Didn't I tell you? That loose woman is showing you her ass. . . . Now you admit it? How many times have I said so and you denied it! Tell me, Ramón, how many times did I tell you?"

"Whatever was said before the hurricane does not count. Now everything has to be reorganized," Arnaud answered, trying to cut the old familiar argument as best he could.

This was not the first incident involving Schultz. It was becoming an everyday occurrence, and Arnaud thought Daría was right: that German fellow had lost his mind. To begin with, after the storm he had developed an animosity against whatever was left of the train and the tracks. Displaying the same dedication with which he had installed and repaired them a thousand times, now he was pulling the tracks off and hurling them like javelins into the sea. When he got tired of destroying things, he lunged indiscriminately at men, women, animals, and the castaways. They especially received the brunt of his violent hostility.

Alicia had her own interpretation.

"This poor man is a work machine," she said. "He was removed from his post, and he doesn't know what to do with all that energy pent up inside him."

Daría Pinzón, in turn, blamed the lack of food.

"White people are used to eating a lot," she explained, "and hunger makes them crazy. Schultz hates the castaways for only one reason: because of them we have less to eat."

"It's not because of them. It's because of the hurricane," Arnaud corrected, not wanting the hostility toward the newcomers to spread.

"It's the same," Daría countered. "Castaways and hurricane, hurricane and castaways. Both came together, and now we go hungry."

In fact, most of the foodstuffs had been lost. Not everything, though, as Arnaud had feared at the beginning. Many sacks of grain got wet and rotted. Of the garden patch and its fruits and vegetables, there was not even a trace, and the ocean had dragged away many cans of food and other provisions. There was no more milk, no sugar, no flour, and very little coffee. But they still had some dry meat, corn, canned goods, and beans in enough quantities to allow minimal sustenance for the old as well as the new inhabitants for two or three months. On condition, of course, that the distribution be made with Calvinist niggardliness and Franciscan austerity. The situation was one of famine, but not of starvation, except for the dramatic lack of vitamin C. They could get by— Arnaud kept reassuring everyone—until the next visit of *El Demócrata* or the *Corrigan II*.

The castaways turned out to be Dutch, even though their ruined schooner—the *Nokomis*—flew the U.S. flag. Her captain was an old salt named Jens Jensen, with whom Arnaud was able to communicate in English. He found out that Jensen trafficked in diverse farm products and that he was taking his cargo to the other side of the world. The night of the hurricane, the *Nokomis* was sailing from Costa Rica to San Francisco, and the story of how the crew had survived did not differ much from what Victoriano Alvarez had guessed.

Jensen's wife was named Mary, like the Virgin, and she walked around, transparent and angelical, on the harsh Clipperton shores, her gaze lost beyond the horizon. The couple had two daughters, Mary, aged six, and Emma, aged four, and in spite of having a pale complexion like their mother's, they joined the children's hunt for crabs in the crevices, as well as their other earthly games.

The twelve Dutch folks were peaceful, well-mannered people. In spite of the pitiful physical state in which they arrived in Clipperton, they were grateful for the hospitality and started to work from the beginning at reconstructing the buildings that had not been hopelessly destroyed. They recovered medications and some clothes from their ship, and placed everything at Captain Arnaud's disposal. They participated as much as they could, and did not ask for more than was given them. They dismantled the wreck of the *Nokomis* and used her timber in the reconstruction of the isle. Even though they did not intend to annoy people, time passed and they were still there, eating. They ate as little as everybody else, but they ate, and that, for this hungry lot, was the worst thing they could do.

One evening Tirsa Rendón took some food to Secundino Cardona, who, despite some setbacks, was recovering after his miraculous rescue, thanks to his animal strength, Arnaud's care, and the prayers and sacrifices Tirsa offered to the Saint of Cabora. She helped him sit down against the wall, and gave him a full plate of beans and tortillas.

"You are lucky after all because, since you are wounded, you are the only one who eats a full ration. The rest of us have only one third of this."

"That makes sense. Otherwise we'll soon die of starvation."

"The others don't think that way. They are saying that the officers and the foreigners have enough food to eat, while the troops don't."

"Then tell Ramón to send me the same amount everybody else gets."

"He already had a fight because of this. He found out that a rumor was going around that you were the pampered favorite. That you weren't doing anything, while they had to work, and that you ate for three."

"Sons of bitches."

"That is exactly what Arnaud called them, he doesn't mince words anymore. He used to speak with elegance; now he's as foul-mouthed as a fishwife, cursing and calling anyone who crosses his path a bastard. The others are not much better. You'd have to see how the people have changed. As if the devil had peed on them. Victoriano is the one who protests the most and commands those who are disgruntled. Last night someone busted the padlocked door of the pharmacy, where the food reserves are kept, and stole a few cans of food."

"What rotten luck. We just had to struggle with the hurricane, and now we have to struggle over food. Who do you think did it?"

"Who knows. Someone left a sign on the wall that says, 'For the people's welfare,' and signed it 'The Hand That Strangles.' "

"Then we're in trouble."

"Yes indeed. At daybreak Arnaud noticed it, and you should have seen him during the closed distribution, his eyes were on fire. He ordered a general inspection and said that anyone who has stored food cans would be whipped raw. He gave the warning that he, personally, with his two God-given hands, was going to squeeze the balls of The Hand That Strangles until the last grain of rice was returned. So the thief better stop stealing and fooling around with signs on the walls."

"And what about The Hand That Strangles? That's funny, all right. Did they finally find anything?"

"No, nothing. The women say it's Victoriano, and others swear that it was the gringo."

"Schultz?"

"Yes, him."

"He's no gringo, he's German."

"What is the difference?"

"You don't know anything about geography."

"Well, gringo or German, the thing is that he's a turncoat. When the Indians here opposed Arnaud and the other white men, Schultz took the side of the Indians."

"What a life! And then an Indian like me takes sides with the white men."

"Schultz is in cahoots with Victoriano. Arnaud can silence the soldier with a couple of shouts, but nobody can control the German fellow. He says that he's a civilian and wipes his ass with military discipline. That no one can order him around. That if it were up to him, he would dump those Dutch people into the ocean and make them leave the same way they came."

"And how come people can now understand what he says?"

"They don't. Victoriano tells them. Maybe that German is only saying Hail Marys and Victoriano translates him the way he wants to. Who knows."

The animosity against the Dutch was growing like a red tide. The Clipperton people closed their eyes when they went past the *Nokomis*, not to see the wreck. They also closed their eyes not to see Captain Jensen's face whenever they met him. Alicia suspected that the source of the problem was deeper than the scarcity of food, and she talked to Ramón about it.

"There is something else," she said. "People don't just hate them, they are scared to death of them."

The fear was growing at night in what was left of the soldiers' barracks. A story had circulated that kept men, women, and children awake and terrified. They didn't know how it got started, but it was repeated in the firm belief that it was true. The story is about a Dutch captain whose ship gets caught in a storm. The crew begins to shout and plead with the captain to look for a safe refuge, but he, in his mad arrogance, refuses, and they all die. For this he is condemned to sail the high seas for all eternity, always trying to weather terrible storms. He is the Flying Dutchman. He feeds himself molten iron and drinks only bile. He can return to land only once every seven years, and wherever he goes, he brings God's wrath with him and death to all who see his ghostly ship.

The Clipperton men put two and two together and it all fit, increasing their fear. It was the year 1914, and fourteen is a multiple of seven: this was the year of the Dutchman's return. It was the *Nokomis* that had brought the hurricane and the hunger: they were God's punishments. Jens Jensen was indeed the Flying Dutchman, and they were all condemned.

Arnaud did whatever he could to assuage their fears.

"What is the problem?" he asked the soldiers at daybreak as they mustered, pale and haggard, at the call of reveille. "If the Dutchman eats iron and drinks bile, so much the better. He won't finish up our food."

But it was useless. The Clipperton people had changed. They were now more mistrustful and selfish, doubly shrewd, eager to take advantage, spoiling for a fight. They had also changed physically: they had the looks now of having suffered damage for life and because of life, and of having been made beggars by nature itself, conditions that were irreversible. It was particularly evident in the children. The hurricane broke their ties with civilization and in twenty-four hours, twenty-four centuries were reversed. Given the emergency situation in which the isle was left, the adults kept forgetting to bathe and dress them, to regulate their schedules, to teach them and correct them, and by the time they realized this, their own children had become an unfriendly lot of semi-wild, naked creatures who ran around the rocks without caring what time of day it was, ate raw fish, and went in and out of the ocean waters with amphibian ease.

Their domestic animals, freed from cages and corrals, wandered at large around the isle, totally unrestrained. Since they stopped receiving any care or food from humans, they lost feathers and fur, did not preen, and became frail. In order to survive, they had to forgo the usual behaviors of their species. They sharpened their hunting skills, and it was quite a sight to see dogs and roosters attacking and devouring crabs. The women put their babies in high places for fear the pigs would bite them. Even the reproductive functions of animals became affected, and some people insisted that there were hens pairing with boobies.

If living beings changed, so did the environment. The Dutch were so industrious in their repair efforts that in a few weeks the home of the Arnauds, part of the barracks, the dock, and some of the depots were again standing. But they could not perform miracles, and the reconstructed Clipperton looked like a caricature of itself. Now the houses were horrendous combinations of varied patches and had been reduced to minimal structures very flimsily held together, when compared to their original condition. Inside they were empty, with nothing left to fill them other than the putrid smell of the lagoon, and outside they looked crooked, tottering. Everything on the isle was diminished and impoverished, trapped in the aura of a nostalgic shantytown.

After the fight between Schultz and Daría, Arnaud started injecting the German with sedatives in doses suitable for elephants, and ordered his men to add to his drinking water a few tablespoons of passionflower extract. In spite of which Schultz stayed calm only when sleeping, and as soon as he opened one eye, he began destroying anything within his reach. Once a pig was sniffing around him and he smashed its head with a clenched fist. Another day it was hens. Sergeant Irra's wife reported that the German had attempted to slash the throat of one of her children, but nobody believed her because she was a notorious liar and because, deep down, everybody knew that Schultz was not a murderer.

One night he broke the rope that tied him to his house, and he appeared in the barracks, naked and screaming, causing more terror than the Abominable Snowman. The soldiers caught him, sedated him, and, instead of ropes, put a chain around his neck. Arnaud ordered that he be untied from the post every morning, and that three men, holding fast to his chain, were to take him for a walk. That dangerous and exhausting task was soon discontinued, and Schultz remained confined day and night.

After a month, he had calmed himself again and spent his time going around the post and repeating the same words: "I'm bored, I'm bored, and I'm bored. I'm bored, I'm bored, and I'm bored."

Then the soldiers brought a bed closer to him so he would not have to sleep on the floor, and those in charge of feeding him were able to take cups of water and plates of food to him without fear that he would smash their heads with them. He showed improvement, and it was decided to assign a woman to take care of him, of bathing and feeding him.

Daría Pinzón didn't even want to know of this. She was not frightened by stories of Flying Dutchmen, and had started a relationship with a fat one, full of warts, by the name of Halvorsen. She fixed up her daughter, Jesusa, who had reached puberty, with Knowles, a lanky one with a big nose.

The one chosen to take care of Gustav Schultz was Altagracia Quiroz.

Altagracia was the young girl the Arnauds had hired the year before at the Hotel San Agustín to help them with their children. She had come to Clipperton with them, with the incentive of being paid a double salary, and for the thrill of getting to know the sea. But she regretted it. The sea did not seem like much, and on the isle the paper bills she could accumulate from her wages were good for nothing. She was fourteen, short and rather plain, though she had that beautiful head of hair. Yet people were not aware of it because she kept it covered.

During the first weeks she had worked so hard at the Arnaud home that she had no time at all to spare. She watered the vegetable patch, ran after the children, washed, starched, and ironed the shirts, shined the silver, helped in the kitchen by grinding corn and washing dishes. After the hurricane things changed. The children did not want to be looked after, there was no starch for the clothes, no patch to water, no silver to shine, and, with all the scarcities that strangled Clipperton, the only thing they had plenty of was time.

Altagracia equipped herself with sponges, brushes, and buckets of water, and step by step, she approached Schultz's cabin. She saw him standing with the chain around his neck, lonely, broken, and filthy, like a big bear in captivity, and right away her fear melted away.

"Come, come," she said while approaching him, as if she were calling a domestic animal.

Schultz growled a little but took the piece of bacon she offered him and allowed her to get closer. Cautiously, she sponged the encrusted dirt off his back. Each time he growled, she gave him a piece of bacon, until she managed to get him passably clean. Then she helped him put on a grungy pair of pants that she found on the floor, tossed in a corner, the first piece of clothing Schultz wore during his period of madness. Then she brought him fried fish and a cup of steaming hot coffee. He ate the fish but spilled the coffee on the floor. She swept around his bed, looked for his best shirts, and took them with her.

The next day she came back with his shirts mended, washed, and ironed, and since it was a chilly morning, she lit a fire to heat the buckets of water. Schultz reacted so well to the warm water that he allowed her to wash his matted hair. Altagracia did it very carefully, massaging the scalp with the tips of her fingers, as she did with the Arnaud children. He also let her cut his nails, which already looked like claws, but growled in protest when she tried to cut his toenails as well.

In a few weeks tremendous progress was made. He allowed her to comb his hair, spruce him up, and even perfume him as if she were playing with a doll. She learned not to take any black food to him because he rejected it, and, once in a while, to smuggle a shot of *mezcal* to him. She polished his boots, darned his socks, brushed his big yellow teeth with ashes. She took him out for a walk, and he accepted being pulled by the chain like a lap dog.

Day by day, the cleaning up and feeding sessions became lengthier and more elaborate. At the beginning she had stayed from six to six thirty in the morning, and it got to be from six in the morning to six in the evening. Altagracia came at daybreak and returned to the Arnauds at dusk. When she left, Schultz was still chained to his post, sitting on his bed, playing solitary chess, updating the Pacific Phosphate books, looking at the stars, and waiting for her return at dawn.

He called her Alta or Altita, and she called him Towhead, German, or gringo. He worked hard to teach her how to play chess, she wanted him to learn Spanish.

"*Caballa,*" he said, holding the horse chess piece.

"*Caballa* to you. It is called *caballo.*"

"*Caballa* to you, too. That's not the way you move that piece."

"And how is it that, before, no one could understand you, and now, suddenly, you talk like a person?"

"Because now I want to, and before I didn't."

That was true. For the first time in his long stay in America, Gustav Schultz felt the desire and the need to communicate with someone.

"And how come you were crazy before and now you're not?"

"I was not crazy before and I'm not crazy now."

His aggressive behavior had disappeared. However, he still had the chain on his neck, and when someone approached him other than Altagracia, he roared and smashed dishes on the floor.

"I'm going to ask for this animal chain to be taken off," she said.

"Don't ask for anything. If they take off the chain and declare me sane, they will never let you come back to me anymore."

"I am going to tell everybody that you can speak Spanish."

"No, don't say a word. I don't want to talk to them."

Their passion started slowly, softly. They felt it coming once she took off the shawl that always covered her head, and her hair, liberated, dropped down to her ankles. It was a yard and a half of natural silk, a black-as-night cascade, a shining animal with a life of its own. Schultz could not believe what he saw. He finally dared to touch it, as if putting his hands into a treasure chest full of precious stones.

"This is pirate Clipperton's treasure. Everybody tried so hard, but I am the one who found it."

"It's just black hair, like everybody else's. Your hair is nicer, because it's blond."

"You don't know what treasure you have on your head, my child."

"I bet you don't know how to braid it."

"I bet I do."

He helped her lose her virginity with tenderness and without any pressure. From then on, he devoted himself to teaching her how to make love with the same patience and wisdom with which he was teaching her to play chess.

Three months had elapsed since the hurricane, and the ship from the Mexican Navy was already two months late. Captain Jens Jensen, who had felt hopeful about the guarantees of government help Arnaud had offered him, came to the conclusion that it was absurd and suicidal to keep waiting. The more he thought about it, the more convinced he became, and he knew that he should have realized this since the day following his forced arrival at Clipperton.

He asked Arnaud's permission to repair a rowboat.

It was a ten-foot boat, big enough for four men. He supplied it with four oars and improvised a mast and a sail. When it was ready, he informed Arnaud of his decision to send part of his crew—his best four seamen—to the Mexican coast to ask for help.

"You are sending them to their deaths," Arnaud told him.

"Perhaps not," answered Jensen.

"They are going to be smashed against the reefs. They'll get lost at sea. The dark nights will turn into nightmares. They'll run out of food and water. And the sharks will attack them."

"You are an army man, Captain Arnaud, and you mistrust the sea. I am a mariner and I can't stay locked on land, doing nothing, abusing your hospitality, and risking the lives of your people and mine."

"Better wait a little longer. The supply boat should come within two weeks, God willing."

"You said it: God willing. With all respect for your beliefs, I prefer to place my trust in my own men."

"Well, then, you have my blessings. May God protect your men."

The following day, June 4, Second Lieutenant Hansen and three crewmen, Oliver, Henrikson, and Miller, sailed toward Mexico in the small sailboat, with some navigational instruments Arnaud had provided, and food and water for twelve days.

The entire Clipperton population—except Gustav Schultz and Altagracia Quiroz, who were in a world of their own—stood at the dock to watch them leave.

On the U.S.S. Cleveland, Heading for Acapulco, 1914

❦

1. On 21 June, at about 1500, while the *Cleveland* was anchored at Acapulco, a small boat approached. It was commanded by L. Hansen, second lieutenant from the U.S. schooner *Nokomis,* with a crew of two. Having left Clipperton Island 17 days earlier, they arrived in very poor physical condition and reported having lost a man en route. The lieutenant also reported that the *Nokomis* had sailed from San Francisco under Captain Jens Jensen and was shipwrecked at Clipperton before dawn on 28 February 1914, with the following crew: Captain Jens Jensen, his wife, and two children; First Lieutenant C. Halvorsen, Second Lieutenant L. Hansen; and J. Oliver, H. Henrikson, J. Halvorsen, and W. Miller, seamen; H. Brown, shipboy; and H. Knowles, cook. Hansen stated that when he left the island, those who remained had supplies for only 17 days.

2. In view of this report, I considered they were in urgent need of help, so I left for Clipperton at 0930 the following morning. I had notified the

British vice consul and the London agents of the Pacific Phosphate Company Ltd., who were sending 200 bales of foodstuffs to their Clipperton representative and to the Mexican troops posted there, consisting of two officers, eleven men, and their families. The *Cleveland* arrived at the island on the 25th at 1100.

3. That afternoon the above-mentioned individuals came aboard, together with the Pacific Phosphate Company Ltd. representative, Mr. G. Schultz, his wife, and daughter. Mr. Schultz, a German citizen who had stayed on the island for several years representing that company, was in a personal situation. His relationship with the officer in charge of the post on the island had reached such antagonism that the commanding officer reported that Mr. Schultz, in his opinion, had lost his mind. From his side, Mr. Schultz reported on the Clipperton shipwreck of Captain Jens Jensen's ship at dawn on 28 February 1914, and Schultz also said that his relationship with the Mexican officer in charge had soured. In consequence, I considered it prudent to take Mr. Schultz and his family to Acapulco.

4. At 1520 I greeted a Mexican boat commanded by the port captain, Ramón Arnaud Vignon, who signed the receipt for the 200 bales of foodstuffs. The port captain departed the *Cleveland* at 1555.

(Signed)
Captain W. Williams

U.S.S. Cleveland, Clipperton Island, 1914

❦

ON JUNE 25 Ramón Arnaud was having some fish with his wife and children when he saw a ship looming on the horizon. His reaction was that of a person watching a loved one return, because he thought the ship belonged to the Mexican Navy. They had finally come to take care of him! Where was Captain Jensen? Ramón already knew what to tell him. He would say, "Don't you see it was better to wait? I knew my superiors would not fail me."

Alicia saw her husband instantly shift from joy to dejection: his face turned paper white as he realized his mistake. The approaching vessel was flying the American flag. It was the U.S.S. *Cleveland* coming to the rescue of the crew of the *Nokomis*.

In spite of the many requests to his superiors that Arnaud had sent through the four Dutchmen, the ship had not come for him but for Jensen's people. Jensen had been right to mistrust his words and to act on his own, Ramón Arnaud thought bitterly.

His disappointment was such that while all the others rushed to the dock, he remained seated without moving a finger for the whole hour it took the ship to anchor on the other side of the reef. A boat landed with two emissaries, and finally a seaman handed him a note from the captain of the *Cleveland*, together with a letter from Mexico.

The note from the captain—named Williams—indicated that his intent was only to take the crew from the *Nokomis* with him, inquire about Gustav Schultz, deliver some provisions, and offer help. The letter was from his father-in-law, Don Félix Rovira, and it was addressed to Alicia. She read it out loud.

My dearest child:

Joy fills my heart. I do not need to tell you that I am leaving for the port right now, and I shall be waiting for you, even though I might have to wait there a whole week for you.

My dream of every single day, during all these years, will finally come true. I am going to see you again—you and Ramón and my grandchildren—and be with you without the threat of a new separation.

I looked for Colonel Avalos to inform him of your urgent needs but he is no longer in Acapulco. He has been transferred, and I was unable to find out his address. The new commander of the zone is Colonel Luis Griviera, who admitted to me that, due to the constant rebel attacks, he is in no position to be able to send ships to Clipperton. He suggested it is best that you return on the Cleveland, *taking advantage of the captain's kind offer to render this service. My impression of Colonel Griviera is that he is too busy with his own survival to attend to anyone else's.*

I have not been able to talk in person with the three Dutch sailors who brought news of you to this port, but I know they reported that there were provisions on the island for three or four more days. I pray to God they last until you get the boxes the British consul is sending.

I am writing this to you in haste, my dear, for I only learned of your situation barely two days ago. I left Salina Cruz immediately for Aca-

pulco, and the efforts on your behalf have not given me a minute to spare. The American ship that takes this missive to you and has promised to bring you back here sails very shortly. For that reason I will not comment on the situation our homeland is going through. There will be time enough to discuss these things (though it seems there is not enough time for anyone to comprehend so many chaotic events).

I am sending you, yes, newspaper clippings about the United States invasion of Veracruz. It has caused an outrage all over the country and, I daresay, in the whole continent. I think that Ramón should be aware of this, since you will be sailing on an invader's warship. As to the personal intentions of Captain Williams, I think they are honest and humanitarian. By all means, I believe it is of the utmost urgency that you return with him, since the possibilities for a Mexican ship to sail to Clipperton seem remote under the present circumstances. My heart will summon the strength that it no longer possesses in order to withstand this period of waiting until your return.

Your father

"Wait a minute," Ramón said when she finished reading the letter. "Let's take this one step at a time, because I don't understand anything. I wrote to the authorities, and your father answers. I ask for a Mexican ship, and we get an American one. And what's this invasion of Veracruz? Let me see the clippings."

They quickly read every word in the clippings sent by Don Félix and concluded that General Huerta was officially in power but without popular support, which was on the side of the revolutionaries, and without the support of the United States, which had invaded the port of Veracruz. The events had come to a climax on April 7. In Tampico an officer and seven men from the American cruiser *Dolphin* had disembarked in order to buy fuel. Once on land they were arrested by Huerta's officials. Two hours later, a Mexican general set them free, apologizing for the mistake. President Wilson demanded that the Mexicans raise the American flag and, in reparation, honor it with a twenty-one-gun salute. General Huerta answered that Mexico would comply with the twenty-one-gun salute provided that the Mexican flag was equally honored by the United States. Seizing upon this as an excuse, Wilson ordered the military intervention he had long prepared, and sent his fleet into Mexican waters. On April 21, the U.S. Marines occupied the Custom House in Veracruz. After the Mexican Naval Academy cadets had resisted the attack for twelve hours and suffered the loss of 126 patriots, on April 22 the post surrendered. Thousands of Mexicans all over the country volunteered to join Huerta's army to fight the invaders. At the same time, the revolutionary forces commanded by Venustiano Carranza, who controlled more than half the territory, also opposed the foreign invasion.

"Why on earth does your father think that we are leaving on that ship?"

"He is taking for granted that Mexican ships are not coming anymore."

"What do you mean, 'not coming'? Nobody has ordered me to leave this post."

"You don't have orders to leave, but you don't have orders to stay either. I think the truth is, Ramón, that nobody cares. With the country in such a chaotic situation, probably nobody even remembers we exist."

"The United States invades, all of Mexico resists, and do you think I'm going to surrender Clipperton without a shot? Is that what you're asking me?"

"I'm not asking you anything. I have never asked you for anything"— Alicia's voice broke, and she began to cry. Softly at first, then emotionally, interrupting to wipe her eyes with a handkerchief and blowing her nose. But the tears rushed out in their own uncontrollable dynamic, making her breathing difficult.

"Have a good cry," Arnaud said. "Let it all come out, all the complaints you have held back for six years."

Finally she was able to speak again.

"I have never asked for us to leave, and I am not going to ask you now. But why don't you realize that it makes me sad to think of my father standing there at the port, waiting for us. How can you expect me not to be heartbroken seeing that those uneducated, underfed creatures running around are my own children? How could I not think that passing up this last chance to leave would force us to stay here forever, and perish. . . ."

Alicia could have kept talking for hours, protesting, complaining about her bad luck, telling her husband all that she had not said in six years about her marriage and her life on the isle. But at that moment Captain Jensen joined them. He was shaved and groomed, and Arnaud felt somewhat intimidated by the other's regained position as a member of the civilized world.

"Better hush, dear, Jensen is coming," he interrupted her. "Tell him that I am not in. I don't want to see him before I know what I should do."

"And if he asks me where you are?" Alicia was still sobbing, her eyes red and her nose stuffy.

"Tell him I am at a Gala Ball. Or at the horse races."

"And what about me? Is it all right for him to see me crying?" she screamed at Ramón's back as he started to leave. "Well, fine! Let Jensen see me, let everybody see me crying! I am sick of pretending to be happy!"

Arnaud escaped through the back door and walked along the beach, taking long strides over the moving carpet of red crabs. He stepped on several of them at every move, and the crackling sound of the crushed crab shells pierced his ears. This triggered the nervous twitch of his upper lip, and at regular intervals his face contracted in an involuntary grimace.

He was trying to think, he needed to understand, but, like a clock without a spring, his mind was not responding. It had stopped. Was the situation as drastic as his father-in-law had made it appear? Was it a black-and-white choice—either to leave now or to stay forever?—or were there intermediate shades that Don Félix as an anguished father could not perceive? Was Huerta's downfall and the collapse of the federal army imminent? Don Félix had always favored the rebels and perhaps that made him overestimate their importance. Or was he right this time? Even so, the foreign invasion had changed everything; it had to, and internal differences would end at the threat from the outside. Wouldn't they? That man Carranza would offer a truce to General Huerta while they fought the invader together. Or would he? If the enemy made the federal army, his army, surrender, what role would he have in Clipperton? Why must he stay if Avalos and all the others went their own ways? However, it is the rats that abandon a sinking ship. Arnaud had no information, and his head was spinning in search of inspiration. He needed to guess right. He read and reread the letter and the clippings, looking for a solution in every phrase, in every word.

Images were flashing fast in his mind, driving him to despair. Two were much more insistent than the others. They were contradictory, irreconcilable; one he would have to reject because there was no room for both, and his head was about to crack like the crabs he was stepping on.

In one he saw Alicia crying and his children abandoned, wild, badly undernourished, and sick.

"I cannot stay here," he said out loud. "I cannot stay here."

In the other he saw himself a few years back, facing the blackened walls of the prison at Tlatelolco and making his solemn promise that "the next time I will stand firm, come what may, next time I will prevail. Better dead, a thousand times better, than being humiliated again."

"I cannot leave," he contradicted himself. "I cannot leave."

He looked for Cardona. He found him standing in the shed, trying to take his first steps using two pieces of wood as crutches.

"Cardona, sit down. And think carefully about what I am going to tell you."

"The gringo ship arrived to rescue the Dutchmen, right?" asked the lieutenant.

"Yes."

"Then the four on the little boat made it to Acapulco—"

"Yes, but only three of them got there."

"That was not a bad deal then. Who didn't make it?"

"I don't know yet."

"Another Flying Dutchman who eats melted iron and drinks bile."

"May he rest in peace."

"Ramón, tell me, do you really believe that someone who dies like that, without a Christian burial, can ever find peace? I would not like to be floating about for all eternity."

"Who knows? But there is a serious matter here, Secundino. Listen to this."

Ramón read his father-in-law's letter, and then the news about the invasion. Cardona did not utter a word until he finished.

"Twenty-one-gun salute? Sure. Right away. Just give me a minute—"

"The captain of the *Cleveland* is also offering to take us to Acapulco. You already know what my father-in-law says— If not now, when? On the other hand, those who are rescuing us here are the same ones who invaded over there. It's not an easy thing to decide, and I would like to know your opinion."

Cardona scratched his head.

"What could happen if we leave? Wait—I mean for a few days, in order to make contact with Colonel Avalos, or with someone who could tell us what's what, who could tell us what the plan is. Hey, we cannot continue the way we are. This looks like an orphanage."

"And if this maneuver is just an enemy trap?"

"It looks more like a friendly trap. Besides, which enemy? The gringos or the French? Aren't we supposed to fight against the French to keep from losing this island?"

"From what I see, now it's the gringos we are fighting against in order not to lose all of Mexico. I don't know, Cardona," he said in a firmer voice and straightening his back. "However, I feel it's our duty to stay in honor of the hundred and twenty-six Veracruz patriots."

"Well, yes," Cardona offered after some thought. "But Veracruz was invaded, and Clipperton was not. . . ."

"But we don't know what might happen."

"No, we don't. But there isn't much we could do anyhow."

"We could offer the ultimate sacrifice for our homeland, like our fellow soldiers in Veracruz. . . ."

"What a darned life."

"Yes, sure enough, life could be better."

They remained in silence for a long time, until Arnaud got up.

"I want to make clear to you that your condition as a seriously wounded soldier places you in a special situation, very different from mine. We cannot take care of you properly here, and you have every right in the world to leave in order to get proper treatment. If you leave, you will not fail Mexico, you will not fail your military honor, you will not fail me or anybody else."

Lieutenant Cardona did not have to think much about it.

"Do you remember what you told me in the cave during the hurricane?" he asked Arnaud. "Either the two of us live, or the two of us die. That was what you said. It was good then, it is good now. If you stay, I stay."

"Let's shake on it."

"Here."

"I must look for Alicia," Arnaud said walking toward the door. "She had never complained, and today when she did, I left her talking to the wall."

At that moment Sergeant Irra rushed in. He had been looking for Arnaud everywhere on the island. He informed him that the captain of the *Cleveland* wanted to meet the port captain to deliver the food supplies; that he had orders from the British consul to take Gustav Schultz to Acapulco, if he so wished; and that Jens Jensen and the rest of the Dutchmen wanted to say good-bye personally.

"You take care of going to the *Cleveland* for the provisions," Arnaud said to Cardona, "and tell the captain that I will make the official clearing later."

"I can barely walk, Ramón."

"Have some of the men carry you."

"But I wonder, wouldn't it be better if you went? In what language do you want me to communicate with him?"

"Find a way. I must talk with Alicia first, the rest will have to wait."

"And what do we do with Schultz, Captain?" asked Irra, waiting for orders. "Do we let him loose, or do we take him in tied up?"

"Set him him free, Irra, and we'll see what happens. If he becomes too nervous, triple up his dosage of passionflower tea, but make sure he boards the *Cleveland*," answered Arnaud, considering the matter closed.

On the other side of the island, Gustav Schultz and Altagracia had not seen the ship approach and were totally unaware of the situation. Everything remained the same, immutable, inside the hermetic bubble where they had taken refuge. Even in his madness, Schultz had the lucidity to understand that the sweet, homely girl was enough of a pretext for him to come to terms with reason and to anchor himself in reality. Thanks to her he did not feel alone for the first time in his life.

That day his warm bath had taken two hours, and according to the ritual they had established, it concluded with the act of love.

Schultz had Altagracia lying by his side, her head on his shoulder. He found serenity in the shade of her extraordinary hair.

"I am going to count every hair on your head, one by one," he would say, "and every day I am going to count them again, to make sure there is none missing."

His heart was at peace, his body relaxed, and the fresh sweep of the trade winds carried away all his past anguish.

"The madman has raped the child!"

The wild shouts of the sergeant broke into a thousand pieces the gentle calmness. Before Schultz could get up, Irra and three other men lunged at him and beat him with their bare fists and whatever else they found handy.

"Dirty gringo, get your hands off that girl!" they shouted.

Altagracia got scared like a little animal and ran into the cabin. Through the cracks in the wall she saw how they tied his hands and took him away, shoving and pulling him by his chain.

She overcame her fear and ran after them.

"Where are you taking him?"

"A ship came for him. Today he goes to hell, the madman."

"Don't take him that way, Irra," she pleaded, "at least let him put some clothes on. Don't you have some respect for a human being?"

"He's more beastly than the beasts."

"You are the wild beasts," she murmured, and while the soldiers struggled at dragging him, she managed to get him into a pair of pants and a shirt.

Schultz roared with a pained blind fury. Everyone could hear his screams, which echoed through the cliffs, but only Altagracia was able to hear a soft, dry cracking sound that escaped from his breast like a sigh.

"They are breaking your soul, Towhead," she said.

On the other side of the island, Ramón Arnaud had met his wife. She was not crying anymore. Broom in hand, she was sweeping the ramshackle porch at home.

"Why are you sweeping?" he asked her.

"Because I already know what your decision will be. And if we are going to continue living here, it might as well be clean."

"Come, I want you to understand something."

They sat on the floor of the eastern terrace where sometime in the past there had been a hammock for watching the sun come up.

"Alicia, do you remember that I told you once I was doing nothing because I felt it was not my war? Well, now I feel this really is my war. I still don't know whether we should leave or stay; the only thing I know is that I have to fight this war."

At the dock Arnaud met Cardona, who was hobbling past the piles of wooden boxes, recording everything in a notebook.

"Two hundred boxes, Ramón," the lieutenant shouted with enthusiasm. "We have dried beef, wafers, sausages, lard, coffee, you name it. Enough for three more months."

"That will give us the option to stay or to leave."

"What I would like to know is who sent this food and for whom."

"Who else could it be? The Mexican Army sent it to us, of course."

"I don't believe so, Ramón. With the little English I know, I understood it came from the British consul for Gustav Schultz."

"Then, let him leave it to us as his legacy. Any citrus fruit?" Arnaud inquired.

"Haven't seen any."

"That's bad news. Very bad."

Arnaud got into a boat and asked to be taken to the *Cleveland*. He still did not know what his decision would be, and he could think of nothing on the way. At 1520 he boarded, and Captain Williams received him in his private office, adjacent to his cabin. It was a small interior room, all paneled in cedar, with the scent of good wood and fine tobacco. On his working table there were writing pens and an inkwell, and a machine of such novel design that it took Arnaud some time before he figured out it was a typewriter. The furniture was sparse but deep cushioned, covered in barely faded, wine-red velour. A Persian rug covered the floor, and a copper and opaline glass lamp lit the room evenly, giving the effect of natural light. In one corner was a trunk in embossed leather, and, in the opposite corner, a heavy iron stove obviously in disuse and covered with books.

Captain Williams's physique seemed more at home in this intimate environment than in the impersonal harshness of his battleship. He was an older man, pale, and so refined-looking that he seemed never to have been exposed to direct sunlight or even a sea breeze. He wore very thin rimmed spectacles, and one could detect a discreet scent of cologne. He offered Arnaud a seat and a cup of espresso along with a glass of cognac. As they exchanged the customary greetings, Arnaud kept fingering the velour, the leather, the warm cup, and took in the wonderful scents of wood, cologne, and tobacco, his body inspired by the memory of these almost forgotten textures and smells. An uncomfortable nostalgia for a better world was beginning to creep over him. He felt dirty, unkempt, smelly, and jarred by a great irrational impulse to leave. He had delayed this interview as much as possible because he knew it would place him in a disadvantageous position. After not even two minutes, and in spite of Williams's politeness, he did not wish to prolong this meeting a second longer than purely necessary.

Arnaud expressed gratitude for the boxes of supplies, and Williams asked about Gustav Schultz. Ramón, who had completely forgotten the German fellow, explained that he was being brought on board because this strange man's altered state, after suffering several mental breakdowns, had made it advisable to sedate him before departure. He spoke ill of Schultz, in too many words and with too many adjectives, which he regretted, noting the detachment in Williams's blank expression as he listened.

Looking at the list of names, Williams said that Lieutenant Cardona had informed him that two ladies, Daría and Jesusa—already on board—would travel with Mr. Schultz as his wife and daughter.

"That is correct, sir. They are his wife and daughter," answered Arnaud emphatically, but realized his error a second later. He understood the sense of Williams's query when he imagined the scene as sharply as if he were actually seeing the two women climbing on board and embracing their Dutch lovers. His face turned red.

"Well, more or less," he stammered, not knowing what else to say.

"Don't trouble yourself, Captain, I understand; it was just a routine question."

The issue of Daría and Jesusa, which he had overlooked, had already placed him in a bad light. And he knew things would get worse. In openly cordial tones, Williams repeated his offer to take him to Mexico together with his family and the rest of the people in Clipperton. Jensen had told him about their hospitality and generosity in spite of conditions. "That kind of conduct deserves a reciprocal gesture," Williams added.

"I am deeply grateful, but I have not received orders yet from my superiors to abandon my post."

"At this point your superiors are in no condition to issue orders, not even to themselves," answered Captain Williams with a kind smile. "The federal army is disbanded."

Arnaud felt deeply hurt. Realizing it, Williams retreated.

"It's just my personal opinion, of course," he said. "Don't take offense."

Ramón Arnaud took time to answer, to feel the weight that each of his words would have, and finally said, "Having to take care of public order makes things difficult for Colonel Huerta, and the arbitrary invasion by your country makes things difficult for my country. Those are two powerful reasons why I cannot abandon my post."

"Everything has changed since you were sent here. Everything. It is not just Mexico's internal situation, it is, above all, the war."

"Are you referring to the war between your country and mine?"

"No, Captain Arnaud. I am referring to the war that is about to break out between one half of the world and the other half. I suppose that you are aware of this," answered Williams, while offering him a Havana cigar. "Would you care for one?"

Ramón felt the rug pulled out from under him. The news had jolted and stunned him like an exploding grenade. It was too much. What war? What world? Why? Which side would Mexico be on? He was dying to know, and his heart began racing like a mad horse. He had to summon all his military pride and all of his willpower in order to lie.

"Of course, Captain Williams. I am fully aware of the imminence of war. But that does not affect my decision."

His own words reverberated in his head: "But that does not affect my decision." He was closing the last door, he felt. This was suicide, and he was condemning his men, his wife, his children. But he contained himself and did not retract. From the corner of his eye he saw the Cuban cigar Williams was offering him. It was a Flor de Lobeto, fragrant and magnificent. For many months he had not seen one. He would have gladly exchanged his little finger for it. But he lied.

"A Havana cigar? No thanks, I just had one."

"As you wish," he heard the other man say.

Time was melting in his head. The minutes stretched with rubbery elasticity, unbearably: "As . . . you . . . wish." Between one word and the next there was an eternity, and meanwhile, the only possibility of being rescued vanished, escaped like the smoke of the cigar that Williams had just lit.

Suddenly, time recovered its usual speed. The Mexican captain felt an unexpected tingling in the pit of the stomach, and an irrepressible urge to live made him speak.

"However, Captain Williams, since this is a question that also affects my men, I would like to ask for some time to consult with them before I give you a definitive answer."

"Of course, Captain. Think about it, and consult with them."

Williams pulled his watch chain and checked the time.

"I wish to sail in an hour, if there are no objections," he said.

They said their good-byes. On deck Ramón met Jens Jensen, his wife, Mary, as evanescent as ever, and the rest of the Dutchmen. They embraced and wished one another good luck.

Once in the rowboat on his way to the dock, Arnaud breathed deeply, relaxed on the seat with a brief smile, and thought: There is an invasion, a civil war, and a world war while I am here, wrapped in my own thoughts, worrying about whether booby eggs are better fried or scrambled.

It was already 1555. Before 1655 he had to make the most serious decision of his life.

After landing, he told Cardona: "A world war broke out. Or is about to. Don't ask me any more. I did not dare ask, I didn't want to concede to that gringo that I didn't know. We'll find out when the Mexican boat gets here."

"If we wait that long, we'll find out who started it and who won, all at the same time."

Arnaud and Cardona summoned the rest of their people, and, a few minutes later, Sergeant Irra appeared on the dock holding Gustav Schultz by the arm. Due to the triple dosage of passionflower tea, the poor German fellow struggled, like a sleepwalker or a drunkard, in an iridescent, blurred, elusive world. He sensed vaguely that something ominous was about to happen to him, but he couldn't figure out what. Even his own anguish dissolved into a nameless feeling. His head was turning around, then it stopped; it rushed forward; it swooped down in a painful and confused trajectory to the depths. His feet tripped forward; he mouthed incoherent words; he was beating Sergeant Irra clumsily.

Altagracia Quiroz ran after them. The moment he saw her, Schultz was able to collect all the loose pieces of his delirium. With a violent jolt he broke free from Irra, embraced Altagracia, and even though he could not fully control his numb, sticky tongue, the words he uttered came from deep inside.

"Come with me, Altita."

"I can't, Towhead. I wish I could. I came with Mrs. Alicia, and I have to stay with her."

Recovering, Sergeant Irra again grabbed Schultz and threw him into the rowboat, where two soldiers were waiting to take him to the *Cleveland*.

The boat left. Schultz defied his condition and the rocking of the waves, and managed to stand up.

"I'll come back for you, Altagracia," he shouted. "I swear to you. I swear to you I'll get you out of here and marry you. I swear!"

The ocean was gray, the sky was violet, and the girl remained at the dock, alone. She heard the German's words, and to bid him farewell she took off the shawl covering her head. Her hair cascaded almost to the ground, sparkling under the afternoon sun, and waved softly in the breeze like a black flag.

In the meantime, Ramón Arnaud ordered the troops to interrupt their tasks and report in formation to the plaza—where their old vegetable garden, now barren, had been—in full uniform, rifles and all. Young Pedro Carvajal made the bugle call, and the men mustered.

"Platoon, charge . . . weapons!" barked Cardona. Arnaud, next to him, just watched.

The ten soldiers who made up the garrison were standing in the inhospitable and harsh wasteland. If a soldier had shoes, he had no shirt; if he had a rifle, he had no sword; if he had a cartridge belt, he had no ammunition. They had only whatever the hurricane had not taken away. Around them in a semicircle, the women stood watching, babes in their arms. They were all battered people in a battered place.

"Present . . . arms!"

They sang the Mexican national anthem and raised the new flag, the one nuns had embroidered. When it was up, Arnaud saw that it was as faded and frayed as the old one. There was no red or green, the white center now extended to the sides. And without the eagle and the serpent, it was nothing but a white sheet in the sun.

Easy come, easy go, Ramón thought, and watched his people. We look like ghosts, and on top of that, we belong to an army which no longer exists. How could he convince them to go on, not to quit? Worse yet, with what arguments could he convince himself? He focused on the tortured nights that he had spent in prison, on his regrets while facing the black walls in Tlatelolco, and as he felt the taste of humiliation in his mouth, he managed to find the arguments he was looking for.

He began his speech hesitantly. About the defeat of their army he didn't say much, not to demoralize them. And about the world war, he said nothing, not to overwhelm them. He picked up energy getting into his historical account of foreign invasions and the national resistance. His enthusiasm rose together with his voice as he informed them of the events in Veracruz, and he waxed poetic talking about the defense of Clipperton. By the time he began to notice it, everybody was crying with heroic fervor.

"In honor of those who fell in the struggle against the American invaders," he announced at the peak of his harangue, "we are going to give them the twenty-one-gun salute President Wilson wanted. But this time, damn it, we'll be saluting our own flag. The Mexican flag!"

Cardona approached him and murmured in his ear.

"Twenty-one volleys is too much, my friend. We'll have no powder left."

"Well, ten then."

"Five?"

"There will be only five blasts," shouted Arnaud. "But with ball, so they reach Washington!"

"And even Paris!" broke in Cardona, who was not forgetting their quarrel with the French.

More or less in unison, the ten rifles fired five times. The thunder of fifty shots was heard, and the smoke from the blasts darkened the sky. Their nostrils felt the burning and their eyes smarted, partly because of the powder and partly because of emotion. All, even the women and children, ended up crying.

They are already mine, Ramón thought. He explained the possibilities and the difficulties of trying to survive on the island, the military and political significance of staying, the personal advantages of leaving, and he informed them of the offer by the captain of the *Cleveland* to take them back to Acapulco, together with their families.

"Whoever wishes to leave has my permission to do so," he added last. "In these confusing circumstances, I cannot decide your fate by asking you to stay."

He gave them some time to think about it and discuss it with their women. They dispersed. Each one joined his own family. Once in a while, someone would go from one group to another. Whispers, laughter, crying, and arguments followed. Some returned to the plaza before the call. When they were in formation, Arnaud called the roll one by one, for each man to report his decision.

"Private Rodríguez, Silverio.
Private Juárez, Dionisio.
Private Pérez, Arnulfo.
Private Mejía, Constancio.
Private Almazán, Faustino.
Private Carvajal, Pedro.
Private Alvarez, Victoriano.
Corporal Lara, Felipe.
Sergeant Irra, Agustín.

Lieutenant Cardona, Secundino."

One by one, each man stepped forward and gave his answer. After the last one spoke, Arnaud ordered them to break ranks.

At 1650, five minutes before the appointed time, the rowboat was delivering their message to the *Cleveland*.

Captain Williams:
On behalf of the Mexican Army, my garrison, and myself, I thank you for the valuable assistance granted. Being in state of war, as we are, we find your attitude to be a worthy model of gentlemanly exchange between combatants. We cordially decline your offer to take us to Acapulco. My men and I, together with our wives and children, will remain here until we receive from our superiors orders to the contrary.

Signed, Captain Ramón Arnaud Vignon,
Governor of Clipperton Island,
territory of the sovereign Republic of Mexico
Clipperton, 25 June 1914.

Back on the isle, sitting on the leaning trunk of a palm tree, Arnaud still did not know whether the correct decision was to leave or to stay. But he no longer cared. Be what may, this had been the best day of his life, the day in which he had recovered his dignity and done something memorable. He was on top of the world.

He saw the *Cleveland* sailing away and felt sorry for Captain Williams, with his little artificial, comfortable corner, his eau de cologne, velour-covered chairs, cognac glasses; Captain Williams, backed by the easy security of his powerful ship. Ramón thought that he did not envy him—or at least, not much—because this time he, Ramón Arnaud, had been the true prince, the dandy, the tough son of a bitch. His decision to stay made him feel pleased with himself, fulfilled, big; and the loyalty of his people—Alicia, Cardona, his men—made him feel like a giant. Fortune did not offer everyone the possibility of playing for all or nothing in the ultimate showdown, of putting to the test each and every fiber in one's body, of lying at the razor's edge for honor and courage.

And this had happened to him. This time he, Ramón Arnaud, had measured up. He was a prince, a warrior, a show-off, a bastard. The old blemish of his desertion had been obliterated, his debt with fate had been paid, and he had finally managed to catch up with his own pride. That Havana cigar, that Flor de Lobeto, was the only thing he needed at this moment to touch heaven with his hands.

When the U.S.S. *Cleveland* disappeared on the horizon, Ramón Arnaud was a man at peace.

Clipperton, 1915

DURING HIS SIESTA, Ramón Arnaud had a nightmare: he dreamed that he was eating mice.

In those times there was nothing much to do in Clipperton besides trying to survive, and that left enough time to sleep. It was almost a year since the visit of the *Cleveland*, the last ship to come to the isle, and people had forgotten everything, even about waiting for the arrival of the ship. They accepted their condition as castaways with a Christian resignation that turned into something close to pagan hedonism as they discovered the advantages of being isolated, the special charm of solitude, and the thousand opportunities for leisure time that their situation provided.

One of them was the deep and pleasant self-absorption of a long peaceful siesta. After lunch, men, women, and children lay down on their straw mattresses or their hammocks. Everything was so quiet and silent during that first half of the afternoon that, rather than siesta time, it seemed like a second night. The bugler Carvajal had the idea of playing reveille at four in the afternoon to awaken the troops, just like he did at dawn. It helped everybody's chronological adjustment. As a result, in twenty-four hours they lived two short days and two long nights, whereby they were awake for ten hours and asleep for fourteen.

Ramón dreamed that he was eating mice and woke up nauseated and with a bad taste in his mouth. He got up, stood in front of the broken mirror still hanging on the wall, and saw that his gums were black.

"Sadness has done this to me," he said. "I've got scurvy."

It was a fatal disease, a curse like those in the Bible, and for years Ramón had feared the day it would come to Clipperton. When people do not eat fresh fruits and vegetables for a very long time, they deprive their bodies of ascorbic acid. It was the scourge of all sailors, particularly of those shipwrecked. Ramón had learned of its devastating consequences during his obsessive readings on the subject. Vasco da Gama had left Portugal for India with five hundred men, and in less than two years, scurvy had taken half of them. Magellan also suffered from it when he spent almost four months in isolation, eating only flour, sawdust, and rats. The British Army, which was kept at seventeen hundred men during the U.S. War of Independence, lost a total of twelve hundred in action, forty-two thousand who deserted, and eighteen thousand due to scurvy.

Ramón had spent seven years trying to detect early symptoms in others, but never thought that he could be its first victim. He moved closer to the broken mirror to examine his mouth more carefully. His gums were swollen, bruised, and in the lower jaw he discovered a tiny infection.

"I have begun to rot away already," he said, and crossed himself.

What a fine moment for the plague to hit him! Just now, when he was enjoying peace at last. Against all odds, in spite of his being abandoned, that year had been a good year. He realized it now. They had not suffered thirst. They often had periods of rain, and since the hurricane had not destroyed the cistern, they had been able to store water for times of drought. Contrary to what usually happens to castaways on deserted islands, the people in Clipperton had been threatened not by the lack of water, but by its excess when torrential downpours flooded the isle and could have easily swept them away. They had not suffered too much for lack of food. They learned to fish and to live off the sea. The food supplies Captain Williams brought had been distributed parsimoniously, which stretched them to last for several months. Ramón had been able to pay attention to cooking, which had always been one of his favorite pastimes. He perfected, to gourmet standards, some recipes like conch and crab stew with coconut milk, shrimp ceviche, and turtle stew in cuttlefish ink. He treasured a few cans of olive oil, and on special occasions he would beat in some egg yolks for making mayonnaise to serve with lobster.

When they ran out of kerosene, used to light the lamps and the lighthouse, the fuel came to them miraculously from heaven—rather, from the sea—in the form of a dead whale dragged in by the tide to rest in peace on the Clipperton beach. They explored and quartered the enormous sea creature, and it yielded leather, meat, and several barrels of some dark oil, thick and smelly, that burned bright with a delicate golden flame.

It had been also a time of revelation in which Ramón learned to be a father. He discovered his children: for the first time in his life he became fully aware of the existence of those three creatures who were growing up freely and unencumbered in adversity as if it were one more element in nature. He spent whole days with them exploring the island, climbing the southern rock, or teaching them how to swim. With fine woods from the *Nokomis* and the *Kinkora*, he made them miniature ships that looked like the real ones. They took them to the lagoon, and by nightfall they were still sailing them. He taught them how to identify stars in the sky, and the different kinds of breezes, and when his children got quickly bored listening to him, he would silently watch them play.

At dusk Ramón, Alicia, Tirsa, and Cardona gathered to keep one another company during that difficult hour on the island when darkness seemed to swallow everything very fast.

"If at least I still had my mandolin," lamented Arnaud.

"That's the last thing we need," countered Alicia.

"Please, Secundino, sing!" pleaded Tirsa.

"I can't anymore. The salty air has dried up my voice."

The four kept together so each one would not feel so alone, though they were not able to see one another's faces and often repeated the same exchanges. Not to be overwhelmed by the enveloping darkness, they tightened the circle of friendship that had been put to all kinds of tests, from the petty annoyances of daily life to great catastrophic upheavals.

Of course they missed Mexico and their families, but as time went on, their nostalgia became more abstract and diffused. Eventually, the most persistent of memories dropped off like ripened fruit drops from trees, and vanished. Ramón had a period in which he talked of nothing else but his mother's virtues. The desserts she used to bake for him, the stories she told him, the wonderful massages she gave him to relax his back muscles. When he noticed that this topic was boring to other people, he went through a period in which he read and reread her letters. Then he wrote poems about his filial love, like this poem recovered by General Urquizo in his biography of the Arnauds.

She was the old lady whose gaze
gave me the greatest joy,
like a virgin full of grace,
completely adored by her boy.

His obsession went so far that Alicia stopped calling him by his given name. "This is for Doña Carlota's son," she would say. "Here comes Doña Carlota's son." Until one night, when they were already in bed, they heard a noise, and Ramón got up to check through the empty house. After a while he returned to bed.

"It was Mother," he announced. "She was in the kitchen."

"What are you saying?"

"That it was Mother, I'm telling you."

"Ramón, you're crazy."

"No, it's not that, it's that she is dead. She died yesterday, and she came to tell me."

And he never mentioned her again.

That was how the preceding year had gone, without any big highs or lows. In spite of their countless needs, Ramón and Alicia were practically contented, almost happy.

Until scurvy appeared. In the past, Ramón's hypochondria had made him think of his own death hundreds of times. He would torture himself in anticipation and imagine its cruelest forms. He barely kept secret his phobias of fire and of water. He felt a faint premonition that he would end up burned alive or drowned. But never, not even in his worst moments of self-pity, did he think he would die for lack of a lemon. My kingdom for a lemon, he kept thinking.

His body had resented the lack of vegetables. Lemon juice was all that he lacked in order to recover his health; a few bitter drops, a caustic cleansing that could burn the decay already existing inside his body, which in no time would show in every pore. Ramón lay back on his bed and began to murmur, like in a litany, first in a low voice and then in a crescendo:

"Lemons, limes, oranges, grapefruit. Lemons, limes, oranges, grapefruit! Lemons, limes, oranges, Brussels sprouts, watercress, green peppers, blackberries, radishes, and parsley! A lot of radishes and a lot of parsley! Beets, mushrooms, plums, tomatoes, coconuts. . . . Coconut, coconut, coconut, coconut!"

Coconut they had plenty of. It was the only food from the vegetable kingdom that the island produced after the garden soil had been swept away. Coconut would be his salvation, the indispensable source of ascorbic acid that could prevent his death. Possibly prevent the death of all the inhabitants of the isle.

He put on a threadbare pair of pants and a poncho the women had patched together out of pieces of sailcloth. He climbed on a raft and rowed across the lagoon in a straight line. He landed where the thirteen coconut palms were. Until then, anyone who wanted to have some coconut needed only to go there. Coconuts were always in abundance, like the fish or the crabs, and one needed only to reach out and grab them.

Ramón took the ones on the ground to the raft. He figured that even in the sorry state of these palm trees, they could still produce about five coconuts a week, which could be painstakingly distributed equally among the twenty-one adults and nine children. He looked for Sergeant Irra and gave him quite an unexpected but peremptory order.

"Sergeant, from now on the palm trees are your responsibility. Make sure they are guarded day and night. Make sure nobody touches the coconuts. If there is one missing, I'll hold you responsible."

He walked away, sat on a rock, opened one with a machete, and drank its milk. During the following two days he tried to control the swelling of his gums with frequent dabs of iodine. However, the swelling increased to the point that he was unable to eat. He did not want to disclose his predicament to anyone, but Alicia discovered it.

"What did you eat that gives you such foul breath?"

He had to tell her the truth. They agreed to keep it secret, so as not to alarm the other people. They isolated themselves in concerted effort to heal the increasing ulcerations in his mouth by cleansing them with some antiseptics left in the pharmacy—methylene blue, gentian violet, iodine, hydrogen peroxide—one at a time, or all mixed into a disgusting, viscous concoction. Since Ramón was not able to chew his food, Alicia mashed the fish and pounded the coconut meat for him. In one week they were able to see some progress.

"I thought that this sickness had no cure, but our plan seems to be working," Ramón said, without daring yet to declare it a miracle cure.

"God willing."

Either God was willing or the coconut remedy did it, but Ramón recuperated. They went back to their disciplined routine as if nothing had happened, but keeping a tight control over the coconuts, several dozen of which they stored under lock and key. And they renewed their gatherings at dusk with Tirsa and Cardona.

"Victoriano is rebelling again," the lieutenant's voice resounded in the dark.

"Is he again agitating the people?"

"No, the trouble now is that he is doing nothing. Does not even light the lantern in the lighthouse. I had to put Pedrito Carvajal in charge of that, because the man refuses to get up from his hammock. Threats don't work. He says we can shoot him if we want to, but right there, lying in his hammock. He does not want to get up."

"Is he sick?" Alicia inquired.

"He doesn't seem to be. It just seems to be lethargy."

The two men walked up to the lighthouse cave to see Victoriano. As soon as Arnaud came in, he recognized the smell: it was the same putrid smell of his own body a few days ago. It was pitch black inside. Arnaud groped the walls to get a sense of where he was going, and found them moist. They were permeated with the unhealthy vapors of the disease.

"Victoriano?"

"Yessir."

"It's me, Arnaud."

"At your service, Captain."

His knees bumped against the hammock, which hung on the diagonal. There was his man.

"My whole body aches," they heard him say. "I think rheumatism got me. It got even my teeth, because they are falling out."

Ramón did not need to see him. He heard his hard breathing and could easily imagine the bruises on his skin and the ulcerations in his mouth. He returned at dawn to apply medications and feed him some coconut mush. He also asked Sergeant Irra's wife to look after him.

Victoriano Alvarez moaned all day, screamed all night, and in the morning he looked like a martyr. His skin was covered with ulcers, as if somebody had beaten him to a pulp. His gums were bleeding, and his mouth was all infected with boils. The news spread all over the island. People came to the lighthouse to see him and gathered at the door of his cabin, their eyes fixed on him. The children sneaked in and circled around his hammock.

A few days later, Ramón summoned his people in front of the room that had been the pharmacy and made them parade in their skivvies to check them out. He found the tell-tale signs on a woman. She was Irra's companion, the one who had been taking care of Victoriano.

The rumor spread like wildfire that this was a contagious epidemic and that it would infect anyone who came near Victoriano Alvarez. Arnaud did everything possible to stop the confusion. He ordered some community meetings and explained the characteristics of the disease, its causes and symptoms. He seemed never to tire of saying that it wasn't catching, and using a stick, even scratched out on the ground crude human figures to explain the body's systemic functions and failures. Despite all his efforts, he could not convince anyone. People did not want to hear anything about "scurvy" and preferred to keep calling it "the plague." The plague, they said, pronouncing the word with more fatalism than hope for a cure. They also refused to believe the citrus story. The disease was contagious, and that was the only truth they were willing to accept. Besides, they needed a more believable culprit than a perfectly innocent looking orange or lemon.

In its secret path, before it became full-blown, the disease altered body humors—fermenting blood, souring bile, poisoning mucus—and brought forth dark passions, and Victoriano Alvarez became the scapegoat. They came to hate him from the bottom of their hearts: they cursed him for being black and for being contagious, demanding that he be isolated and placed in quarantine. Nobody wanted to take care of him. Or even to get close to the big rock, or to turn on the beam in the lighthouse. Ramón agreed to isolate him, in part so as not to agitate the crowd even more, in part for fear they would end up by lynching their chosen victim.

During the days that followed, many people began to look yellowish, like Asians, and suffered attacks of rash and rancorous apathy that made it difficult to get them to do anything or to follow any discipline. Ramón knew how to interpret this: as the first signs of the disease that was spreading to everybody. He devoted himself, together with Cardona, to rebuilding the pharmacy. He inventoried the few medications left, had the women wash and boil rags, and in the depository that had once been ransacked by The Hand That Strangles, he continued storing coconuts, after he fixed some locks and bolts. He had everybody receive a coconut ration together with their daily food.

Scurvy spread with implacable speed anyway, and rashes, sores, brown spots, and hematomas proliferated. Women and children were less affected; the disease attacked the men with particular virulence.

The sickly coconut palms could not produce enough, and the portions of coconut were reduced to ridiculous amounts. Ramón ordered the pulp to be grated and mixed with fish, and the coconut milk extended with rainwater. But even so, the remedy was not enough. In desperation, Tirsa Rendón thought of using the shells also. They tried to boil them in a big pot and prepared an infusion that they started to distribute in their pewter bowls, a ladleful at a time. Since the taste was awful, people refused to drink it, and Ramón made it compulsory to have it under threat of punishment.

The soldiers thought he had lost his wits.

"Our good Captain Arnaud blames everything on the oranges and wants to stop us from dying with coconut milk!" Since no one wanted to take care of the agonizing Victoriano, Alicia, who was still healthy, volunteered to do it. He was in a sorrowful state. His body emitted a putrid odor, his sores were oozing, and he could not get up from the hammock even to relieve himself. Making a big effort and trying to control her nausea, she fed him and tried to alleviate his suffering as best she could. Once, during wash time, she lifted the dirty serape that covered him. His body was naked, emaciated, and ghostly, but between his legs, in full erection and apparently in good health, Alicia saw his large-sized member. She was stunned. She let go of the serape and searched his face as if expecting an explanation. His eyes were gazing at her without shame, with some amusement, in fact. For a moment she felt paralyzed, then stepped back. Victoriano grabbed her hand, but she escaped and ran away as if Lucifer himself had touched her. She did not stop running until she met Ramón in the infirmary, on the other side of the island.

"I'm not taking care of Victoriano anymore," she announced, still breathless from her moment of panic and her racing away from it. "It's a man's job."

"Why?"

She did not dare tell the truth.

"Because he is too heavy and I cannot handle him."

Alicia never went back to the lighthouse lair, and with so many sick people to take care of, Ramón completely forgot about Victoriano Alvarez. The soldier was left forsaken in his cave, dreaming of revenge while seeing his body rot away, piece by piece.

But the scurvy continued spreading around. The ulcerated sores and bursting boils increased, and some of the infections were so bad as to be swarming with worms. The antiseptics ran out, and Ramón had to resort to drastic old ways. With cold-blooded Tirsa Rendón as his assistant, he filled the wounds with gunpowder, added a wick, and let them burn out.

The rainy season came suddenly, and the deluge seemed like the sky wanted to wash away the miasmas from the plague. The floods forced people to disband. The sick became isolated, with only their own horror to face.

On one stormy dawn, someone knocked at the Arnauds' home. Alicia got up to open the door and met face to face with a monster. It took her a while to realize it was Irra's wife. She had lost all her teeth, and her face was purple and disfigured. Her gums were swollen beyond any possible imagining. From the opening gap that was now her mouth came a rancid odor that Alicia recognized: it was the odor of death.

"I came to ask you where I can bury my two children," she mumbled. "They died last night."

The burial was scheduled for that afternoon, next to Jesús Neri's grave, Clipperton's first fatality, the old soldier who was attacked by sharks. But Irra's wife died before then. They placed her body in the same box with her two children, and a sad procession dragged along under the downpour, all the way to the cemetery by the southern rock, with the makeshift coffin on their shoulders. Their heads were bent, and they avoided looking at one another: it was too hard to see their own disaster reflected in the others' faces. There was no ceremony, either religious or military. They did not have the strength. Whatever strength they had left was spent by the sick in keeping themselves on their feet, and by the healthy in digging into the rock, the rain pounding on their backs.

The dead disappeared underground, and the living scattered in the storm. Only a small group of men stayed by the grave, keeping company with Sergeant Irra, who had just buried his whole family. Without a word, they knew what they wanted to do. They walked slowly toward the lighthouse lair, all with a single aim, a single will. They found Victoriano lying in his hammock, still alive, and bludgeoned him until they felt he was dead. "We did the right thing," they wrote on the earth floor of the cabin.

Doña Juana the midwife, Jesús Neri's widow, had become an ill-tempered, mad loner. She had no home—nobody remembered whether her house had collapsed or had been blown away by the hurricane or dragged off by the floods—and she wandered around with her belongings on her back. Life in the open had shrunk, wrinkled, and darkened her skin like a raisin. During the day she kept mumbling, and at night she lulled herself to sleep as if she were her own child. The others forgot about her and would greet her only in passing, "Morning, Doña Juana," or "Good morning, Doña Juana."

"What's 'good' about it?" she would mumble, though nobody paid attention. "There are only bad ones and worse ones."

When the scurvy condition worsened, they remembered her.

"The midwife could help us with our sores!"

They looked for her by the lagoon, under the pile of rubble and garbage where she had taken refuge, and she came out dressed in rags. She stood on a mound of rocks and spoke about the devil. Clipperton was living in sin, "like Sodom and Gomorrah," she preached, "and the plague was God's punishment. Men and women were living together without the sacred sanction, and the children were growing up without being baptized." She would take care of them, she promised, provided they first achieved peace with their consciences. It was easy for her to convince them. She conducted marriage ceremonies, blessing the pathetic brides and grooms ravished by disease. She held communal baptisms, making the little ones go into the rotten waters of the lagoon up to their knees. Her regalia as priestess for these occasions was really striking. To the various rags, she added pelts from dead animals, and on her head she wore an old lamp shade decorated with tassels all around. At one end of a long stick, which she used as a bishop's crosier, she had attached a porcelain doll.

Notwithstanding their repentance, their prayers and sacraments, the faithful continued to writhe in pain. The midwife then complemented her mysticism with medicine. She prepared infusions with turkey feathers, sea urchin shells, bat pee, and toad milk. She applied leeches, vents, and guano poultices. The sick stopped going to the pharmacy for their daily ration of coconut, and established themselves at the shore of the lagoon, all around the midwife's hovel. Their days and nights were divided either between moans and agonies, or prayers and processions.

The death toll kept increasing, and the living became impatient waiting for a miracle cure. The midwife expanded her gospel repertoire. She told them that there was poison in the air, and ordered people to light bonfires to cleanse it and to feed the fires with the belongings of those who died. So, into this purifying fire went scapulars, combs, petticoats, shirts, love letters, toys: the last remaining family memories, the few friendly objects that were left, minute traces of a bygone world.

But nobody was getting better; they all got worse. Their skin fell off in scales, and their flesh was raw. With their lowered defenses, other diseases took hold: anemia, rheumatic fever, bronchitis, leukemia, diarrhea, depression.

The faithful were losing patience.

"You lying hag, if you don't cure us, we'll throw you into the lagoon," the people shouted at her one day in the middle of one of her rituals.

Then she demanded sacrifices. She said that the sins had been so numerous that only blood could wash them away. Dutifully, they threw into the fire a whole litter of newborn piglets. A new brotherhood of flagellants was formed, and they went around the island flailing their backs.

The flagellants, led by Sergeant Irra, punished themselves and everything around them. Weak and in pain, they were nonetheless a pitiful horde of hooligans and predators. Their emblem was to carry a handful of hair that each had pulled out from someone's corpse; their slogan, "Long Live Death"; and their hymn, the "Salve Regina, Empress of Heaven." Using the same whips and heavy sticks with which they mortified their flesh, they killed all the animals and destroyed all structures and water tanks, as well as ransacked the food depot. They would have cut down the palm trees with their machetes, had Arnaud and Cardona's gunshots not prevented them.

As long as Ramón was in control, burials were made in the cemetery. But when Clipperton became a no-man's-land, each one dug a hole for his dead wherever he could. The island was dotted with graves. Sometimes—though not often—their presence was indicated by a wooden cross or a heap of stones. At the end, when the living were fewer than the dead, and the presence of death became overwhelming, they threw the corpses into the lagoon or into the sea.

Arnaud's authority had collapsed. He and his military orders and coconut milk could not compete with Doña Juana's magical, mystical influence. In one last attempt to bring this pandemonium to some semblance of order, he walked to the lagoon with the clear intention of confronting the old woman.

"You are no priestess, and no doctor. You're nothing!" he shouted in the presence of her followers. "You're nothing but a deranged old woman, and I forbid you to keep on driving these people mad."

"You are not in charge anymore, Arnaud," she countered. "And neither am I. This is the reign of death. Go and die in peace, and let others die the way they want to."

Ramón walked away from the place without a word, and resolved to keep to himself at home with his family, Altagracia, Tirsa, Cardona, three widows, and one orphan. The isle became two domains—the midwife's colony and the Arnaud home—that had less and less contact with each other, each side finally ignoring the other as if they were an ocean apart.

Those who stayed in the house organized a guard duty day and night to prevent an attack from the flagellants, and, against all hopes, they kept eating coconut and drinking an infusion made with the shells. Not even Arnaud did it out of conviction. For him this irrational gesture only embodied the remnants of his will to live.

Though the curtain of water falling from the skies did not abate, some signs from the other side were perceived. Laments from those dying, smoke from the bonfires, hymns from the flagellants. At night the sounds became weaker, more surreal, like voices from the other world that were growing fainter. Like the echoes from a nightmare when one is about to wake up.

Then the rains suddenly stopped. The sky changed colors, like a snake changes skins, and the color it finally acquired was a limpid, innocent blue. The Arnauds and their three children, the Cardonas, and the rest of those in the house were still alive. Besides, they were healthy. They were the only survivors on Clipperton Island.

"Blessed are the holy coconuts," Ramón said, and went out with his children to the beach to welcome the sunshine.

Clipperton, 1915

❦

"SECUNDINO, A SHIP is going by!" shouted Ramón Arnaud one quiet, gray morning.

Everything seemed to be at peace, except for the ocean. In between the lazy stillness of the sky and that of the land, the sea in frantic waves exploded on the reefs.

Ramón Arnaud and Secundino Cardona had been sitting on the beach for hours, just killing time. The smell of death still lingered and reached them once in a while, but they did not notice. They had become inured to having their noses tickled by mellow, rotten scents, and no longer remembered the smell of pure air. A few weeks before, when the rains stopped, they had ventured to the midwife's hill and found only corpses. Together they piled them up and set them on fire. They killed a few pigs that had been eating here and there and burned them also. They did not want to eat animals that had eaten human flesh. Then they left that place, never to return.

Death had made the island a profane, polluted wasteland, and the survivors stayed around the Arnaud home, the only clean spot. They even forgot about the lighthouse, for they did not want to go there. They only ventured far from the house once a day to collect coconuts. Whatever else was left, they had close by, and they still had the habit of keeping together in a compact group, as if anyone who strayed would be exposed to greater perils than the rest. As if the spirit of the plague, or of impending disaster, were still around. They were alive but had felt death too close, and that had left its mark. They turned fearful and superstitious, and in their minds they found room for the god they had worshiped in another time. The one and only god, all powerful, magnificent, beginning and end of everything: a ship that would rescue them.

Relaxing on the beach by the house, Arnaud and Cardona were playing with pebbles. When the waves receded, so fast that for a moment they left a smooth film of water, they were casting pebbles horizontally so that they would skip on the surface several times. Cardona always won. His stones would rebound four and five times; Arnaud's, only two or three.

"A ship, a ship!" Ramón suddenly shouted.

"No kidding!" piped in Cardona. "Where—?"

"I don't see it anymore, but I swear I saw it."

They both rose to their feet in order to look, cupping their hands to protect their eyes from the sun's glare.

"There it goes again!" Arnaud said quickly. "It's a big one! Look at it: How come you don't see it? It's sailing from east to west . . ."

"I don't see a thing. . . . Is it coming?"

"I'm afraid not. . . . It's sailing away, damn it!" Arnaud was beside himself. "Let's light a bonfire, Cardona! Let's make some smoke signals."

"All right, but I do not see any ship," Cardona said, and began to start a fire. Alicia, Tirsa, and the other women came, attracted by the hollering.

"Bring rags, pieces of wood, whatever you can find that will burn," Cardona asked them. "We are signaling to a ship."

"What ship?"

"The one Ramón is looking at."

Arnaud had walked away, but he came back running. His heart was bursting, and the excitement made him stammer.

"Now I'm sure!" he screamed. "There is a ship out there, I swear to God."

"Are you really sure, Ramón? Do not joke about this," Cardona said.

"Let's go, Cardona, let's not waste any more time with bonfires. Let's follow the ship on the raft."

"On the raft?" The one screaming now was the lieutenant. "On those four tied boards? We could not follow a ship on that, even if there was one."

"It's still far away. If we go straight out, we can intercept its course. Let's go, or we'll miss it! It's now or never!"

"We'd better keep making a bonfire, Ramón. . . ."

"Are you insane? A ship is passing us by, our only hope for survival, and you want to keep burning rags?"

"But I don't see any ship and to go into that rough sea is hell."

"Now's the time!"

"Wait, brother, let's not die—"

"Nobody is going to die, and least of all now. If people on the ship see us, we'll be saved!"

"Excuse me, aren't you seeing the phantom ship of the Flying Dutchman?"

"Damn you, Cardona. You are more stubborn than a mule, and dumber than a Chamula Indian!"

"Stop the insults, you're overexcited."

"Forget I said it. But please bring the blasted paddles, damn it!"

Lieutenant Cardona complied. "Here, but I really don't see any ship. I don't know, Ramón, I asked Alicia and Tirsa, and they don't see it either."

"Don't mind them. Women see well up close but very badly at a distance."

"You're seeing just what you want to see."

"No sermons now. They are going to see us, and they will rescue us. We are saved, Secundino. Let's go!"

"But the sea is too rough, my friend."

"It doesn't matter. Let's go!"

"But look at the ocean, it's a killer!"

"No more words," said Captain Arnaud, now calmly and with authority. "We leave on the raft, and that's an order. Where are the women? Where is the bonfire?" He was shouting again. "What does everybody think, that this can wait until tomorrow?"

The women, bringing rubble to light the fire, took a look at the horizon. They moved without conviction, like robots.

"Nobody believes me, is that it? You'll see. Let's go, Cardona."

The two men hastily reinforced the ties that held the boards together.

"It's ready," announced Arnaud.

"Jesus Christ! You're really insane now, Ramón. All right, I'll go with you, but I insist I don't see any ship. I'll do it for what you said before about us both living or—"

"We both live or we both live," interrupted Arnaud. "We'll all live, little brother. Our misery is over."

Ramón went to his wife.

"I'll be back right away," he told her. "Get the children ready, because we are leaving today. Do you hear, Alicia? Yes indeed, today. I'll go to your father's, we'll send the children to school. You'll have the life you deserve."

"I don't understand," she said, her voice tight.

"It's easy. Once I wanted to stay, and I did it for Mexico. But now I want to leave. I want to leave for you."

"But in what—"

"In that ship, look at it!"

Ramón spoke with conviction, his words carried his fervor, and Alicia, who had not seen the ship, did finally see it. All iron, enormous, and close. Reflected in the depth of her husband's pupils.

He kissed her quickly on her forehead and went into the water dragging the raft. Alicia did not move, did not say a word, frozen in her anguish.

While he limped on the beach trying to catch up with Arnaud, Secundino Angel Cardona turned back to look at Tirsa.

"Good-bye, my pretty one," he hollered. "Love you forever!"

The Last Man

Colima, Today

COLIMA IS A SMALL CITY, white and peaceful, with the same palm trees, the same air and rhythm of so many cities by the sea. But Colima is far away from the sea: two hours inland from the port of Manzanillo on the Pacific Coast. I am now at the bus station in the outskirts of town. It is very hot, and I don't have any specific target address. I came here in search of Victoriano Alvarez's past, and I have only a few details on the black soldier's life before Clipperton: that he was born here, that he left in his youth and never returned, and that he had no children. That's all. I tell the cabdriver to take me to the *zócalo* because the main plazas preserve, as if in formaldehyde, the old town stories. I walk along the streets around the plaza, where little has changed since the turn of the century. The heat is oppressive, and I can't help but think that it would be easier to try to find a needle in a haystack. Seventy-one years after his death, who's going to recall anything about this unknown soldier? Who's going to remember one of the least memorable of its citizens?

At the Portal Medellín there is a place that seems to have witnessed several generations of townspeople. It is a general store with an over-sized and weathered dark wood counter. Outside, a sign reads, "Here is the traditional, renowned, and prestigious Casa Ceballos, open since 1893." Inside you can find anything, from hardware to underwear. The owner, Don Carlos Ceballos, inherited the business over fifty years ago. He is a well-educated, polite gentleman, like those of yesteryear. I tell him what I am looking for and ask for his help, and he suggests that I come back in the afternoon. He is going to gather a number of people who might have some information.

Hours later, Don Carlos has assembled a group of friends and towns-people about his age at the Hotel Ceballos, next to the store. They are important local people, and a few historians and journalists.

"Last name Alvarez, from Colima, and black?" they want to be sure. "There is only one family, the illegitimate descendants of our illustrious leader, General Manuel Alvarez, our first state governor."

"But the Alvarezes from Colima are not pure black," they point out, "they are mulattoes."

In the center of Villa Alvarez Plaza, cast in bronze and ruling over the town from his pedestal, is soldier Victoriano Alvarez's paternal grandfather, General Manuel Alvarez. In the assembly room of the Co-lima town hall, there he is again, in an oil painting with his name in gold. He is a thickset man with sharp features. And he is milky white.

At the corner of Venustiano Carranza and 5 de Mayo lie the ruins of what was his home, a one-story colonial structure. The facade is still standing, but the interior has crumbled down due to the Colima earth-quakes. The bases of the walls, like a blueprint, are still visible, indicat-ing where the patios, the kitchen, the bedrooms, and the sitting rooms were. The family rooms were toward the front of the house, next to the street. That is, the general and his successive wives lived there—he became a widower three times and married four times—together with his numerous offspring.

At the back of the house, surrounding the patio, is where the help lived: servants, chambermaids, grooms. The general, great patriarch and stud, fathered children everywhere he went. Willing or not, no female escaped him. At night and in haste, he used to sneak across to the back side of the house, to ravish the young servants, take care of the older ones, and make love to a black maid called Aleja, who was faithful to him all her life.

His wives did not live long; three of them died in childbirth. But not Aleja. She prevailed, surviving her childbirths, and bearing him count-less children. The general recognized some and gave them his name. They were his illegitimate, mulatto descendants, among them Victo-riano Alvarez, father of the Clipperton Victoriano.

General Alvarez was named governor on July 15, 1857, and five weeks later, during his siesta, his political enemies rioted and gathered at the plaza shouting their slogan, "Law and Religion." Annoyed, the general woke up, and when informed of the news, he was furious. Livid with rage and without waiting for anyone, he loaded his guns, jumped on his horse, and rushed toward the plaza to end the revolt all by himself. He didn't get past the first intersection. A gun blast re-ceived him, and a bullet nested in his heart. The family went to the church and asked to let him have the last rites and absolution adminis-tered postmortem, as was the custom when Christians died suddenly or violently, and to allow his being laid to rest in the cemetery. The parish priest denied the request because the general, a liberal through and through, had been excommunicated for supporting the federal constitution. Finally the priest acceded, in exchange for two thousand pesos, provided they let him whip the demons out of the dead body. So after receiving the bullet that killed him, General Alvarez had to withstand a whipping, and then he was able to go down peacefully into his sepulcher.

His fourth wife, Panchita Córdoba, was young when he died, and soon married Filomeno Bravo. Good-looking Filomeno, reputedly the handsomest man in Mexico, held fast to the household's same macho and big-daddy traditions practiced by the deceased general. His blue eyes and golden beard made him resemble Emperor Maximilian himself, which served him well in order to reach Empress Carlota's bed no less. After this, there was no woman he could not claim. He was shrewd and resourceful enough to court them and deceive them all. One afternoon he picked up an unknown, pretty woman all dressed in red. He pulled her onto his horse and took her to the outskirts of town, where he made love to her in an open field. He was seen by neighbors passing by. Before anyone could relay the story to Panchita, his wife, Filomeno rushed home, ordered her to put on a red dress, pulled her onto his horse, and took her on horseback to the outskirts of town, where he made love to her in an open field. That way, if anyone came to her with the story, she, blissfully innocent, would believe that "the mystery lady in the red dress was no one but me."

When the great Benito Juárez, then president of Mexico, came one day to Colima, he was about to be shot by Filomeno the Blond, who decided to spare his life. Benito Juárez, in gratitude, signed a card for him that read: "You have reciprocity for your life." So once when Filomeno, imprisoned in Zacatecas, was about to be executed, he showed the card promising "reciprocity for your life," and was let go. Years later, like General Alvarez, he was also killed by a bullet to his heart, and the people of Colima thought up an epitaph for him: "Filomeno's pax is a relief for everybody's ass."

Miguel Alvarez García, General Manuel Alvarez's grandson, was also a governor, and a great-grandchild, Griselda Alvarez Ponce de León, was a governor as well. Pomp and circumstance accompanied the Alvarez family for several generations. At least for the white, legitimate Alvarezes, those who lived in the front part of the house.

Victoriano, the mulatto grandson of the general and his black servant Aleja, shared the fate of those who lived at the back of the house. He learned of the family history through the maids' gossip. He was an invisible, mute witness to the economic success, the political struggles, and the military adventures of his grandfather, uncles, and his white siblings and cousins. Through the cracks he spied on their amorous conquests and their forced ones. Until he got tired of lusting after the women they possessed, got bored with their feats, that is, with admiring and envying their style of life. He wanted to live his own life, so he joined the army and ended up in Clipperton.

Clipperton, 1915

❦

THE RAFT THAT WAS TAKING Arnaud and Cardona became unreal, like a faded memory, as it entered a zone of greenish fog. The
women and children were watching it from the beach. They saw it moving away with difficulty toward the reef, bobbing up and down, fragile
and tentative, in the treacherously contradictory ocean waves. The effort
exerted by the two men rowing diligently made the raft advance, but
the force of the waves kept pushing it back. It moved away, grew
smaller, darker; it approached, became more visible, and then disappeared again. From the beach, the women kept it afloat with the power
of their eyes, they saved it through their prayers to the Saint of Cabora,
they brought it closer to shore with the power of their thoughts. When
the image became more blurred, they waded in up to their knees to
bring it nearer and to hold it back, to rescue it.

"Do you think they'll reach the ship?" Alicia asked Tirsa. Their
soaked petticoats entangled their legs and they had to hold on to each

other's arms in order to withstand the waves and the wind. "Say yes, please say yes."

"I don't see the ship anymore."

"But Rosalía sees it. And Ramón was sure—"

"Maybe it's behind the fog. Maybe they can get to it, Tirsa."

"There is nothing, and you know it. Shout with me."

They shouted together—they all shouted, the children shouted—but the noise of the churning sea swallowed their voices.

The raft was getting close to the reefs and was being jostled about. It would ride up to the crest of a wave and then fall. The women lost sight of it, and then it appeared again, floating amid the greenish vapors or on top of another mountain of water. A big black wave pulled it back toward the beach.

"They're coming back! They heard us, and they're coming back!"

"Yes, they are returning."

The women were screaming until their voices became hoarse. Speaking at the same time, they cursed, they prayed, they argued. Another wave caught the raft and threw it against the rocks.

Alicia covered her eyes with her hands.

"Tell me if they went over the reef," she pleaded.

"I don't see them. Yes, I do! There they are—"

"Do you see them?"

"Yes, over there."

"Thank heaven. . . . Are they all right?"

"I think so. But look . . . look at that dark thing that is coming out of the water."

"A dark thing—"

"It's a manta ray. The ray is attacking them!"

"Shut up, Rosalía. Those are rocks. Tirsa, do you see them?"

"I only see shadows."

"Our Father who art in Heaven, hallowed be—"

"Stop praying, Alta, and take care of the children."

The seven children had forgotten all about the raft and were mind-lessly splashing about in the water.

"I am telling you it is a manta ray. It overturned the raft!"

"Open your eyes, Alicia. Help me look."

"No, I see them. They sank! Can anybody see them?"

"There they go, there they go, I see my papa!"

"Children, hush!"

"My daddy is struggling with a manta ray."

"Shut up! Don't you understand? Altagracia, I'm telling you to get the children out of the water. Tirsa, do you see them?"

"No, Alicia, I don't see them."

"Altagracia, do you see them?"

"No, ma'am."

"Rosalía, anybody! How come nobody sees anything?"

"Oh, Jesus, the sea swallowed them."

"You shut up, too! Come, Tirsa, come with me." Alicia waded deeper into the water. Ramoncito clung to her neck.

"Ramoncito, you must go back to shore."

"No."

"Go away, you're going to drown, and you're drowning me. Some-body come and get this child!"

Altagracia pulled the screaming Ramoncito away. The rest walked away also. Only Alicia and Tirsa remained, getting deeper into the water until they couldn't touch bottom. So they floated for a while, swallow-ing water each time the waves went over their heads.

"Tirsa, do you see them?"

"No, I haven't seen them for a while. I see shark fins."

"Sharks? The sharks got them!"

"Wait. Let's go to the beach to look for them, maybe they came back on the other side."

They got out of the water. The children were running, all wet, their teeth chattering with cold.

"Alta, you stay with the children. Take off their clothes and put them out to dry. Everybody, help us search for Ramón and Cardona. Rosalía and Francisca, you go that way. Tirsa and I will go this way."

They spent the rest of the morning walking over the ground coral all around the shore. Sometimes one of them seemed to see something, and they both would go into the water, calling their men in loud voices, and then they would come out of the water and continue walking. By midafternoon their feet were bleeding, cut by the broken coral. Occasionally they met the other women.

"Did you see them?"

"Nothing."

"Keep looking. Keep looking until you find them."

They met Altagracia and the kids. Ramoncito ran after his mother and clung to her legs.

"Not now, child."

Ramoncito cried. He did not want to let go.

"Alta, take this child away. Give them something to eat. They must be hungry."

"What do I give them?"

"Whatever you can find."

"There is no fish."

"Give them eggs. Give them water, they are thirsty. Get them dressed, they are cold."

"Their clothes are all wet."

"Then light a bonfire. Let me go, Ramón. Help Alta make a bonfire."

"And Daddy? I know where Daddy is."

"Where?"

"At home. He got there already."

"How do you know?"

"I know."

Alicia ran home. The child ran after her, and Altagracia after the child. When they arrived, they found the house empty.

"Didn't you, ma'am, have something to look at things from far away?"

"Ramón gave it to the Dutchmen."

"If they could reach Acapulco, maybe the master can also."

"On a few tied-up boards? Don't be silly. Take this child with you, Alta. Play with him, put him to sleep, feed him, do anything, but take him away from me. I must find Ramón."

Alicia and Tirsa ran toward the southern rock. Seeing them go away, Ramoncito screamed, and with so much crying and hiccups, he could barely breathe. The other children, meanwhile, were playing blindman's buff. The two women climbed up to the lighthouse and searched in all directions until their eyes hurt. The fog had grown thicker, and it was like a veil occasionally parted by the sharp fins of the sharks. Nightfall found them still there, battered by the wind's frozen eddies, and they were still there at dawn, eyes fixed on the horizon. The sun was coming up strong, dissipating the phantasmagoric mists, and the sea woke up in shades of yellow, rose, and orange, without even a shadow to darken the limpid sunshine.

The following days were like one another, and brought no changes. Alicia wrapped her wounded feet in rags to protect them from the coral, and she wandered about the beaches incessantly, in an anguished, irrational agitation. Once in a while, she would mutter in passing.

"Alta, the children are hungry. Feed them."

"What do I feed them, ma'am?"

"Whatever you can."

Or else it would go like this:

"Alta, it's very late. Put the children to bed."

"They don't want to, ma'am."

"Then, let them stay up a while longer."

She didn't go to bed at all. She would wander around the isle like a soul in purgatory, always looking at the sea. Ramoncito, whimpering and with a runny nose, would trot behind her.

"Mommy, I know where Daddy is."

"Listen, let's not pretend."

On the third day, Alicia sat in a corner of the kitchen, her feet full of blisters. She could no longer move and remained there, silent, catatonic, until Rosalía came with the news that she had seen the raft buried in the sand toward the north shore. Forgetting about her feet, Alicia rushed out, with the child tagging behind her as usual. The raft was there, but not the men. Not even a trace of them.

"Tirsa, do you think they are dead?"

"Yes."

Alicia lay down on the sand as if she had decided to stay there forever. More than a widow's sorrow, she felt the spite of an abandoned bride. A painful kind of anger and unreasonable jealousy consumed her. It was the sorrowful rancor of a woman whose lover leaves her for another woman, or of a man betrayed by his friends. There was no letup in her anxiety, like a woman demanding of her lover to come back, or like a man expecting a well-deserved apology. To leave and abandon her had been Ramón's betrayal. If he ever returned, she would throw that in his face. What right had he of dying in such an absurd manner, so senselessly, and leaving her so desolate? If he ever returned, she would tell him: Didn't you think of your children before taking such risks? If he returned—of course she would pardon him. She would embrace him, adore him, she would dry his feet with her hair. If he returned—perhaps he would return, surely he would. And Alicia lifted her head again to search the horizon.

The rest of the world no longer existed for her. She did not see, hear, or understand; she did not touch the food prepared for her. She was not even aware of Ramoncito's presence as he clambered upon her shoulders, pulled her by the arms, and fluttered around her, constantly talking to her.

"Mom, look at this conch. Mom, it hurts here. Mom? Can I tell you a story? Mom, I saw Daddy a while ago. Could I make a necklace for you, Mom, with this shell?"

Alicia did not respond. She had drifted far away without wanting to return. The child caught a crab and began playing with it. It had fiery pop eyes, and a red shell with white dots. It would open and close its pincers and had hair on its legs and antennae on its head. In an attempt to escape, it ran backward, sideways. Ramoncito blocked its way with a log. He pricked it with a stick and harassed it with his foot.

"Mom? Look at this sea monster, Mom."

The animal suffered, got angry, went mad; it was fascinating in its desperation. The child got his face closer to see it better.

His screaming and his bloodied face pulled Alicia from the bottomless pit of her loneliness. The crab had bitten Ramoncito on the lip, parting it in two. She picked up the child and ran home with him in her arms.

"Did you see, Mom? The sea monster got furious."

She hugged him, kissed his hair and his eyes, asked him for forgiveness.

"I'm sorry, my son, I'm sorry. Forgive me, it was my fault, I am to blame, mea culpa, mea culpa, mea maxima culpa."

Back at home, Alicia cleaned the wound, took out her sewing basket from the trunk where she kept her valuables, and threaded a needle with the last strong, long blue strand left.

"Where is Tirsa?" she asked Altagracia.

"She's not nearby, ma'am. Do you want me to go get her?"

"There is no time. Alta, hold the child."

Alicia took a deep breath, controlling the tremor in her hands, and summoning a courage she did not have, she started to sew the wound, stitch by stitch, with the needle and the blue thread. When she finished, she lay the child on his bed and kept caressing his head until he fell asleep. Then she called the other women. The five came: Tirsa, Altagracia, Benita Pérez (Private Arnulfo Pérez's widow), Francisca (who was Pedrito Carvajal's girlfriend), and Rosalía (who belonged to all and to no one in particular). Alicia glanced at them—they were all disheveled, undernourished, dressed in rags—and she thought they looked ten years older than they actually were. I must look like this, too, she thought. Like a witch. If Ramón had returned then, he would have been scared to death. She asked the women to sit down and hear her out.

"The men here have died, but we are still alive. The children are alive, and we have to feed them. It's not going to be easy. We must work hard, so the mourning period is over. We must stop crying for our husbands because we have to take care of our children."

As a result of this meeting, the first one headed by Alicia, the wearing of skirts was forbidden.

"No rags to get in the way," she said. "And we must learn how to fish."

She distributed the pairs of pants left by the men. Cutting them above the knee, they cinched them around their smaller waists with hemp. All had been living on the isle for seven years but had not learned how to fish: to provide food had been solely a male endeavor. From that day, come early dawn, they were working by the ocean, setting traps among the corals, and toiling with nets, fishing poles, and hooks. They hurled sharp sticks at anything that moved underwater. Hours later they would lie on the beach, enervated from overexposure to the Clipperton sun, completely exhausted and demoralized after so much fruitless effort. The first week they went hungry; they caught only a couple of eels, an octopus, and a small ray.

The discovery of an easier way to fish came to the children. One day when the women returned from the seaside empty-handed, they found the children sitting around a half-dozen sardines still alive and flapping.

"Who gave those to you?"

"Nobody. We took them away from the birds."

They saw how the children, golden and supple, disbanded and rushed to the beach. When a booby darted into the water and got a fish in its beak, the children zigzagged after it, prancing around, and then lunged forward to grab the bird and shake it by the legs until it let go of its catch. The children came back bursting with pride, shiny fish in hand. The women laughed—it was cute to see them run, and funny to watch them shaking the ugly birds—and then tried to imitate the children but couldn't, lacking their agility. Alicia and Francisca ran after one bird, got entangled with each other, and fell to the ground. The bird started to fly away. Alicia managed to stand up, lunged, and, still holding on to a few feathers, fell again. Lying down and with the children shouting and clapping around her, she understood what a minute before would have seemed inconceivable to her. She realized that, in spite of everything, she could still feel happy. She felt ashamed of herself on account of Ramón, got up quickly, and shook the sand off her hair. That night the women lit a bonfire by the seashore and roasted more fish than they could eat.

In time, they perfected other practical ways of fishing. The most effective was to lie facedown at the dock with a sharp stick ready, and then wait until a big fish came around looking for shelter underneath. It was easy to mount a surprise harpoon attack through the broken deck boards. With this method they obtained sawfish, sea bass, tiger fish, and moonfish. Alicia regained her role as a schoolteacher, and the children and the rest of the women had to attend her classes daily. For paper and pencil, they wrote on the sand with sticks. Since all the books had been lost, the readers used were the accounting records of the guano company and some old newspaper clippings about the invasion of Veracruz. They conjugated verbs in English and in French, and learned religion, good manners, and civics.

Long ago, Ramón had solved the lack of a calendar by carving lines on the veranda of their house. After his death, Alicia completely forgot to mark the days. Now she wanted to keep track, but she had no clear notion of how much time had elapsed. She thought it was about a month and Tirsa believed it was only twenty-five days. So they compromised, and marked twenty-eight lines.

"I have no idea what day is today in the rest of the world," Alicia declared, "but here it is Tuesday, June 24, 1915."

Between teaching, taking care of the children, and the intense, indispensable survival activities, they managed one day at a time, without the leisure of wondering about the days gone by or the days to come. In that way, without realizing it, they overcame the nightmare in which they were living and made it bearable.

All that was during the day. But when night fell, their fears and sorrows came back to overwhelm them. The children were so frightened that they clung to the women and would not fall asleep unless cuddled in their arms. In spite of being so tired, the women could not sleep either. In the dark, memories weighed so heavily that the past became present, and the dead returned, first one and then another, until they filled the house, and those still alive had to nestle in the corners to make room for them.

The moans of the flagellants were heard again, and the cries of Irra's young sons, struck down by scurvy. Jesús Neri would appear, bitten by sharks, together with Juana, his wife, smelling horrible. Some of the visits were pleasant, like those of Ramón and Cardona, who would talk about their own death. Their voices came out of the dark as in the old happy times when they gathered at dusk.

"Ramón, I say there is no ship."

"You don't see it, Secundino, but it's there, all lit and silvery, waiting for us."

"It's not a ship, Ramón, it's a manta ray, the one that killed us."

"It was not a manta ray, Secundino. It was sharks."

During the day Alicia understood and accepted Ramón's death. But come night she allowed herself to be confused by these apparitions, and she would often sit looking at the sea in the moonlight and awaiting his return. Not even Tirsa, the strong one, who did not know about poetry or believe in the afterlife, was able to escape this collective delusion where the living and the dead coexisted.

"Secundino came last night to console me," she told Alicia once.

"And what did he say?"

"Evil does not last forever, and neither do we."

"He's right."

The souls of Pedrito Carvajal, Arnulfo Pérez, Faustino Almazán, and the other soldiers would come in at midnight through the holes in the roof, and, after extending a gray serape on the floor, they played cards, drank pulque, and filled the house with their loud shouts.

"You can kiss your money good-bye, I have the king and the jack."

"Then you can shove them you know where, because here comes the ace."

Besides those who had died, there were the private ghosts. These had come from everybody's hometown or were inherited from loved ones. The women started talking about them in order to pass the time, to re-call their lost childhood fears. But the darkness of night in Clipperton was so desolate that it naturally evoked all sorts of phantoms. Alicia summoned the dead dwarfs that people called chaneques; an image of Our Lady of Sorrows pierced by seven daggers; and the legendary Ensign Nun, whom Death did not carry away in a horse carriage, like in Orizaba, but in the ship of the Flying Dutchman. Tirsa dragged in all the specters Cardona had left with her, brought to Clipperton from the land of the Chamula Indians. The one that terrified them most was Yalambequet, a flying skeleton that made his way into people's homes to steal their souls, announcing his presence by a thunderous clattering of bones that pierced the air.

"There goes Yalambequet. May God have mercy on us," the women and the children soon learned to say when there was a storm, and even when there wasn't one, just in case Yalambequet came unannounced.

They saw La Llorona, beautiful and phosphorescent, her arms full of lilies and her naked body wrapped in a *rebozo*, always wandering, always howling about the loss of her children and sweeping her long hair against people. They saw Doña Carlota, Ramón's mother, who appeared in a white nightgown and with her bonnet of black feathers, complaining about how undernourished and uncared for the children were. They frequently saw a silent, nice lady dressed in brown, whom nobody had met before. Clipperton itself had its own ghosts, like Ferdinand Magellan, the mariner who gave it its name, Isle of Passion, because of all the pain and sickness his crew had suffered when sailing close to it. Or like the pirate John Clipperton, who retired to his favorite refuge in order to relive orgies of old, keeping the women awake with the noise of wineglasses shattering on the floor, harlots' laughter, and swords clashing.

The ocean was dotted with ghost ships. The Flying Dutchman's was joined by a black schooner with her sails forming a cross, and another one that was just drifting, enveloped in flames. It was common belief that Arnaud and Cardona had been deceived by the *Marie Celeste*, the infernal ship that attracted death and ill fate the way a magnet attracts iron.

Supernatural incidents were on the increase in quantity and quality; they ceased being individual events and turned into collective experiences. Night after night when the temperature lowered, a throng of ghosts formed at the southern rock to begin the pilgrimage around the isle, carrying lighted torches, praying, dragging their chains, and leaving behind letters and messages for the living. They were the souls of all those who had died in connection with Clipperton, from those who had been condemned and marooned by the pirates to the Dutch sailor who drowned on his way to Acapulco. At first, the women ran home, bolted their doors, and covered their heads with their arms, in order not to see the river of lights or hear the *thump-thump* of their footsteps. But later they dared kneel on their balconies, waiting for the procession to pass by. The next morning they went out early to pick up the messages from the other world, and if these contained any orders or wishes, they would fulfill them faithfully. It did not take very long for the living to join the nightly wanderings of the spirits. Against Alicia and Tirsa's wishes, Francisca, Benita, Rosalía, and sometimes Altagracia marched all night behind the dead, and the next morning, bedraggled, they also looked like ghosts and had no energy to deal with their daily chores.

The spirits became capricious and demanding. Their orders took up all the time of those still living. They asked for stone altars, ceremonies, offers of food, and even goods impossible to obtain on the isle, like cigarettes and bunches of the fire-red *cempaxuchitl* flowers, which feed the insatiable hunger that tortures the dead in their tombs. The isle looked like a primitive holy land. Everywhere there were stone altars surrounded by plates of food, yellowed photos of the deceased, and a few remaining personal possessions: a straw hat, a sandal, a razor, a handkerchief, an image of the Virgin.

One night Tirsa and Alicia stayed home with all the children while the other women marched in the procession. Tirsa told Alicia that she had discovered Benita and Francisca flagellating themselves and wearing hair shirts and tight pieces of old rope around their thighs.

"Things cannot go on like this," warned Alicia, "or we are going to end up burying each other alive."

Alicia and Tirsa agreed to take drastic measures for all, beginning with themselves. The only way to survive was to stop this delirium. They bid farewell forever to the souls of Ramón and Secundino, explained the dangers of the situation, and wrote five commandments. They swore to enforce them until common sense prevailed and things returned to normal, for which they might have to impose penalties on those who would not comply. With a knife, they carved these commandments in big letters on the wall, and when the others returned at dawn, they were surprised by the following pentalogue:

First: From now on it is absolutely prohibited to pray, to build altars, and to perform religious sacrifices.

Second: Only what we see and the people we can touch are real. All others are hereby banished from Clipperton forever. It is forbidden to deal with the dead.

Third: No one is allowed to go out of the house at night, unless it is for a short task and after obtaining permission. The hours of the night are for resting, and for protecting the children and keeping them company.

Fourth: Nobody can scare a child, or say to a child things that are not true.

Fifth: She who violates any of these laws, in word or deed, will be thrown out of her house, separated from her children, and condemned to live in isolation.

Alicia and Tirsa went all around the isle toppling altars and burning idols and fetishes. Alicia's moral authority and her imposing personality, Tirsa's courage and physical strength, plus the unwavering alliance between the two, ensured their leaving behind these ominous times in which the dead invaded Clipperton and made slaves out of the living.

In spite of heading the struggle against the threat of the incorporeal,

Alicia began to have strange experiences, to feel inexplicable presences. She felt she was weakening, and that something inside her was depriving her of energy, something that hoarded the food she ate, that sucked the liquid with which she calmed her thirst. Someone who took away the air she breathed and robbed her heart of blood. She seemed to have a strength inside of her, smaller but more powerful, which existed and thrived at the expense of her own stamina, as her body, already ravished by malnutrition and fatigue, became weaker.

Two months after her husband was swallowed by the ocean, Alicia realized the nature of her problem. It was simple and obvious, and if she had not understood before, it was just because of her panic over accepting it. She called Tirsa.

"I am pregnant," she told her.

"This is incredible," Tirsa responded. "I didn't want to tell you because I wasn't sure, but I think I'm pregnant, too."

That night, hiding in her kitchen, Alicia cried all that she had not been able to cry when Ramón died. Violating her own commandment, she talked to him again, which she had not done for a long time.

"I called you many times, and I begged you to come back," she told him, "but not in this way. I needed your company and your protection, and look at what you are sending me instead of you: another baby."

Altagracia realized what the situation was and came to offer her consolation.

"Don't worry, ma'am, someone will soon come for me, and I'll take you with me, and all the others also," she told her.

"And who is going to come for you?"

"It's a secret."

"Don't come to me with stories of the dead. It's forbidden."

"He's not dead, he's alive."

"Alive? Tell me who."

"The German fellow."

"Schultz?"

"The same. He promised me he would come for me."

"Stop dreaming, my child. You're in worse shape than the ones who believe in ghosts."

"He is going to come. He promised me."

"He promised that to you because he was crazy."

"He was not crazy. He was just too lonesome. I cured him."

"Enough! All that you would need is to make an altar to your blond saint and pray to him for a miracle!"

"It's not a miracle, ma'am. It's that he loves me."

"It's over a year since he left, and he has not come."

"But he must be looking for me, I know."

"He was probably locked up in a nuthouse."

"Then he will escape and come for me."

"All right, you can believe anything you want. You might be right. You better keep on believing in Schultz's love, since you are lucky he's alive. Hold on to your memories so that despair does not dry you up, as it has done to us."

Mexico City, Today

THERE ARE CONFLICTING DETAILS regarding the deaths of Captain Ramón Arnaud and Lieutenant Secundino Cardona.

The first is the exact date: the day, the month, the year they occurred.

The second has to do with the kind of fish that overturned their raft, or that killed them when they fell in the water. Did it exist, really? If it existed, was it a manta ray? Or was it sharks?

The third is more complex, and it refers to the vessel that appeared that day on the horizon, the one they were trying to intercept. Was it a real ship? Was it, on the contrary, a mirage produced by a man's anguish, or a product of the Clipperton survivors' collective wish?

The four direct testimonies that I found about this event are contradictory, and do not dispel our doubts. Quite the opposite.

First: Letter of the nurse María Noriega, Lieutenant Cardona's legal wife, dated July 1940, in which she claims her widow's pension from the Mexican government.

Division General Lázaro Cárdenas

National Palace

By Hand

I am the widow of Infantry Lieutenant Secundino Angel Cardona, who under orders of the Secretary of Defense and of the Navy, with a detail of the Thirteenth Infantry Battalion commanded by Captain Ramón Arnaud, left the port of Acapulco on board the Mexican steamship Cor-rigan II.

My deceased husband informed me before parting that his stay on Clipperton Island, where they were headed, would last only a year; but after the year was over, he never returned, leaving me and my children without economic support, and restlessly waiting for him while locking in my heart the joy of ever seeing him again.

But fate or misfortune decreed to keep us apart forever. At dawn, on May 4th, 1915, they saw a sailing ship headed from east to west, to the northeast of the isle, and Captain Arnaud and my husband, in the hope of being rescued, started out in an improvised rowboat to follow the ship, which did not meet with success, and they perished at sea.

The persons who had stayed on the isle feverishly followed the fugitive ship, which became more and more distant, and observed anxiously and with despair the frantic efforts of the little boat, which was being left behind without managing to be seen. The ship finally disappeared on the horizon; only the boat could be seen, advancing with difficulty, and then disappearing behind some clouds. When these dissipated, the boat had vanished, swallowed by the ocean [. . .].

Yours truly,

María Noriega, Cardona's widow

Second: Logbook of Captain H. P. Perril, of the gunboat *Yorktown*, of the U.S. Navy, dated Wednesday, 17 July 1917. Captain Perril heard the story of the events that day from an eyewitness.

Captain Arnaud considered himself responsible for the desperate situation in which the people on the isle found themselves and worried so much about it that his mind lost its balance.

One day, *imagining* that he saw a ship at a short distance from shore, he forced his men to launch a boat and row out to sea to intercept it in order to seek help. *The men refused to give in to the whim of their captain, well aware that the ship existed only in his imagination.* Finally they obeyed his command and started out in the boat against heavy seas.

Shortly after, through her binoculars, Mrs. Arnaud saw the boat capsize and the men disappear in a sea full of sharks.

Third: Report filed in 1982 by Ramón Arnaud Rovira, Captain Arnaud's eldest son, who was about six or seven years old at the moment of his father's death.

One day at the *end of May 1915*, [. . .] my younger sister Alicia came in running and announced, addressing my father, "Dad, a ship!" [. . .] *In fact, a small shape was seen approaching* from the northwest. We all ran to the dock. [. . .] About one hour after we saw it, it was in front of us, its steel-gray gleams indicating its position in full sunlight.

In spite of all our signals and shouts, the vessel seemed not to be stopping, and continued on its course, ignoring us, [. . .]

"The ship is leaving! Why? How could this be? O Lord, have pity on us! Don't abandon us!" my disconsolate mother was shouting. [. . .]

The threatening tide was beginning to rise. By then the sea was already dangerous and our boat was not in very good condition. A strong wind was already blowing. The boat struggled

against the thrust of the waves. In the meantime, the ship continued on its course. [. . .]

Suddenly, a big thing made them capsize. It was a gigantic sea
animal, *I suppose it was a manta ray* that made the canoe capsize!"*

Fourth: Version of General Francisco Urquizo, written in 1954 and
documented in the Annals and Archives of the Mexican Army:

Captain Arnaud is already at the edge of insanity. . . .

It was October 5 of that fateful year of 1916.

The sun was already out, promising a clear, peaceful day, one
of those days when the sun dazzles [. . .]. The watchman at the
lighthouse called out that there seemed to be the silhouette of a
steamship looming on the horizon.

Everybody went up the tower in the avid hope of confirming
the news.

*It was true. This was no mirage or delusion. There was a ship in
the distance.* It might be headed toward the isle or it could just
hold its course, but it was there.

Arnaud thought that he was losing his mind; this was the opportunity he had been waiting for, the only opportunity to liberate
his people. Afraid that the ship would pass them by, he decided to
start out and try to intercept it. They boarded the only boat they
had and started out rowing to the limit of their physical strength.
He was carrying a long pole with a white flag to make signals.

Nervousness, desperation, hope: all contributed to give the
men enough energy to row.

---

*In: María Teresa Arnaud Guzmán, *La tragedia de Clipperton*, Editorial Arguz, Mexico,
1982. See also Charlotte K. Perril, *Forgotten Island*, U.S. Naval Institute Proceedings, Washington, 1937, vol. 63, no. 42, pp. 796–805.

From the tower on the cliff, Alicia, her children, and the rest of the women saw the boat grow distant and silently prayed for success.

"Let them be seen, O Lord! Let them be seen! [. . .]

Impossible.

It was written.

That day, October 5, 1916, was a fatal day. [. . .]

Those who were watching saw with anguish and desperation that the boat had stopped and that there was a struggle on board.

A big black mass had taken hold of the boat, and the men were furiously trying to hit it with their oars.

It was a manta ray!

It all happened in a matter of seconds. The sea monster was more powerful than the weak men and their little boat. It quickly overturned the tiny craft and it sank. The men never came back to the surface. [. . .]

The sea was calm as if nothing had happened. The ship's silhouette, indifferent, continued on its course.*

*Francisco Urquizo, *El capitán Arnaud*. Editorial del Río, Mexico, 1954.

Acapulco, Today

❦

I COME TO ACAPULCO to find out what happened to Gustav
Schultz after he left Clipperton on the gunboat *Cleveland*, of the U.S.
Navy. In a newspaper of 1935, I found the first trace, the thread that
would lead me to unravel the story: the German fellow never returned
to his native country.

After Captain Arnaud threw him out of the isle, Schultz stayed for
the rest of his days, which were many, in the Mexican port of Acapulco.
What tied him to a country that, besides being foreign to him, was being
torn asunder at the moment by a violent revolution? There was only one
thing: a deep, sworn commitment. The one that he had screamed at the
Clipperton shore, a few minutes before his departure, to the woman he
loved, whom he was being forced to leave behind against his will. With
his blond locks prey to the winds and a stormy expression in his madman's eyes, he had promised Altagracia Quiroz that he would not rest
until he could rescue her, that he would marry her and make her happy.

And if there was a reason he had remained in Mexico, it was to fulfill his impossible promise.

I have been able to find the address in Acapulco of one of the houses in which he lived. It's an adobe structure on a large piece of land in the colonial district of La Pocita. I talk to the old local neighbors, those who had heard about him and still remember his name. I ask them if he was insane when he arrived or if he was ever crazy.

"No, not crazy, never," they answer me. "Mr. Schultz was a great man here in Acapulco. A respected and beloved person, who gave us drinking water here in our port. We owe our first aqueduct to him. Did you already visit the Water House? It is a tourist attraction, but it was his home for years. At first he lived here in this house, but after he brought the water, he moved over there."

In the Water House one can still see the tanks, the pumps, and the hydraulic equipment that Gustav Schultz brought, installing them himself and making it all work, certainly applying the same meticulous care that he had taken with the Decauville train tracks in Clipperton.

A few years later he became a Mexican citizen and accepted a public office which he served with honesty and Teutonic perseverence: that of the port captain.

"Had he any children?" I ask people.

They say no, but he adopted a newborn Mexican baby from an orphanage, and gave him both his first and family names.

So now I'm looking for Gustavo Schultz, his adoptive son, at the place I am told he works. He is the owner of a poultry business in the Acapulco Central Food Market. The passageways have been recently washed with buckets of water mixed with a disinfectant. I get lost in a labyrinth crowded with all sorts of colors and smells. I pass by the striking piñatas in the shape of stars, ships, bulls. I pass by the mangoes and the custard apples; the fifty-eight varieties of chiles; the images of baby Jesus on a throne, donning crown and mantle; the kiosks of the clothes menders waiting for customers in front of antique sewing machines. I circulate among the ears of corn, the sweet potatoes, and the prickly pears; and in between the tables with benches where one can eat tacos, flautas, and burritos prepared by sweaty fast cooks. I see the *huitlacoche* and the incredible variety of mushrooms; someone offers me colorfully striped serapes, neck scarves, and hand-embroidered *huipiles*. They want me to buy paper cutouts, candy skulls, and *cempaxuchitl* flowers for the dead. Pumpkin flowers to make soup, and Jamaica flowers for *agua fresca*. I cross through the meat kiosks shouldering past legs of beef and heads of lamb. Until I finally reach the chickens.

They hang by the legs, all in a tight row, ugly and featherless, a hostile look in their dead eyes. There are thousands of chickens in more than two hundred kiosks, with at least one vendor in each kiosk. I go one by one, asking, "Are you Gustavo Schultz, or do you know him?"

"He had a business here, but he died about three years ago. His son, who has the same name, lives in Chilpancingo, state of Guerrero."

Gustav Schultz, the German fellow, Gustavo Schultz, his son, Gustavo Shultz, his grandson. I search in the Chilpancingo phone book, make a long-distance call, and talk with the last Schultz, the only one still alive. His voice sounds young, and he tells me he's in politics. He remembers his grandfather as very blond, with a light complexion and bushy eyebrows. He says that neither he nor his father, who are both dark-haired, resembles him physically because they had no blood connection. He confessed not to know any details of the Clipperton drama because the family does not like to recall such a painful past.

He does not have more information, he acknowledges, but in order not to disappoint me, he reads on the phone from a clipping he has kept for years. It is an interview of his grandfather by the journalist Hernán Rosales, published in the Mexico City newspaper *El Universal* on May 14, 1935. In it Schultz tells more about other people than about himself. His grandson reads with some difficulty because, as he explains, the clipping is now yellowed and faded. On the phone I get the story of the first Gustav Schultz, succinctly told by himself.

He says that in 1904, when he was twenty-four, he embarked in San Francisco, without much thought, for a place he had never heard of, Clipperton Island. He was going there to work for an English phosphate company. When he arrived, the uninhabited and barren isle filled him with melancholy: "I was living there like Robinson Crusoe." Eager to see and touch something green and alive, he sailed from Clipperton to the island of Socorro in the Revillagigedo Archipelago to bring back thirteen young and tender coconut palms and forty tons of topsoil in which to plant them. As man cannot subsist on coconuts alone, he also imported some company for himself: a young woman, Daría Pinzón, and her only daughter, Jesusa Lacursa.

On his return to Clipperton, he shared his life with that woman, watched the palm trees he planted grow, and made his employees work like slaves. He worked like a beast of burden himself. "I fell in love with my life in that desert seascape," he says. About his conflicts with Ramón Arnaud and his violent and crazy days, Gustav Schultz chose to keep silent. About the appearance of Altagracia Quiroz in his life, he confesses: "Her presence relieved my great sadness."

He refers to the arrival of Captain Williams at Clipperton, and confirms that he agreed to travel to Mexico aboard the *Cleveland* out of his own free will, not forced to do so by anyone. Once on the continent, it seems he recovered his sanity, if it is true that he had ever lost it, and he dedicated himself to try to rescue Altagracia. In the midst of the revolution that was rocking the country, she was merely a blade of grass lost in the storm, like so many other Mexicans. To reach Clipperton was not easy; a trip could not be improvised on a small vessel. He had to obtain the collaboration of a government that would be willing to make a large vessel available for the sole purpose of rescuing the remaining survivors. It was wartime, when thousands of people were dying, and a rescue mis-

sion for a few soldiers left in an enemy camp was certainly not among
the priorities of the Mexican government.

But Gustav Schultz did not forget his promise. On the contrary, his
steadfast determination became an obsession. He traveled regularly to
various places with the purpose of making inquiries about Altagracia
Quiroz before the proper authorities and the rebels, those of the de-
posed administrations as well as the elected ones. In the interview he
tells how he spent a year going from one government office to another,
and from one department to the next, uselessly making his request over
and over again to bureaucrats who would ask him to present it in writing, just to bury it in their archives, or who, insisting on protocol, would
then shut their doors in his face for good. Convinced that he had tried
all possibilities on the Pacific coast, in June 1915 he went to Veracruz,
on the Atlantic side, to speak with a government official who was known
to be a humanitarian, generous person. His name was Hilario Rodríguez
Malpica. This kind man listened to the whole story, worried about the
situation of those forsaken on the isle, and commissioned Schultz to go
to Clipperton to rescue them. For days they contacted people high in
government and some who were influential with the navy, until a plan
was agreed upon. Gustav Schultz was to travel to Salina Cruz, a Pacific
port, and there would board a ship, the *Corrigan III*, for the isle.

He had finally secured governmental support and help from the
navy, had received a commission, money for the trip and essential crew,
and a set departure date. Perhaps he even had a bouquet of roses to give
to his fiancée at the time of their meeting. "But fate," Schultz recounts,
"determined that upon my arrival at Salina Cruz, I found the *Corrigan III*
aground at the dock."

Since it was impossible to repair the *Corrigan III*, the only available
ship, the trip was called off, and the poor German fellow had to start all
over again. For two more years he continued in his efforts, to no avail,
and in January 1917 he traveled again to Veracruz to visit the only man

who had ever listened to him. This time, however, even Rodríguez Malpica discouraged him.

"My advice, Mr. Schultz, is that you face reality. You need to look at things with more pessimism. I regret having to tell you this, because I consider you my friend. But you must realize that all of them must have died by now. Your Altagracia Quiroz, and all the others, are dead."

"I don't agree, my friend. I can assure you that woman is alive and is going to marry me. Someday. Besides, I am certain that day is not far off. And you, who have always been so kind to me, you are going to be my best man."

Clipperton, 1915–1916

WITH A RAG ATTACHED to the end of a stick (brooms had disappeared long before) Alicia was trying to sweep the sand out of the house. This chore, which she had done every day for seven years, was an obsession with her still, now that they were living in rubble. The effort exhausted her, and she had to sit down to rest. In the past, each time she was pregnant she had been full of joy and bursting with energy. But not this time. Malnourishment had greatly affected her. She felt old and dispirited, and her disposition had turned sour. She was tormented by the thought of her body having to compete with her own offspring for the scant nutrition she was receiving. It was obvious that the baby resented the lack of food even more than she did, since the size of her belly after five months of pregnancy had not reached the volume of her previous ones at three months.

Tirsa Rendón was not doing much better. Her pregnancy had started a month later, but she was also looking wasted. Tirsa, the brave one, the strong one, the one who managed to collect, all by herself, three-fourths of all the food they ate, had become quite a different Tirsa: distant and listless, covering up her infinite fatigue with an indifferent exterior.

Alicia got up to finish her chore. Every time she swept a room, the children would come running in and bring the sand back.

"I tire myself less if I sweep again than if I scold them," she would explain.

She went into the small room next to her bedroom. Instead of a stained-glass window, there was now a big gaping hole that allowed the wind in. Instead of the wicker chair, which the hurricane had carried away, there was a wooden box, and she sat on it. She opened the trunk where she kept her most precious possessions. She took out Ramón's gala uniform, his woolen jacket with the double line of buttons, epaulets and chevron still golden; his military hat, flattened sideways, with its braid unstitched; his sword; his black boots. She took out her wedding gown, with its twenty yards of lace, and a dozen tablecloths and bedsheets, among them the wedding-night saintly sheet. Two little sailor suits that had belonged to her older children but could still fit the younger ones. Some clothes she had bought (but never got to wear) on her one and only trip to the Mexican capital. Carefully wrapped in tissue paper, there was a bar of Ivory soap, already half used. She took it out, smelled it, and wrapped it again. There was a silver frame, with its glass missing, from which her father smiled at her. He was young and wore a white suit. She untied the silk ribbon around a huge wad of bills and counted them: there were four thousand two hundred pesos, all the money she and Ramón had saved. She took out his hairbrush, the one with the silver handle, let her hair down, and brushed it for the first time in months. It was coming out in handfuls, and she rolled a ball with the hair left entangled in the bristles.

"When Tirsa comes," she said to herself, "I am going to tell her that tomorrow we'll get our hair cut. This long hair is of no use to us; on the contrary, it's sapping away our babies' calcium and iron."

She opened her jewelry case. In it she saw her ring and the diamond earrings, a sapphire brooch, several gold hoops, chains, and several twigs of black coral that the children had gotten out of the sea to give to her. In the bottom she found what she was looking for: the gray pearl necklace that Ramón had sent her from Japan. She put it on, caressing it for a long time: she seemed to want the tips of her fingers to memorize even the tiniest irregularities in each pearl.

She folded everything back in, arranging things inside the trunk, except for the sheets and the tablecloths. She needed them to cover herself at night, to use as towels after her bath, to make clothes for the children and diapers for the babies to come. She took off the crude tunic she was wearing, made out of real sailcloth, and wrapped herself in the saintly bedsheet like a sari. She closed the trunk tight and dragged it out to the veranda, making rest stops. When she managed to bring it to the edge, she gave it a big push. The trunk fell about five feet, sinking somewhat into the sand. She went down and spent the rest of the morning digging a hole around it.

Ramoncito came to help her.

"What are you doing, Mom?"

"I am burying the trunk."

"What for?"

"To protect what is inside."

"And what is inside?"

"The clothes and the money I am going to need the day we are rescued."

"Are we going to be rescued?"

"Perhaps."

"I don't want to leave. Do you?"

"I do."

"Why? Is it better somewhere else?"

"Much better. Perhaps."

"And why do you need clothes the day we are rescued?"

"I don't want to be pitied."

"And you also saved clothes for me?"

"No, not for you. Your old clothes are too small for you."

"Then I am going to be pitied?"

"No. I am going to buy you a new suit as soon as we land. And a pair of shoes."

"I don't like to wear shoes."

"When you are there, you'll like them."

"I don't like it over there. I don't want to go."

The rest of the women were still on the cliff side. Every day they clambered down the steep rock, competing with the waves in order to take away the ocean's bounty of oysters, squid, and crayfish. Tirsa, the most skilled at this task, could not do it anymore and limited herself to offering instructions from higher up. Alicia heard their voices.

"They are coming," she told Ramón. "Let's hurry and finish burying this. They're coming back early. They must have made a good catch."

They were coming at a gallop, bolting like colts, but carrying no food. They stopped in a circle around Alicia, without saying anything. She saw them panting, extremely pale, a wild look in their eyes.

"What's the matter, for God's sake? Someone fell down?"

"No, ma'am."

"What happened? Why won't you tell me?"

"Because you will scold us if we tell you, ma'am."

"The children! Something happened to the children?"

"No, nothing to do with the children. It's because up on the cliff we saw— We saw Lucifer."

"Are we going to start that again?" barked Alicia, making no effort to conceal her fury.

Tirsa, who had lagged behind, came then.

"It's true, Alicia. This time I saw him myself."

"Did you see the devil? You, too?" There was more sarcasm than surprise in Alicia's voice.

"Yes," Tirsa said. "Me, too. I don't know if it was the devil, but it was some horrible being."

Then, all started talking at once: he was tall, big, his red hair standing out, hairy all over, hairy only on his back. His eyes spewed fire, no, they were human but he had a snout instead of a mouth. His face was that of a man. He walked on all fours. He didn't walk on four, only on three. In any case, he was on two legs, but he did not walk like other people. His skin was dark, dried up, he had scales like an iguana. He smelled putrid, and before he appeared on top of the cliff they had perceived his stink, like a rotten corpse. He was naked, and his private parts were the devil's, or at least very big, and anyway, he was truly male, no doubt about that.

"The devil surely he's not," Alicia decreed. "So he is a man or a beast. Or he's nothing, like so many other ghosts around here."

"He's a beast," some women said.

"He's a man," said the others.

"Could he be a shipwrecked sailor who got here?" Alicia asked.

"Well, if he was shipwrecked," Tirsa answered, "he must have lived at the bottom of the sea for years."

They decided that a few women, armed with sticks and headed by Tirsa, would go around the isle. They would go to places they had not been since they had set essential perimeters of action for themselves.

"We'd better not go today. It's already late and darkness will soon close in on us," Benita pleaded.

"Yes," agreed Tirsa, "we'd better do it tomorrow when it's light."

"Better never," Alicia said. "Let's not look for him, but wait and see if he appears. There is no hurry, since he has caused no harm so far."

The women had a restless though quiet night. At dawn Alicia summoned all to the beach. When they arrived, they saw in Tirsa's hands two kitchen knives, which she was sharpening on a stone.

"Are we going to hunt that demon we saw?" they asked.

"No. We aren't hunting any demons. We are going to cut our hair," Alicia announced, "because it's interfering with our tasks. Besides, we cannot take care of it anymore, and, unkempt like this, our manes look frightful. We have all discussed this several times, it was decided long ago, and we're finally doing it. Who will be the first volunteer?"

Rosalía was first, then Benita and Francisca. Alicia and Tirsa would grab the long tresses and shear them just below the ears, throwing the cuttings on a single pile that started to look like a sleeping hairy animal. Then Alicia and Tirsa cut each other's manes. Someone brought the broken mirror; they looked at their short haircuts, and they all laughed.

"Let me see how you look," Francisca said to Benita. "I bet you will not get any beaux with your hair like that."

"And whom did you have in mind for me? The cliff monster?"

"I'll wait for this child to grow up and marry me," Rosalía said, lifting Ramoncito up in her arms and smacking kisses on his face. "And by then, my hair will be long again."

"We are already shorn," Alicia said. "All but you, Alta."

"Not me, ma'am, I'm not cutting it."

"Come on, you're not eating enough for you and your hair."

"No, ma'am, I can't . . . because my German friend likes it."

"Let it be, then. This girl is really in love."

The little girls came running with their porcelain doll all battered and ragged.

"Alta! Dear Alta! Make a real wig for the doll," they begged her, "she is tired of having no hair."

"No hair, no hands, and only one eye. The poor thing is hopeless," Alta said while choosing a good chunk of hair for the wig.

That afternoon Benita separated from the group to go salt the fish. She came back breathless, her face all flushed.

"The monster appeared, ma'am," she told Alicia. "He's— It's Victoriano Alvarez."

"What do you mean? Victoriano Alvarez died months ago."

"No, ma'am, he didn't die."

"Of course he did. Scurvy did him in!"

"No, it didn't kill him. He's disfigured, but he didn't die."

"It must be another apparition. Did you touch him?"

"He touched me. He really did touch me."

Benita said that she was cutting the fish in fillets and separating the bones when she smelled a strong, unpleasant odor. She thought of the fetid lagoon, or that maybe there was still an unburied corpse. The monster then came up behind her without making any noise. When she realized it, she jumped up and screamed, and he told her not to be frightened, that he was Victoriano.

"Victoriano Alvarez? Are you dead?" Benita asked him, almost in a whisper.

"I almost died, but I came back to life all by myself."

She looked very carefully at the ghost who was facing her and recognized in him a remote resemblance to the lighthouse keeper, to the big and strong soldier of old. His legs were now bent and full of boils. In order to stand up he needed to support himself on a stick. His skin was spotty and his thin mat of flaming red, spiky hair continued in hard corkscrew tufts all down his back. He had toadlike eyes, and his gums had shrunk. He had no teeth.

"What happened to you that made you so ugly, Victoriano?"

"Hunger and disease did it."

He said he lay dying in his hammock for many days in the lighthouse lair, and when his soul left him, the crabs invaded his den. When he woke up, he was able to catch and eat them by simply reaching out, and that had saved his life because he was so weak he could not even get up. When he was very thirsty, he dragged himself across the floor and lay faceup in the rain. As time passed and there were no signs of other human beings, he thought they had all died and he was the only survivor. He recuperated some and began hunting and eating boobies. They were raw, slimy, and reeking of iodine. As he could not get to his feet, he lay there, dead still, waiting for hours at a time until a bird got close enough to be hit. It took him quite a while to be able to stand up. Then, leaning on a stick, he would take a step, two steps, and fall. He needed to wriggle like a snake in order to reach the hammock and rest, to catch his breath before trying again. Days and nights went by, and he was finally able to wade on the beach and harpoon fish, hurling his regulation bayonet. He began to notice signs that he was not alone, to suspect that there were other survivors, and in his search for them he ventured a bit farther each time. He also said that the pain in his legs tormented him and that walking was torture. Two weeks before, he had discovered the other survivors, the women, and he spied on them day and night without being seen. He found out that the rest of the men had died: he knew that he was the last man on Clipperton Island.

"Why didn't you ask for help?" Benita asked him.

"When I did, you all tried to kill me."

Victoriano told about the beating he had suffered the day Irra's family was laid down.

"Those who beat you up are all dead," the woman said. "Come home with me. Mrs. Arnaud and the others will welcome you."

The man accepted, but on the way he drew a knife and pressed it against her neck.

" 'First I need to have a woman, so lie down,' " Victoriano demanded, Benita said.

"Oh, my God! And what did you do?" Alicia asked, terrified.

"Lie down, ma'am, what else could I do?" answered Benita, without offering any explanation. "He's here now, around the corner, waiting for permission to come in."

Alicia sent for him. First they perceived the stink of someone who, though reprieved at the last moment, still had the smell of death. When he crossed the threshold, the women found themselves face to face with the cliff monster. It was all true: scurvy, arthritis, and rickets had turned Victoriano Alvarez into a fright. Yet they were glad to see him, and after a while they got used to the way he looked. He was in a sorry state, but it was good to have a man around.

"You're in bad shape, but you are alive, Victoriano," Alicia said to him.

"But not thanks to you."

"We are not alive thanks to you either. But this is no time for recriminations. We can help you, and you can help us. Provided you behave. You abused Benita, and that was evil. If you want to live with us, you cannot do that again, ever."

"I needed to be with a woman, after so much loneliness."

"Next time, you have to ask her whether she also wants to be with you."

"And if she doesn't want to?"

"Then you have to do without, as we do."

They brought him food, and he spoke again of his struggle for survival.

"In the end, we are the only ones left, you and us," Alicia said. "It's not so strange, women and blacks are the most resilient races on the planet."

"And you have turned black."

"Why, yes, that's true, we're dark like you now. The sun made us all look alike."

"The sun and the suffering, ma'am, have toughened our skin."

"If suffering darkens people, Victoriano, our souls must be coal black."

As he bid farewell to return to the lighthouse, they brought him one of the bedsheets, a spoon, and a few other utensils he had asked them to lend him. They saw little of him during the following days. They knew sometimes that he was around because they could perceive his deathly stench, and because they learned to recognize the rattling of his bones and his limping steps. Alicia and Tirsa suspected that the purpose of his visits was to meet furtively with Benita. Once in a while he came by the house, bringing seafood or fish. The women would feed him, and he would sit around to ruminate the food in his misshapen mouth, without saying a word. They gave him any available remedies and some cod liver oil that they had extracted themselves. Rubbed in well, this warmed his body and offered some relief for his rheumatism. They made a paste out of ground mother-of-pearl to treat his old scars, which he complained still itched and burned.

Late one night they realized that Benita had not returned home. They searched around calling her, but she did not respond. They thought she probably was in the lighthouse lair and went for her. Victoriano was at the door, blocking their entrance.

"We have come for Benita."

"She is staying with me, and you're not taking her away from here."

"Benita, do you want to stay?" shouted Alicia.

"Yes, ma'am, I'm staying," came her voice from inside.

For several weeks the women did not meet either of them, until one morning while collecting shrimp by the ocean-bathed cliff. It was Rosalía who found Benita's body. Her head was split, and she had red marks all over her body.

"She fell off the cliff and broke her neck, poor thing!"

"What are those things on her body? All those red marks."

"They are Judas kisses."

"An octopus sucked her dry."

"No," Tirsa said slowly and with sorrow. "Victoriano beat her up, then killed her. And he's coming to take another one of us with him."

That same night, they heard him come near, invisible in the dark. When the air turned rancid and they heard femurs and tibias clatter, Alicia and Tirsa came out to face him, pushing their big pregnant bellies ahead of them.

"You are a murderer, and you're not coming into the house."

"I can go in anywhere I want to, because now I am the governor."

The clouds that were hiding the moon parted like a curtain, and a chalky light spread over everything. They were then able to see the ferocious aspect of the tattered leper pirate: he had three daggers tucked under his belt, a rifle in bandolier, and he was wielding a heavy club.

"Why did you kill her?"

"I killed her for being a disrespectful lazybones. Now I am the governor, see. I'm in command, and all the women are mine for whatever I want. I'll take you two with me after you give birth."

"You will pay for your crimes, Victoriano," Alicia threatened.

"Oh really, ma'am. And who will make me pay? You?"

"Justice, when we are rescued."

"Nobody is going to come, and if they do, I'll kill all of you first, so there will be no tattletales left. If you don't want a beating now, don't stand in my way, because I'm going in."

With a hard swipe of his left arm, he broke into the house and grabbed Altagracia. He jostled her, brought her down, and dragged her by the hair. Her long, blue-black, shiny hair.

"I'm taking this one with me," he said, "so she can cook for me and be my woman."

He walked away, tottering painfully on his shaky legs, with Altagracia on his shoulder. Eyes closed, ears and mind closed in order not to see, not to hear, not to feel, she let herself be carried like a sack of flour. Her hair was dragging, sweeping the floor and leaving a track through the pebbles and seashells.

A few hours later, Alicia went into labor prematurely. It was a baby boy, ethereal and fragile like a sigh, and no one doubted that such an angelical face would soon return to heaven. In order not to let him be held back halfway there, suffering in purgatory, they baptized him immediately with water on his head and salt on his mouth, and they named him Angel Miguel after Ramón father. Alicia was not even able to breast-feed him.

"You're so anguished the milk cannot come down," Tirsa told her.

The baby was kept alive with teaspoonfuls of coconut water and booby egg whites until Tirsa's delivery. She had a baby girl, big and strong, and named her Guadalupe Cardona. Tirsa breast-fed both babies and neither was ever satisfied. They cried all the time. Lupe screamed loudly, and the boy squealed like a sick little bird. But neither wanted to die, and both consciously clung to life.

Alicia and Tirsa knew that the time had come to face Victoriano. They had some weapons, a few guns and regulation rifles, but no ammunition. They had run out of that years before.

"It is as useless as still keeping your mother after she's dead," Tirsa commented.

In spite of his condition, Victoriano was still powerful and an excellent shot. Adversity had made him evil, cruel, and fierce. He presented a terrible challenge for them, like an unconquerable mountain.

"We must kill him, no matter what. It's our duty." Tirsa was really firm on this.

"Our only duty is to stay alive, for the sake of our children," Alicia countered, equally firm.

Their disagreement and their fright paralyzed them, and even though they were overwhelmed by the certainty that for Altagracia each minute could be her last one, they spent evenings discussing what to do, but without taking any action. They finally found a compromise. They would try to kill him, but without risking getting killed by him.

"Poison," Alicia said, running in search of whatever remained of Ramón's pharmacy. Most of the bottles were broken, empty, or dry, but the blue flask she was looking for was intact. It had never even been opened. It still had its original label: *"Agua zafia (Arandula vertiginosa),"* and Arnaud's handwritten red label, which read, "Potentially lethal," and included instructions for its use: "One drop dissolved in a half cup of water taken after meals, good for heartburn; two drops, at eleven, improves appetite; five drops, excellent aphrodisiac; ten drops taken daily, great tonic for the heart, prolongs life; but thirty drops taken at once endanger it; two tablespoons of agua zafia will kill anybody."*

They needed Altagracia's complicity, and they were looking for a way to communicate with her without Victoriano's knowing. They discovered that the best time was early in the morning while he was in deepest sleep. They found Altagracia turned inward; protected, aloof, and untouchable in the fortress of her dreams.

"Is he hurting you much?" they whispered, not to wake up the man.

"He only hurts my body," she answered, "because my mind thinks of the one who loves me, and it escapes with him very far away from here."

"The memory of your German fellow saves you," Alicia told her, "and you are the one who is going to save us."

They prepared two full tablespoons of agua zafia dissolved into a thick fish soup and explained to Altagracia that for him to die, she had to make him eat it. That she should not taste it, not even a sip. She could tell him she had prepared it especially for him.

"He's not going to believe me," protested Altagracia. "I don't cook for him, even when he hits me for it."

---

*Jorge lbargüengoitia. *Dos crímenes* (Two murders). J. Mortiz, Mexico, 1979.

They convinced her, embraced her, gave her their blessings, and returned home. For the following two days they had no news, either from
Altagracia or from Victoriano, and they tormented themselves with the
possibilities.

"He must have swallowed only enough for the dose to be an aphrodisiac, and he's going to come now and rape us all."

"Or maybe he took the dose that prolongs life, and then not even a
bolt of lightning could touch him."

"Or the poison opened his appetite, and he wants more soup. . . ."

On the third day he reappeared, furious like a wild beast, more haggard and horrible than before because, he growled, he had eaten the
soup and kept vomiting, nonstop, for three days. He beat up all the
women, dragged them by the hair, and then took away all the rifles,
guns, tools, and even kitchen knives so that they could not use any of
them against him.

"Bitches, you wanted to kill me! I'm going to kill you all, and save
your tender daughters for later. I'll teach them to love me while they are
still young, and not to stab me in the back."

One day Alicia woke up quite determined. She could find no rest after Victoriano had threatened the girls. She had a responsibility, even
though it meant doing something horrible. At dawn, she prepared her
children's breakfast. She wrapped Angel in a rebozo and slung him on
her back as the women had shown her. She grabbed Ramón by the hand
and called Alicia and Olga.

"Where are we going, Mom?"

"To the southern rock."

The children were happy, remembering the times their father used
to go on outings with them. Though their mother did that frequently
now, it was not the same. When they got to the top of the rock, she
would stand at the edge of the cliff in utter silence. She did not show
them the stars, as he used to, or talk to them about the direction of the

winds. She just stood there, lost in thought, while they played. Then suddenly she would say, "Let's go back home, children, our excursion is over," and it was of no use to plead with her to stay a little while longer, or to ask her to let them go down to the bottom of the rock through the center hole. But it didn't matter: they were happy to go anyway.

The girls ran ahead, and Alicia had to run to catch up with them. When they were close, with the sun already out, she asked them, as usual, to be silent so as not to wake up Victoriano, and to crouch as they walked so he could not see them in case he did. Nervous but with shiny eyes, the children obeyed, trying to hold back their laughter with their hands.

Alicia was climbing up with the baby, but he was so small that she didn't feel his weight. Her older boy guided her, told her where to step. She trembled, determined to do what she had not dared do on other occasions. It was different now, they were running out of time. It was now or never; if she waited any longer, it would be too late.

The girls clambered up the cliff, holding on to the rocks. They were naked, suntanned, electric, and agile like monkeys.

When they reached the top, Alicia looked down, and her heart shrank. This is utter madness, she thought. She had stood there several times, reviewing all the proceedings in her head, rehearsing it all mentally in order not to fail at the moment of truth. Night after night she had prepared herself for this moment. But now, when it was real and there was no turning back, nothing seemed according to plan, even in her darkest forebodings. The cliff felt more hostile, more merciless. Its height, which had seemed tolerable to her, opened into a black void, terrifying and abysmal. It would take them ages to fall to the bottom, they would hit the rocks on the way down, their bodies would be mangled before reaching the water. They would not die quickly, as she had thought, but, instead, descend slowly through the morning mist, and the children would have time to realize what was going on, to feel the panic, to scream at her for help, and not to forgive her for all eternity. "Let's forget it! This time we'll go back the same way we came," Alicia said, but then she remembered Victoriano, his threats to kill them and rape the girls. If he ever touched her girls, if he mistreated them, could she ever forgive herself? Would Ramón forgive her? I'll jump with the children now. There is no other solution, she thought.

Then she realized that the children were not going to stand still waiting for her to push them. They were going to run helter-skelter, to squeeze by and defend themselves. She would have to run after them. This had not occurred to her before, perhaps because it wasn't ever real. She had imagined them holding hands with her and jumping into the void, unaware, half asleep, tired of living, resigned to their fate, accepting death. But the creatures ahead of her, playing and jumping around, were full of vitality. They were life itself, and they would cling to her with overwhelming energy. "Oh Lord, forgive me for planning such a stupid atrocity. What I must do is kill Victoriano." She felt strong and determined. She had been hiding Ramón's sword. She would do it. She and Tirsa would kill him. Could they do it? Would the enormous and rusty sword be serviceable? No, they could not do it. What would probably happen is that he would kill them first, and that the children would be left at his mercy. There is no other way out, she thought. Today there is no turning back.

The extent of her pain surprised her. Even though in her soul she knew, or wanted to convince herself, that this time they would not jump either, she suffered as if they were going to. She firmly believed that she had suffered all the pain that a human being could withstand, that she knew suffering deep and wide, that it was already familiar terrain with no surprises. But her suffering now was a hundred times, a thousand times worse than all she had been through before. She was horrified at the intensity of the anguish her heart could tolerate.

The children found the hole that led to the interior of the big rock, used by Ramón and his men in search of treasure years ago.

"Look, Mom! Look at all the bats!"

"Come here, Mom, the toads are so ugly!"

"Mom! Help me catch one, Mom."

Alicia suddenly realized that her children were happy. Many times before, she had watched them behaving in the same way, saying the same things, playing in the same manner, but she had not realized that. Now she saw it clearly: that all her years of tragedy were for them just everyday life. They had nothing to compare it with; they missed nothing. Like other times before, she convinced herself that she should go down the cliff, walk back home, and forget about demented solutions. How was she going to kill her own children, when neither hunger nor Victoriano had yet been able to? It made no sense. It was absurd. Horrible. She was not going to do that. She wouldn't do it for anything in the world. Her pain diminished, allowing her to breathe again. An unexpected joy of life came over her, and to see the children alive, alive in spite of everything, made her happy.

She almost told them, like often before, "Let's go back home, children, our excursion is over." But she remembered the three years they had been abandoned on the isle without hope. They would be in the same situation after three more years, and in three more, six; and three more, nine, and three more, twelve, and three more, fifteen. The words died in her throat. It was better to jump and be done with it.

Over and over she made up her mind, got close to the abyss, looked at the children, and changed her mind, anguishing in her doubts. Her heart could not take it any longer. The sun had not reached high noon yet, and there was still a layer of green mist over the ocean.

Behind the fog, on the horizon, Alicia saw a radiance. Points of light were moving, shining. They twinkled, died down, they reappeared suddenly, to disappear again as quickly. She remembered watching the sky as a child in Orizaba when sometimes she had been able to see, very high and far away, the fireworks celebrating a neighboring town's patron saint. But now the lights were low, at water level.

"The last thing I need," she said. "A ghost ship."

She felt light-headed, and shivers went down her spine.

"Oh, Ramón, don't do this to me. Don't send me mirages also; we had to pay so dearly for yours."

She rubbed her eyes, bit her lips, but the brilliant points of light were still there. They were compacting, becoming a solid mass.

"Please, Ramón, don't make fun of me, not now. Take away this vision and give me strength to jump, before the suffering makes me hesitate again."

The children, lost in their world, were making a lot of noise, holding on to her legs, pulling her to and fro. As usual, they wanted to go into that hole inside the rock, catch a toad, or wanted to know if it was true that bats could smoke. She remained mute, motionless, and stunned, without being able to free herself from her hallucination. A big gray thing was advancing toward the isle, cutting through the waves and dispersing the fog.

"Ramoncito!" she summoned her son. "Come here. Tell me, what do you see over there? But don't lie to me, don't pretend. Just tell me what you see."

"It's a ship, Mom."

There it was, facing them, in the water. Metallic and solid, identical to the one she had seen reflected in her husband's eyes before he died.

"Make some signals, son," Alicia ventured in a weak, brittle voice.

The boy waved his arms. Alicia did not dare to, she did not want to fall into that trap. Her body was paralyzed, but her heart was racing. She would not make any signals. She would not shout at a ghost to ask for help. It was all a dream, and she was bound to wake up. Since everything was lost, at least she would keep her composure, her reason. She remembered her own dictum: only what one can touch exists. That ship was intangible; it did not exist. Ramoncito was screaming: "Here, we are heeeere!"

The two girls came to see what was going on, and they went crazy when they saw the ship. Ramón took off the piece of material he was wearing as a loincloth, and waved it over his head. The girls soon imitated him. They let themselves be carried away by their enthusiasm. They were running in every direction, yelling for help, waving their rags as if possessed.

"Help!" Alicia heard herself shout, to her surprise.

This first shout was like a door opening in her throat, letting out all the hopes she had held back, after so many years of stifling them, of not giving them wings. Now she, too, was running, screaming, laughing, and praying, kissing her children.

"This is the real thing, Ramón. This is really it!" she repeated, looking upward, more in an effort to convince herself than to inform her husband.

The ship was closer now, and she could see the flag: it was the U.S. flag. A sharp panic stunned her: What if nobody on board saw them and the ship went back? It was not a Mexican ship, and therefore it would probably just cruise by. Unless they could manage to make it stop.

"Let's yell loud and clear, so they hear us!" she told the children, and she herself put her whole soul into each yell.

In the furor of all the clamor, Alicia tore off the saintly bedsheet she had wrapped around herself. Naked like her children, with Angel on her back, and brimming with the joy of her renewed desire to live, she waved the white sheet in the air.

"You rag, better be good for something," she commanded. "Make them see us!"

High Seas, Aboard the Gunboat Yorktown, 1916

❦

IT WAS STILL AS DARK AS night at six fifteen on Wednesday, 18 July when Captain H. P. Perril came to the bridge. He was hit by a milky curtain that, at first, he could not decipher as fog or as the nebulae in his still-sleepy brain. Nobody on board the *Yorktown* had been able to sleep due to the choppy seas and the extreme heat. A few of the men had tried to sleep on deck, until various scattered but recurrent rainstorms forced them to go back in. At four o'clock, even the captain had managed some light sleep, which had just become deep sleep by the time he was awakened, as usual, at six.

Slowly he began to connect with the real world: a strong wind was blowing from the southwest, and an impatient sea jolted the ship without mercy or rhythm. He asked the helmsman if he could see anything, and he answered, "Only the fog, sir." There was no visibility until nine fifty, when the lookout shouted that he had sighted land.

"That boy has an eagle eye," commented Perril, uselessly trying to see it.

Not until fifteen minutes later was he able to see a gray shadow in the distance. As they got closer, the shadow darkened and took first the tall aspect of a ship's sails, and later that of a castle. It was Clipperton, no doubt. It was the big rock on the southeast coast, according to description. Captain Perril felt uneasy. Neither he nor his men had entertained any desire to sail there. Before they left San Francisco, however, Admiral Fullam, commander in chief of the U.S. Pacific Fleet, had informed them that Clipperton was to be included in their itinerary. They were in the middle of the world war and there were rumors that the Germans, taking advantage of the tense relationship between the Mexican and U.S. governments, had installed radio stations or submarine bases along the Pacific coast of Mexico. The gunboat *Yorktown* had to engage in a meticulous surveillance trip.

It was a monotonous, routine job, and his crew was anxious to be in action, so he received the news reluctantly. Before the gunboat parted from the continent, they had determined their ports of call carefully. Admiral Fullam had placed the quadrant on top of the map and traced an appropriate itinerary from Honolulu to Panama. Clipperton was just underneath the black line.

Captain Perril protested. "I am going to make a foolish request, Admiral. You know the men don't like to get near that isle. I know there are superstitions, of course, but if possible, it would be better to avoid it."

"I'm sorry, Captain, it can't be done. It is well within our area of operation." Fullam was explicit, knowing well what Perril was referring to. Clipperton was one of those places sailors consider bad omens, in part because of the difficulties they present for navigation, in part due to superstition. In the case of Clipperton, there seemed to be a good basis for both, since the number of shipwrecks around it was strangely elevated.

The ship's itinerary had been, in fact, slow and boring, and as they had suspected, it had been only a rumor, they did not find even a trace of the Germans. Accustomed to matter-of-fact issues, Captain Perril felt uncomfortable about this wild-goose chase. To make things worse, now he also had to pass by Clipperton. After Perril read his navigation instructions and the unfavorable information about access to the atoll, he was convinced that he should not make any attempt except in broad daylight.

Therefore, that Monday afternoon of 16 July, he reduced speed in order to reach the isle at dawn on Wednesday. On Tuesday, at 2000, he veered the gunboat slightly east so that, maintaining course during the night, their position in the morning would be five miles east of the isle. However, a night squall had altered his plans somewhat, and by 0600 Wednesday, Clipperton was still not in sight as expected. The isle had not yet appeared by seven, nor by eight, and Captain Perril, convinced that it had been left behind, decided with some relief not to reverse course. He was troubled to learn then, at 0950, that against all odds, Clipperton had suddenly emerged from the mist dead ahead.

The encounter had been a matter of chance rather than willingness, or, perhaps, it had been due to the isle's willpower rather than his own. In spite of his Anglo-Saxon phlegm and pragmatism, Captain Perril could not help but feel disturbed by the idea that this undesirable place had willed him to its shores. Notwithstanding, the *Yorktown* approached the coast without any difficulty. The ship circumnavigated the atoll while Perril watched through his spyglass without finding anything abnormal. On the contrary, it was sort of a deception, since everything he saw was small, barren, quiet, insignificant. Nothing that could suggest a black legend. The only signs of life seemed to be some people with handkerchiefs waving good-bye. Just the usual. A while later the people were still waving handkerchiefs, and it seemed to the captain there were perhaps women, and also children, running on the beach waving good-bye.

They keep doing that, Perril thought. They must have nothing to do.

He considered his mission accomplished, and was about to give orders to set sail, when something made him change his mind. Nothing specific, just an impulse, the stirring of a premonition. He ordered his second in command, Lieutenant Kerr, to get ready to disembark. Kerr looked at him in surprise. A risky landing would have to be made by boat because of the choppy seas, and there was no apparent justification for it. Perril noticed his bewilderment and tried to formulate an explanation.

"I want to know whether the lighthouse I see over there is working," he said without conviction. Lieutenant Kerr nodded, but his bewildered expression did not change.

Taxco, Today

⬥

I AM LOOKING FOR ALTAGRACIA Quiroz, the chambermaid at the Hotel San Agustín who left for Clipperton as nursemaid for the Arnauds' children. I find out she died last year at a very old age, but I meet with her cousin, who was close to her and knew her well. Her name is Guillermina Yamada. She had a Japanese father and a Mexican mother, and lives in the town of Taxco. She is tall and slender, her fingers are long and aristocratic, and she has deep circles under her Asiatic eyes.

I interview her on July 5, 1988, a day before the presidential elections. All of Mexico is papered with posters, and the faces of the candidates jump out from all the walls and around every corner. Aside from the election din, the place where she lives looks like a tourist postcard. It is a small house with balconies and bougainvillea, squeezed in with other houses on a narrow, uphill street: Number 9 on Benito Juárez, a few yards away from the Taxco *zócalo*.

Guillermina's manner is deliberate and aloof, and she apologizes for her failing memory. She explains that after her husband's death she suffered a brain seizure that erased all the past from her mind. She never recovered and even forgets the present, she says, her daughters have to help her find her things, because she does not remember where she places them.

At first, sometime after Altagracia returned from Clipperton, they had been like mother and daughter, because of their age difference. Altagracia was born in 1901 and Guillermina in 1918. But later, as time went on, they became friends, confidants.

I inquire about Altagracia's life after her return from Clipperton. "Tell me, Doña Guillermina, did your cousin ever get married?"

"Yes, of course she did, with a man called—you are not going to believe this—"

"Yes, I believe you. I have been told already. His name was Gustav Schultz, and he represented a foreign company dealing in guano at Clipperton."

"Exactly. Isn't it unbelievable? The love story of those two is like a soap opera."

"Why don't you tell me about it."

Guillermina remembers more than she believes; she is more lucid than she claims to be. Between one apology and another about the weakness of her mind, she tells me about her cousin, the woman who had been like a mother to her, and who later became her best friend, Señora Altagracia Quiroz Schultz.

"Alta died a year ago, I accompanied her in her last days. I had a debt to repay to her, because she had accompanied me in my life. For many years we had talked and talked, but at the end she could not hold a conversation. She had lost her mind by the time she died, due to all the beatings she had to endure from that sick soldier. He damaged her for life. She had an inoperable tumor that gradually made her insane. In her last days she could not make any sense, but only at the end, when she was very old. Not before. Before, she only had memory lapses once in a while. During those times she got desperate when all her memory went, but afterward she recovered, and the rhythm of her life continued.

"Altagracia must have suffered a lot on the isle," says her cousin and goddaughter, Doña Guillermina, "because that man tortured her mercilessly. He was what is called a sadist. She could never have children with her husband, the German fellow, and that was also the result of the damage done to her by that evil man who raped the women. He beat all the women on the head, grabbing them by the hair and dragging them on the ground. Alta had the most beautiful, longest hair that I have ever seen in my life. But you are not right when you say that all the women cut their hair in Clipperton because it interfered with their work, with doing the men's jobs that life had forced them to do. It did not bother them, because they kept it in thick braids tied up on top of their heads. That was not the reason. They cut their hair so nobody would use it to drag them around, and knock them unconscious."

"Then they cut their hair to spare their heads."

"That's right. That Victoriano Alvarez, Alta used to tell me, was so evil that he held the isle in a spell so that ships would not get close to it. They knew it was he who kept them isolated, and that as long as he was alive, that spell on Clipperton would not be broken. That was why, and also because he beat them and raped them, they wanted to kill him. Altagracia told me that when they could not stand it anymore, they had once prepared him some poison, mixed with marmalade, in order to do away with him. He realized it was a trick, and that day they were the ones almost done in. His fury turned him into a more cruel beast than he usually was. He grabbed them by the hair, one by one, and beat them all unconscious. It was then that they decided to cut their hair short."

"Did they attempt to poison him with marmalade?" I ask her. "Wasn't it with soup?"

"With marmalade."

"Where did they get the fruit and the sugar?"

"I don't know, but Alta said it was with marmalade. My cousin's bad luck started when she met Mrs. Alicia Rovira Arnaud at a hotel in Mexico City. That lady already had three children and was looking for a nursemaid to take to the isle when she realized that her chambermaid, Alta, was an educated person who worked there only because of the situation in which the Mexican Revolution had left her family. Our family. Alta's father was a schoolteacher and had taught her to write with good spelling and good penmanship. They lived in Yautepec, state of Morelos, which was the zone of the rebel Emiliano Zapata and of the peasants in arms. The Quiroz family was running away from the fracas when they were almost killed in a shooting. Alta was saved by a soldier who galloped by, pulled her up onto his horse, and got her out of there. She never knew to what side he belonged. The family disbanded after leaving their home, and all had to fend on their own. Alta had to earn her living as best she could in the capital. She accepted the Arnauds' offer, and when the family went back to Clipperton, she left with them. I suppose she did because it was her best prospect. She was fourteen years old and making five pesos a month. The Arnauds offered her ten and promised her that she would be on the isle only for four months and could return with the next ship. They were able to provide the double salary, but not her return in four months. Not that.

"Alicia and Altagracia were together in their predicament. One was the mistress and the other the servant, but fate treated them, I mean, mistreated them, equally. They were both forced to be Victoriano's lovers, like all the other women in Clipperton. None was saved from that. He was the king and they were his slaves, and there were no privileges under this tyrant.

"But the more you suffer, the faster you get to heaven, and that was what happened to Altagracia. Heaven on earth, because when she returned from the isle, she met the German fellow again, who had never stopped looking for her, and they married. She had the good luck then of having an adoring husband who had established himself in Mexico in order to be with her, and who was totally devoted to her. He took her with him to live in the Water House in Acapulco, and since he always treated her like a princess, the local people called her 'the Princess of the Water House.'

"So she never had to work again, Schultz put three servants and a gardener at her disposal. He bought her the best imported dresses and the most expensive shoes from incoming ships overflowing with merchandise. For her, mind you, who had been dressed in rags and had run barefoot for so long in Clipperton. Since she had been deprived of food, he gave her all the food she wished. It was usually German food, it's true, like sausages and cabbage, which were the only things he liked, but she hid in the kitchen to prepare her Mexican mole or stuffed chiles, and shared them with the three servants and the gardener.

"That German fellow, Gustav Schultz, became the most beloved foreigner in Acapulco, because he was the one who brought drinking water to the port city. He probably did this to compensate her for all the thirst she suffered, and the many mouthfuls of seawater she had to swallow when it did not rain.

"I have always asked myself why Altita—that was how her husband called her—was able to inspire such love in a foreigner. Surely it was because of the way she was. There is no other explanation. She had a sweet but strong temperament, and he always liked to see her happy, in spite of all she had suffered. She was not pretty, we might say she was rather ugly. Her best feature was her precious hair. It was quite unusual. But in everything else she was quite ordinary. She was thickset, short, with peasant features, and I especially remember her fat fingers," Guillermina tells me, looking wistfully at hers, so long and graceful, and she smiles when I tell her that it should have been the other way around, that she should have been the one named Altagracia, since she was so graceful, and her cousin, Guillermina.

"Alta told me many times about her life in Clipperton, without hate, without regrets. She did not mind her sad past anymore because her present was so happy. She would talk about it because she liked to reminisce. She lived to an old age and was a bit crazy, but she was happy. Her life was like a fairy tale, with a lot of suffering, but a happy marriage afterward. I cannot tell you any more, because I had a brain seizure that made me lose my memory," Guillermina Yamada tells me once more, wringing her beautiful hands.

Clipperton, 1916

TAKING HER LAST CHANCE against death, Alicia climbed to the lighthouse to make signals to the approaching vessel. She heard voices coming from below, from the beach. The rest of the women had already seen the ship and were frantically shouting for help. If we all see it, she thought, then it must be real. While she was waving the sheet, the idea of a rescue became a real possibility. Her father, Orizaba, a school for the children, and so many ghosts that had become parts of an abandoned dream were suddenly taking substantial form again. Nobody could keep that ship from reaching the shore. The only thing to do was to pray for time to pass quickly, to precipitate the end without her having to go through the preliminaries: the wait that burned her throat, the smarting anxiety that made her eyes hurt. This time nobody could prevent it, it was enough to extend her arm to reach salvation. Nobody would stand in the way. Nobody.

Except Victoriano Alvarez. Like a vulture flying low and hitting her with its wing, the thought of Victoriano threatening to kill all of them before they could be rescued—so they couldn't denounce him—jolted Alicia like a bolt.

She let herself go downhill, running without looking where she placed her feet, without stopping, and still struggling to keep her body wrapped in the sheet, getting up quickly every time she stumbled, without feeling the sharp rocks cutting her ankles, her legs, her knees. After reaching her three children, she untied Angel from the sling on her back, and laying him down on a safe spot, told her son Ramón:

"Now you stay here and keep an eye on the baby and on your sisters. We might be rescued, but we'll have to do things very carefully. Swear to me, Ramoncito, that none of you are going to move away from here until I come back."

She kept on going down without waiting for the child's reply. *I always climb this rocky cliff full of reasons to stop living, and I go down again full of reasons to keep on living,* was what came to her mind as she descended, half running, half sliding. She saw Tirsa trying to light a bonfire on the beach, surely in order to make signals, and she called her, catching her voice, not daring to shout. Victoriano's lair was on the other side of the rock, and he should be there if he was still sleeping. She was afraid the wind would carry their voices and wake him up.

"Tirsa," she said when she got close to her, "we must kill Victoriano. Right now, before he kills us."

"He wouldn't dare, the boat is too close."

"Yes he would, because he's insane. He will shoot us, as he promised, and then he will hide, or he will leave, he alone. Let's go, we have no time to waste."

"How do we kill him?

"I buried Ramón's sword next to the house—"

"No, we can't use that. It has to be something we can hide so he doesn't see it. We better hit him on the head with a rock."

They chose a medium-sized rock, sharp-edged, with a pointed end.

They got close to the lighthouse lair and called Victoriano. Tirsa hid the rock behind her, and Alicia walked in Tirsa's shadow. They could feel the irregular pounding of their blood, and everything seemed unreal, like someone else's nightmare. Nobody answered, and they called again. Altagracia came out and said the man was not there. She had not seen the ship, nor heard the shouts. She was not aware of anything.

"Do you think Victoriano has found out?" asked Alicia.

"No, surely he hasn't either. A while ago he took his harpoons and walked north to go fishing."

"Will you help us, Alta? We're going to kill him."

"How?"

"Whatever way we can."

"But look at your legs, Señora Alicia, you're bleeding. You'd better wash first, and calm down. If he sees you like that, so nervous, he's going to suspect your intentions."

"That's right," Tirsa said, "to kill him, we have to trick him. We have to think this out better."

"We have no time to think anything. We have to go and hit him, and that's it." Alicia did not want to say more and started walking. "If you're not coming, I'll go alone."

Tirsa grabbed her arm.

"Do you want us to commit suicide at the last minute? Calm down, Alicia, you need a cool head. While you tempt him, I'll kill him."

"I tempt him? In five minutes? What do you want me to do?"

"You tell him you'll marry him, or that he is looking very handsome, or you ask him to kiss you. Tell him whatever you want: you distract him while I hit him."

"He's not armed. He locked up the knives and guns before he left, but he left this out," Altagracia said, and handed Tirsa the mallet Victoriano used to open coconuts.

They agreed that if they were going to speak to him of love, Altagracia should not accompany them. Alicia alone should face him, and Tirsa should sneak up later from behind. Altagracia should instead go and bring the children down, before they fell off the cliff.

Tirsa tied a rope around her waist to hold the mallet hidden in back while Alicia rinsed her legs in seawater and fixed her hair with her hand. They walked north as they discussed how best to approach him: together, alone, together, alone. Together. This continued until they saw him, about seventy feet ahead, sitting on the beach, with his reddish, corn-husk hair, his ashen skin, and his arthritic, bent legs. They slowed down, held and squeezed each other's hand, and letting go, moved closer to him.

"He is going to know because when I speak to him my voice will tremble," whispered Alicia.

"Your voice will not tremble when you speak to him, and my hand will not tremble when I hit him. All these months we have behaved like idiots. Now it's time to act and do things right."

Victoriano was baiting his fishing hooks when he sensed their presence.

"What do I tell him, Tirsa—" Alicia asked between her teeth.

"Anything, it doesn't matter. Go on! Now!"

"Victoriano!" Alicia shouted. "I need to talk to you."

"Go ahead, ma'am."

"Aren't you going to invite me to sit down?"

"Since when do you need permission to sit on the ground?"

"It's something important, Victoriano."

"Sit down, then," and he made a pompous gesture with his arm, pointing at the sand.

"I'm coming to tell you that I want to marry you."

"That you what?"

"That I want to marry you."

"Oh, that's good. Until yesterday we were ready to kill each other, and today, we're ready to get married."

"That's true. We have been thinking, Tirsa and I, that since we are going to live out all our lives on this isle, it's better we do it like civilized people and put an end to this war between you and us. I mean, for us to solve our problems peacefully."

"And what problems do we need to solve?"

Alicia sensed that her proposal was not being well received. She felt ugly, old, disheveled, and thought, Nobody would want to marry me in this condition. Better try another tack.

"Well . . . you want to be the governor, right?"

"I am the governor already."

"Not true, you are a tyrant, and you only dominate by beating us. You have no authority over anybody. But I, I am indeed the governor, because Porfirio Díaz conferred that title upon my husband."

"Porfirio Díaz is dead now."

"And so is my husband, and so many other people, but that does not change anything. If you and I get married, everybody will recognize you as the governor, as well as me, both of us. That way we could command the isle in peace, the way God intended, and not through violence, which is bad for the children, and for everyone."

"Does a man who marries a lady governor also become governor?"

"That's right, like he who marries a queen becomes king."

"I like that, to be the legitimate governor, like my grandfather."

"Which grandfather?"

"My grandfather General Manuel Alvarez. He was a real governor, of the whole state of Colima. Not like Captain Arnaud, only governor of this shitty isle."

"It's not so bad. Don't you see that France wants to take it away from us? And the United States. Even the Japanese want it, there must be something."

"Oh well, heaven knows why. What I don't understand is why there was so much hate between us and now so much sweetness."

"I already told you. If we are going to live here for the rest of our lives, we better do it in peace."

"But why do I need to marry you? Don't be offended, ma'am: you're very pretty and quite a woman. A little skinny, but you pass, and I am grateful for your deference. What I mean is, when I need you, I just go and take you home with me without asking for any permission, and that's it. That's how my white grandfather, the governor, used to do it, and that is what I do."

"But that way I am never going to love you."

"And if I marry you, you will not give me any more poisoned soup?"

"No. There is no more poison."

Tirsa, who was sitting facing Victoriano, stood up, careful not to show her back to him.

"I don't trust this. It doesn't sound good to me," Victoriano said, and hearing this, Tirsa sat down again.

At sea on the other side of the isle, from the bridge of the *Yorktown*, Captain Perril was looking through his spyglass at the strange behavior of the women and children who were making signals. It all seemed too urgent, too emotional to be only a greeting. He sent for Lieutenant Kerr, who was readying the landing boat together with two bluejackets.

"Lieutenant," he said to him, handing him the spyglass. "Watch. Those people are in trouble. An emergency, maybe. Take Dr. Ross with you, in case they need a surgeon."

Kerr, Dr. Ross, and the two bluejackets left on the boat. It was noon. They tried to get close to the coast through very heavy seas, and Captain Perril, who kept a close watch on them, feared they would be overcome by the waves and ordered to signal them to return.

On the beach, Altagracia, Rosalía, and Francisca, their lives hanging from a thread, saw the approaching boat and gesticulated, trying to encourage the four men who were on board to row even faster and reach them. According to Alicia's instructions not to shout, or else Victoriano would be alerted, they were making desperate gestures in silence, like mimes. Suddenly, when the men were only a few yards away from crossing the barrier reef, the women saw the boat turning around, heading back to the gunboat. Was it possible they would be abandoned again? What kind of abominable joke was this, for the boat to have come so close and then to head back, leaving them behind? Were they going to meet their deaths anyway, after almost being rescued? The women went all out, shouting, crying, pleading hysterically, wading into the sea, wanting to fly, swim, run, anything in order to reach the boat. But their nightmare was not over; there was no way to stop it. The rowboat reached the gunboat, and the men went aboard. They all saw them. It was not a mirage. The only mirage was the possibility of a rescue. It had been just another cruel joke, like the one that took Captain Arnaud and Lieutenant Cardona to their deaths. The women stopped shouting. They remained in the water, silent, vacant, suddenly lifeless, waiting for the ghost to disappear from view. The gunboat started to move away. They saw it going northwest and waited until it was engulfed in green mist.

Lieutenant Kerr went up to the bridge and discussed the whole procedure again with Captain Perril. They agreed to attempt a landing farther to the northwest, where the sea seemed less aggressive.

Sitting on the beach, worried and puzzled by the conversation, and unaware of what was happening on the other side, Victoriano Alvarez continued baiting his hooks nervously, trying to figure out what was behind Alicia's words.

"What you are proposing, ma'am, sounds good to me," he said. "For us to become husband and wife, both to be governors, and to live in peace. What I don't understand is why now, when you never wanted this to happen before."

"I always treated you right."

"Yes, in a condescending way. But you never treated me like a man."

"I had my husband, Victoriano, and I loved him very much."

"But then you became a widow, and you didn't change."

"Then I had the baby, and besides, I was in mourning."

"Are you through now?"

"I think so."

She noticed that Tirsa had stood up, walked away, and was moving her hands behind her back. Alicia guessed she was pulling loose the mallet secured with a rope, and made a superhuman effort not to follow her with her eyes so that Victoriano would not turn around.

"And your children, will they accept me as their father?" he asked.

Alicia had begun to tremble, and her mouth turned dry. "If you treat them right, of course—" the tension strangling the words in her throat as she felt Tirsa's shadow approaching.

If I look at her now, Alicia knew, Victoriano will kill her. But her eyes did not obey and moved on their own, her pupils dilated, fixed on the mallet that Tirsa had raised over the head with the red hair. In Alicia's glance Victoriano saw the reflection of his own death. He recognized it immediately: he had faced it many times before. Once more he fought to evade it by trying to escape. He lurched to one side, but his sick legs responded very slowly. His movement was clumsy, his attempt faltered, and the descending mallet hit him on the nape of the neck. He was stunned for a fraction of a second, then recovered his reflexes, now sharpened, and instinctively reached for one of the harpoons. Tirsa was retreating, surprised that her attempt had failed, while Alicia watched the scene in a daze, numbed, as if she herself had received the blow. She felt like running away but restrained herself. She saw how Victoriano had taken the harpoon and was aiming it between Tirsa's eyes, and saw her flex her legs, recover her position, and wait for the attack, ready to defend herself with the mallet. If I don't do something, the harpoon will go through her, Alicia thought, and she lunged at the man from the side, far from the harpoon's point. An arm curled around her neck and squeezed. She felt the sudden lack of air in her lungs, but remembering to use her mouth, she opened and closed it, digging her teeth in up to their roots. She recognized the taste of blood, and focused her whole being on the strength of the bite, aware that no earthly power could force her to let go. Tirsa took advantage of that moment to raise the mallet again, letting it fall where it would, and she heard Victoriano roar. She laughed, suddenly fascinated by her own strength.

"This time I will kill you, Victoriano," she told him without anger, almost joyfully. "So that you learn not to go around raping women."

With self-assurance and precision, without haste, repulsion, or remorse, she dealt a final blow right in the middle of his head and heard an abrupt, muffled dry noise, like that of a machete splitting a coconut.

"Let him go now," Tirsa told Alicia, who was still biting. "He is dead."

Alicia had to make an effort. Her jaws were rigid, as if welded together after pressing so hard. She pulled back, prying her teeth away from the inert arm around her neck, and stood next to the other woman. The body on the ground shook with a tremor, its bones clattered, and its eyes turned. Tirsa held the harpoon, took aim, and thrust it deep into the corpse's chest.

"Enough! Why did you do that?" Alicia screamed.

"Just in case."

"That's enough. Let's go, we'll miss the ship."

"And what about him? Do we leave him lying here, without burying him?"

"Let the sea take him away at high tide."

They left, running as fast as their legs would permit, passed by the southern rock, and reached the little beach where they had left the other women, but there was no one. The ship was nowhere to be seen. Farther north on the isle, there seemed to be some movement, so there they headed, arriving just when the four men were landing.

"Could you take us on your ship?" Alicia begged, half in English and half in Spanish, while extending her hand in greeting. "Pleased to meet you, I am Alicia Rovira, Captain Arnaud's widow. Could you take us to Acapulco or to Salina Cruz, please? These are my children, and these are my friends and their children. We are five women and nine children. We have been here eight years already, and we want to go back home."

Lieutenant Kerr, who was looking at them wide-eyed as if they were from another planet, nodded and indicated they could climb on the boat.

"Give us one hour," Alicia pleaded in English, "*just one hour, please,* to collect our belongings."

They dispersed, and Alicia went home and dug up her trunk. She took out her bar of Ivory soap, put her four children into a tub of rainwater, and washed their hair, their faces, their bodies. She dressed Olga in a sailor suit that had belonged to Ramoncito, and for him and her oldest daughter, she found two of her blouses, of embroidered organza, that covered down to their knees. She combed their hair, made them sit where they would not get dirty, and ordered them not to move while she got dressed.

She called Tirsa, who was chasing after the only two remaining live pigs in order to take them also, and told her that she had stored enough clothes for both of them.

"No, Alicia. Thanks, but I never dressed that way, and I think I would look strange."

"And don't you think you look strange with that sailcloth sack, so thick it can stand up on its own?"

"I feel more comfortable because I look more like who I am."

Alicia took all the time she needed to bathe. She covered every inch of her body with white foam from the Ivory soap, and then poured jugs of water to rinse herself off, feeling that the very cold water was purging all of her old anxieties and dead memories, besides Victoriano's splattered, dry blood. She dried herself carefully, allowing no moisture to remain. From a nail care box she took out an orange stick, saved from floods and hurricanes for years, and removed the cuticles from each finger. When her hands seemed acceptable, she placed the wedding band and diamond ring on her left hand. She looked at herself this way and that in the broken mirror, trying to recognize from some angle the perfect features of the woman she had been. Putting on her earrings, she got distracted for a moment by the violet gleams of the diamonds in the sunlight. She slipped into her corset with copper eyelets and shiny braids, but when she wanted to adjust it, she realized how big it was on her and how many pounds she had lost. She chose a silk blouse in a rosemary color, pleated in front, with high neck and puff sleeves, which closed with a long row of tiny buttons. She shivered as her skin felt the fresh contact of the silk, and she buttoned the blouse slowly, enjoying the touch of each button, one by one, as it passed through its buttonhole. She clasped her gray pearl necklace, making sure the brooch was in front, to show it off. Out of her trunk she chose a floor-length taffeta skirt, black and smooth, then gathered her short hair under a woven straw hat with big muslin flowers, petal pink. She pushed it to the front, to the back, to one side and then the other, until she found the exact position that suited her best.

Last, she put the wad of bills into her pocket, lifted Angel, and took her other children by the hand. Dressed in that manner, although barefoot, they all walked toward the boat. Alicia asked Lieutenant Kerr to allow the bluejackets to help her by bringing her trunk on board.

"All right," said the lieutenant, "provided it is only one."

Tirsa and Altagracia were already on board with the other children, a barrel full of things, and the two pigs. Rosalía and Francisca came last. They stood in front of Alicia, their eyes downcast.

"Hurry up, we're ready to leave," said Alicia.

"No, ma'am. We are not leaving. We are staying."

"How come?"

"Here is where our dead are, and we cannot leave them."

"Our dead," said Alicia, "have been blown by the wind, swallowed by the sea, and by now they must be flying over Africa or sailing around Europe. So, come on, quick, let's go."

The bluejackets first carried the children and the women, then brought the trunk on their shoulders, climbed on their boat, and rowed toward the *Yorktown*. It was already four o'clock when they left Clipperton.

From the sea, Lieutenant Kerr looked at the empty atoll, barren, inhospitable, disquieting, and wondered how it was that these people had been able to survive there for so many years without dying of loneliness and boredom. He saw the ruins of miserable huts; a sad cemetery with a half-dozen fallen crosses; an unhealthy lagoon; a ragged, jagged, uninviting cliff; and some debris on the beach, among which was the hull of a sunken ship, an old mattress full of holes, some rags, and the battered body of a bald doll. Alicia was also looking at Clipperton, but it presented itself before her as full of joys and sorrows, the stage where her life had been played. She bid farewell to the invisible wooden houses with cool verandas still resonating love words that she could repeat in their entirety by heart; to the mild prehistoric monsters at the bottom of the lagoon; to the caves that hid from the heavens the sickness and suffering of the scurvy epidemic; to the magnificent chalices that the English pirates had buried after desecrating them with Jamaican rum; to the live rock that cradled the bones of loved ones as well as hated ones; to the tablecloths and bedsheets embroidered lovingly days before her wedding; to the walls guarding against the hurricane's fury; to the wrecked ghost ship that brought the twelve Dutch sailors; to her daughters' porcelain doll; to the lamb's wool mattress where her children were conceived, and brought into this world. To Secundino Angel Cardona's seductive laughter and the heroic and violent battle that her husband, Captain Ramón Arnaud, had undertaken against no one, ultimately at the cost of his life.

From the ship's bridge, Captain Perril, who had been alarmed by the delayed return of the boat, was astonished at the spectacle of women and children from the isle climbing into the gunboat. He had to keep his curiosity in check for twenty minutes, until Lieutenant Kerr came on board, explained the visitors' presence, told him whatever he had been able to understand of their tragic story, and relayed their petition to be taken to Salina Cruz.

Perril asked all the castaways to come aboard, welcomed them warmly, gave them boxes of chocolates as gifts, and ordered the preparation of the watchkeeper's quarters, which had sanitary facilities. He personally supervised a menu, palatable enough but appropriate for their digestive systems, which were unaccustomed to oils and spices. About two hours later, the Clipperton survivors were taken to the dining room, where the children became the center of attention for the sailors, who joked with them and made faces. This resulted in their crying and running for cover behind their mothers. They were served chicken breasts Maryland, mashed potatoes, salad greens, milk, and apples.

After dinner, Captain Perril took Alicia to his cabin for the customary official questioning, with the help of Dr. Ross, who spoke some Spanish.

"Could I serve you something to drink, a liqueur perhaps?" he asked to break the ice. She said no thanks.

"I would like to know what day is today," Alicia asked.

She was told it was Wednesday, 18 July 1917.

"How strange," she commented, "we thought it was Monday, 16 July 1916. We were off by only two days, but we obliterated a whole year. I do not know how this could happen."

"Don't give it another thought," Perril answered. "If according to you we are in 1916, we shall make it 1916. I like that number."

She was asked for names, dates, events, and motivations. They found out all the hows and whys. She answered as accurately as she could, in the English she had learned under the nuns' guidance in her adolescence, and which up to that moment she had only used to write love letters to Ramón. Perril wrote everything down, and when they finished, he asked if she would like to accompany him for some fresh air on deck, to take advantage of such a pleasant evening. Dr. Ross decided to retire, concluding that they no longer needed his services as translator in order to understand each other.

Looking at the ocean and enjoying the evening breeze, Captain Perril wished to express to Mrs. Arnaud the profound sympathy he felt for their misfortune and his admiration for the courageous way in which they had preserved the lives of adults and children. He put phrases together in his head, he had them at the tip of his tongue, but he could not articulate any of them. He was surprised to find himself insecure and bashful in the presence of this woman dressed in such an old-fashioned way and who, in spite of everything, still impressed him as beautiful.

"Don't you have a special desire, or wish for anything in particular?" Perril managed to say. "I would like very much to be able to please you, after the many years of deprivation that you had to suffer."

She thought about it for a moment, and told him there was something, that she would like to have some orange juice. The captain ordered a tall glass for her, and while drinking it, Alicia commented that if they had not lacked this on the isle, many lives would have been saved. From there, she told him about the scurvy episode. Then he told her about the world war, and she spoke about Victoriano; he informed her about the Russian Revolution, and she explained how they used to catch boobies. So he told her about the death of Emperor Francis Joseph I, and time went fast without their realizing it. They had engaged in a conversation that lasted until one o'clock in the morning and which they ended just because it grew too cold on deck. Before going in, the captain confessed his worries of that morning about approaching the atoll.

"Those underwater reefs," he commented, "make navigation in that area a very delicate matter. I am happy we are already far away from that place."

"However, I have already begun to feel nostalgia for it," she said, smiling.

While he accompanied her to the cabin where the other women and the children had already retired earlier, Perril had one more question.

"Please tell me, Mrs. Arnaud, were those nine years a real torment for you?"

She gave it careful thought, weighed the good and the bad, and answered him with honesty.

"They were bearable, Captain. Thanks."

After wishing her happy dreams on the first night of her new life, Perril went to the radio room. Together with the radio operator until three in the morning, he tried to send a radiogram to the British consul in Acapulco, who was also in charge of U.S. affairs, with the notification of the ship's expected arrival at Salina Cruz in four days' time, and of the survivors he had rescued from Clipperton Island. This accomplished, he retired to his cabin, but since he was not able to sleep, he made some informal notes in his diary.

Captain Arnaud's widow is the only white survivor in the group. She is only twenty-nine years old, and, even though she seems older, she still is a beautiful woman, and very intelligent, as her conversation proves. She must be. Otherwise, she would not have been able to help the group through the extreme hardships they were subjected to. Her clothes are very old fashioned but of excellent quality, and she wears some splendid diamonds that speak of more fortunate times. She showed me the money she has accumulated and protected, which she intends to put to good use upon her return. I did not dare confess that even though that money could have represented a fortune in the times of General

Huerta, now it is worth almost nothing. Except for her and her children, all of the others are Mexican Indians, but at first I thought they were black, they are so suntanned. Dr. Ross examined them and informed me that he found all in reasonably good health. He told me also that he had talked with the women and learned that when our boat returned to the ship after the failed first landing attempt, they felt so desperate that they thought of killing the children and then committing suicide by drowning in the ocean. The one who seems to have the strongest resolve and a most energetic personality is Tirsa Rendón, widow of the lieutenant at that post. As soon as she came on board, she asked if we would lend her a sewing machine from the quartermaster and without any time to waste, she started to make garments out of some drill material for the children.

The children are very timid, but very curious. Everything seems strange to them, and they want to see and touch everything. They cried when the bluejackets carried them to the gunboat because they thought they would be separated from their mothers, who were still on the boat. The men paid much attention to these children and gave them boxes of candy, although the children had no idea what it was. I spent some time watching a young Indian girl trying to open a box of marshmallows. When she succeeded, she walked to the guardrail, threw the marshmallows in the water one by one, then closed the box and took it with her, satisfied with her new toy. She placed it on the deck, and let it slide back and forth with the movement of the ship. At dinnertime, the younger ones did not want to eat even a bite of anything they were served because, I heard them say, they wanted to eat booby, which is the kind of seagull they used to eat on the isle. The women, on the other hand, said that they hoped not to have to eat more seagulls as long as they lived.

They brought on board two desolate pigs, the scrawniest I have ever seen in my life. The men say they look like the original pair just out of Noah's ark, and even though they were offered to the cook, no one wants to kill them. It would be cruel for them to lose their lives right after being rescued, after such a hard struggle to survive.

At four in the morning Captain Perril closed his notebook and fell asleep. Two hours later, the radio operator woke him up with the British consul's reply. He said he would go personally to welcome the survivors and had already notified some of the relatives who had maintained contact with him as part of their rescue efforts.

On Sunday, 21 July, at 1700, the gunboat *Yorktown* dropped anchor in the Mexican port of Salina Cruz. Three men stood waiting at the dock: the British consul; Alicia's father, Don Félix Rovira; and the German fellow, Gustav Schultz. Captain Perril ordered the admittance of Don Félix to the cabin where his daughter awaited him. That night he wrote in his diary that he saw them embrace with such emotion that, for the first time in many years, he could not hold back his tears. That they sat together, in silence, looking into each other's eyes, very moved, and holding hands tightly. Perril also wrote that he left them alone in the cabin, and when he returned, half an hour later, they were still in the same position he had left them, unable to utter a word.

Epilogue

CLIPPERTON CEASED BEING under Mexican authority in 1931 due to a decision favorable to France by King Victor Emmanuel III of Italy. Aside from crabs, boobies, and a French flag, which flies like a faded bedsheet hung out to dry in the sun, the only things standing on the isle are the thirteen coconut palm trees planted by Gustav Schultz.

Acknowledgments

IN ORIZABA:
Alicia Arnaud (Mrs. Loyo)

IN COLIMA:
Carlos Ceballos
Genaro Hernández

IN MEXICO CITY:
Colonel N.N.
Rodrigo Moya
Carlos Payán
Paco Ignacio Taibo II
Roberto Bardini

IN BOGOTÁ:
Carmen Restrepo

Acknowledgments

Helena de Restrepo

Guillermo Angulo

Mireya Fonseca

Alvaro Tafur

Ramiro Castro

Gonzalo Mallarino

To Alex Knight, wherever he is.

To Chiqui, wherever he hides.

To the Teacher, in the desert.

To Eduardo Camacho, forever.

To Fernando Restrepo, from afar.

To Dolores M. Koch, for her impeccable translation.